WHEN I KILL YOU

ALSO BY B. A. PARIS

Behind Closed Doors

The Breakdown

Bring Me Back

The Dilemma

The Therapist

The Prisoner

The Guest

WHEN I KILL YOU

B. A. PARIS

ST. MARTIN'S PRESS
NEW YORK

This is a work of fiction. All of the characters, organizations, and events portrayed in this novel are either products of the author's imagination or are used fictitiously.

First published in the United States by St. Martin's Press, an imprint of St. Martin's Publishing Group

EU Representative: Macmillan Publishers Ireland Ltd, 1st Floor, The Liffey Trust Center, 117–126 Sheriff Street Upper, Dublin 1, D01 YC43

www.stmartins.com

Designed by Omar Chapa

The Library of Congress Cataloging-in-Publication Data is available upon request.

ISBN 978-1-250-28944-5 (hardcover)
ISBN 978-1-250-44253-6 (international, sold outside the U.S., subject to rights availability)
ISBN 978-1-250-28945-2 (ebook)

First U.S. Edition: 2026

First International Edition: 2026

10 9 8 7 6 5 4 3 2 1

For Chloé

Thank you for proofreading my novels before anyone else sets eyes on them. I'm eternally grateful for your diligence in deleting my (many!) double spaces and errant commas, and for correcting all my typos.

WHEN I KILL YOU

It's the lamp going out in the living room that alerts me the electricity has been cut. I jump to my feet, knocking my empty mug onto the floor. A crushing fear tightens my chest. It's too early, I'm not ready.

If they come for you, it will be in the dead of the night, Alex had told me.

But it's not the middle of the night, it's barely 9:00 PM.

What if they come earlier, when I'm still downstairs? I'd asked.

Focus on getting to your bedroom where you can lock yourself in, Alex had said. *Don't let fear muddle your thinking.*

Remembering his words, I take a breath to calm myself, then grope my way to the door. The hall is in complete darkness. I'm about to run to the stairs when a dark shadow peels itself from the wall. I cry out in shock; they're already inside.

What if I can't get to my bedroom? I'd asked. *What if they're already inside?*

Scream, Alex had said. *Use your voice. Take a deep breath and scream as loud and as long as you can. You'll have a couple of seconds before fear numbs you. Use them well.*

I open my mouth to scream but fear has already wound its steely grip around my lungs, squeezing the breath from me. My eyes pick out a looming mass advancing down the hall toward me. I scramble back as fast as I can and feel the kitchen door behind me.

If you can't get upstairs, don't let yourself be backed into the kitchen, Alex had said.

But what if there isn't anywhere else to go? I'd asked.

Then try and arm yourself with a weapon. You have knives on the counter.

I grapple for the handle and as the door swings open, I stumble backward into the kitchen. They follow me in and kick the door shut. The room is in total darkness, confusing me for a moment, because there should be at least some light from the light well. I recover quickly and step to my right, visualizing the knife block next to the stove. But as if they can read my mind, they bar my way, forcing me to move to the left, my feet tripping over each other as I back around the island, until I come to the far end and can go no farther.

Whatever you do, Alex had told me, *don't let yourself be cornered behind the island, because if you do, there will be no way out. You cannot let it happen. Do you hear me, Nell? You cannot let it happen.*

Yet here I am. My legs tremble at the implication. As my eyes adjust to the inky darkness, the looming mass defines itself as a black-clad figure standing on the other side of the island. There's a movement, followed by a swish in the air. My throat constricts; they have a blade.

"Stop!" My voice rings out and to my astonishment, the air stills.

"Before you kill me," I say, keeping my voice strong. "I need to know who you are."

PART ONE

NELL

PRESENT

His thigh presses against mine as I sit on the bus. I don't think it's intentional—the seats are small and he's a large man—but still, it makes me uncomfortable. I'd like to move my leg, cross it over the other one and turn my body away from him, toward the window. But I don't want to cause offense.

The bus lurches around a corner and, thrown against me, the pressure of the man's thigh increases. My throat tightens and, overwhelmed by cloying claustrophobia, I stand up abruptly, needing to get away from him. I wait for him to stand and move into the aisle, or at least move his legs to let me past and when he doesn't, my only choice is to clamber over him. My navy coat brushes his face and, hot with embarrassment, I mumble an apology. I want to see his face but from where I'm standing, gripping the metal bar, I can only see the top of his shaved head and the tattoo on the back of his neck.

I'd had my face turned to the window when he'd sat down next to me but as I make my way to the exit, I notice that the bus is only a quarter full. There would have been other empty seats, double seats, when he got on two stops back, so why had he chosen to sit next to me? The bus brakes to a halt and I move to the door. It's not my stop but I prefer to walk the rest of the way to work than sit with doubts crowding my mind.

I step quickly off the bus then hang back as it pulls into the road, the wheels splashing in yesterday's puddles, wanting to be sure that the man hasn't followed me off. He's sitting at the window, in the seat I vacated, his head turned away, toward the interior of the bus. Is it on purpose, so that I can't see his face? I try to guess his age from the little I can see of him and think he must be in his forties. Some of the tension seeps from me. He's not the right age.

I take my water flask from my bag and sip from it slowly as I walk to the office. This feeling of being followed began a couple of weeks ago, out of nowhere. There's been nothing to back it up, no footsteps behind me, no strange man lurking in doorways, just a sense of eyes watching. Sometimes, when the feeling intensifies, I spin on my heels, hoping to catch someone ducking their head, or doing a quick about-turn in the street. There's never anyone there, just ordinary people going about their everyday lives.

My mind, as I walk toward Brixton, is full of the day ahead. Fridays are always busy at Drop In, the charity I work for, and apart from a hair appointment at lunchtime, I plan to keep my head down until I leave to meet Alex, my—boyfriend? lover?—I'm never sure how to categorize him, even to myself. It's too soon to call him my partner. I've only known him a few months and for half that time, he's been in the US. At our ages, thirty-six for me, forty-four for him, "boyfriend" seems too casual. He's definitely my lover, but that reduces our relationship to sex and although that is a huge part of it, given that we only see each other every two weeks, it's so much more than that. Simply put, he's my everything.

The sky is a palette of grays as I cross the street at a green pedestrian light, breathing in the cool morning air. There's a sudden hiss from somewhere behind me and a bicycle comes hurtling out of nowhere, narrowly missing me. A cry of fright escapes from me and I quickly cover the last few steps to the pavement, where I stand for a moment, my heart pulsing in my chest, my eyes following the rider until he disappears from sight. The swish of his tires as they passed inches from me is still loud in my ears but I push down the anxiety bubbling inside me. I cannot—I will not—start thinking that every such incident is suspicious.

I don't usually arrive at work at seven in the morning but Alex had a late dinner last night and had gone back to his hotel to sleep there. I'd felt uneasy all evening in the too-quiet house, and had slept badly without him beside me. I'm already dreading Monday, when he'll return to the US for his usual two weeks there.

Despite the man on the bus and the man on the bike, my spirits lift at the thought of seeing Alex tonight. If someone had told me, just a few months ago, that for the first time in twelve years I'd soon be in a meaningful relationship, I wouldn't have believed them. But the proof is there; since meeting Alex I've begun, tentatively, to make plans for a future I never thought I'd have. *A future you don't deserve to have*, a voice reminds me, and immediately, my mood slumps again. I shouldn't be surprised. I always knew that my past life—when I was still Elle Nugent, before I became Nell Masters—would one day catch up with me.

ELLE

PAST

"Hey!"

Disturbed by the shout from the street below, I put my book down and moved to the window of the first-floor flat, glad to have something to break the monotony of an afternoon without my boyfriend, Jaz, who'd gone to see a friend. Looking out, I saw a young woman standing on the opposite pavement.

"My phone!" she cried, pointing to farther along the road.

I pushed my head through the open window to get a better look and saw a man on a moped disappearing down the road at high speed. I was about to call to the woman to tell her I'd come down but she was already running after the moped, calling for it to stop, come back. Then, realizing the futility of both her actions and her words, she stopped and burst into noisy tears.

She was younger than I'd first thought, a student I guessed, from the way she was dressed, in jeans, sneakers, and tee. I felt bad for her; it wasn't the first time someone had had their phone snatched by a guy on a moped and it wouldn't be the last.

I was about to go down and do my good deed for the day, offer her my phone to call someone, when a car screeched to a stop beside the young woman.

"I saw that!" The driver's window was open and I saw a dark-haired man lean toward the passenger door. "Quick, jump in, we'll go after him!" He sounded American and I gave a sigh of relief that he had taken over and I could get back to my book.

"Great, thanks!" The young woman dashed the tears from her eyes and began to get in the car.

I suddenly felt uneasy. The car had appeared from nowhere. What if it was a setup, and the guy in the car was an accomplice of the thief on the moped?

I leaned further out of the window, my body prickling with alarm "Hey!" I called. "Wait!"

But the young woman was already in the car. A sense of foreboding coursed through me. "Hey, you!" I shouted louder, addressing the driver. "What are you doing?"

At the sound of my voice, he swiveled his head toward me. I just had time to register the look of irritation on his face before he gunned the engine and roared off down the street.

"Nooo!" My breath whooshed out of me as I pulled myself back through the window, hitting my head on the wooden frame in my haste. Cursing under my breath, I snatched my phone from the table, ran out of the flat, and took the stairs to the ground floor two at a time. With a bit of luck, the car would be stuck at the end of the street, waiting for a gap in the traffic before pulling onto the main road. Spilling through the front door and onto the pavement, I looked to the right. The car was there, indicating left, but as I ran toward it, it moved forward and disappeared around the corner.

I came to a standstill, my breath coming in short gasps, not quite sure what I'd hoped to achieve by running after the car. Even if I'd managed to open the passenger door and had yelled at the young woman to get out, she might not have listened. And if the man had driven off while I was hanging on to the door, I could have fallen under the wheels, or been dragged onto the busy main road. I walked slowly back to the flat, wondering what I should do. Maybe it was completely innocent and the man really was a knight in shining armor. But what if it was something more sinister? What if I'd just witnessed a kidnapping?

Aware that I was probably wasting their time, I called the police and while I waited for someone to pick up, I sifted through what had happened. During the whole incident, something had been niggling at me, something to do with the man driving the car. It took me a moment to realize that I'd seen him before, only a couple of hours earlier, when I'd gone to buy a jar of honey from the local supermarket. While I was leaving the shop, my head bent over my phone as I messaged Jaz to tell him the washing machine had sprung a leak, I'd walked slap-bang into a guy. The jar had slipped from my hands and smashed onto the pavement.

"Oh geez," the man had said, coming to stand beside me as I looked in disbelief at the gooey mess. He was holding a cup of coffee in his hand and some of it had spilled through the sip-hole onto the lid as a result of me crashing into him. He raised a hand to his head and scratched absentmindedly at his hair. "I'm sorry."

"No, it's totally my fault. I wasn't looking where I was going." I looked toward the shop. "I'd better go and see if they've got something I can clean it up with."

"Can I help?"

I'd given him a smile, looking properly at him for the first time. Despite being on the old side, he was seriously good-looking. "No, it's fine. Thanks," I'd added, struck by the color of his eyes, which matched the blue shirt he was wearing.

"Right, well, hope your day gets better," he'd said, moving away.

I was sure it was the same man that had been driving the car the young woman had gotten into. Doubts about my call to the police set in. The man I'd bumped into had seemed nice. What if the police stopped his car and accused him of kidnapping the young woman when he'd only been trying to help? What if he and the young woman knew each other? When I thought about it, the woman had gotten into the car without hesitation. But before I could hang up, my call was answered and to my relief, my worries about what I'd seen were treated with concern. The responder took details of the young woman (average height, slim build, long blond hair, dressed in pale blue jeans, a white T-shirt, and carrying a black tote bag) who'd climbed so recklessly into a stranger's (white male, dark, neatly parted hair, pale blue shirt, American accent) car (large, black). I kicked myself for not having gotten the car's registration number but as I explained to the responder, everything had happened so fast.

"I think he might be local," I added. "I saw him in the street earlier today. I live near Waterloo and he was walking along The Cut."

The responder thanked me for my call and said that it would be looked into. I tried to put it out of my mind but found it hard to go back to my book because my thoughts kept slipping back to the young woman. By the time Jaz came home, the need to speak about what I'd witnessed was overwhelming. But he was full of a new app he was going to design with the friend he'd just seen and wasn't as invested in the story as I hoped.

"You did everything you could, babe," he said. "Stop stressing."

So I'd given a mental shrug and stopped stressing. Best-case scenario, the young woman had been reunited with her phone and was safe and well.

Except that the next morning, when I opened the news app on my phone and saw the headline article, my heart plummeted, then almost stopped. The body of a young woman, as yet unidentified, had been found in a burned-out car, not far from Wimbledon Common.

NELL

PRESENT

I arrive at the building where Drop In, the charity I work for, is situated. Taking my keys from my bag, I unlock the security door, checking that a regular isn't hovering nearby, waiting to be let in even though the doors don't officially open until nine. Sometimes it happened and I always allowed them in. To my relief, there's no one waiting.

In the reception area, I switch on the light, lock the door behind me and wait until the silence settles on my shoulders like a warm blanket. This is my territory. This is where I feel safe.

The charity's offices are simple. There's a reception desk and behind that, the main room where computer stations have been set up on the left-hand side, a kitchen area to the right and two smaller rooms, one we use for workshops and the other for coffee and conversation. We've had two workshops running this week, one on returning to the world of work and the other on acknowledging and dealing with grief. Both were oversubscribed and the feedback has been excellent. I make a mental note to ask Sadie, my wonderful but slightly scatty assistant, to book them in again.

My office, the only office, is to the right of the reception desk. It's small but has a door I can close and a window that looks onto a tiny paved courtyard at the back of the building. I go in, flick the light switch and press the button to open the steel shutter which protects the window. The sun hasn't fully risen but I drop my bag on the chair, return to the main room, wind up the shutter on the back door and step outside. I love this time of the morning when the city hasn't fully woken from its sleep and the sounds of its awakening are only a distant murmur. I sit for a while on one of the wooden benches, huddled in my coat, my head tipped back against the wall, absorbing the calm, knowing that once the doors open at nine it will be manic until they close again at seven this evening.

I started working at Drop In four years ago, as a volunteer at weekends, until I was offered a permanent post doing the job that Sadie does now. When my boss left to work for a larger charity, I was offered the job of overall manager. My main role—securing funding to keep the charity afloat—isn't something I thought I'd enjoy. But approaching corporations, local and national, big and small, and getting them to agree to a sponsorship, or making a donation, has turned out to be surprisingly satisfying.

I check the time on my phone and leave the courtyard, wanting to catch up on my emails before Sadie arrives. On the way to my office, I switch on the kettle and make myself a cup of instant coffee. I'd love a proper coffee machine, and although I'd be happy to buy one for the charity at my own expense, it would be misplaced to have such a luxury item in our humble workspace.

In my office, I begin the laborious task of going through my emails, a part of my mind on seeing Alex tonight. I'm tempted to phone him, just to hear his voice, and the pull is so strong that when the office phone rings I think telepathy is at work and that he is calling me—until I remember that he would call me on my cell phone. Going through to the reception area, I answer the call, presuming one of the volunteers is sick and is letting Sadie know so that she can arrange cover. No one replies to my questioning "Hello?" nor to the second one. But I'm sure there's someone there.

"Hello, can I help you?" I ask gently, because some people who call the charity need encouragement to speak. But no one answers. I must have received a hundred such calls over the past four years but after the man on the bus this morning, this is the first one to make me anxious. I cut the call and return to the sanctuary of my office. I'm still answering emails when Sadie comes in.

"What time did you arrive?" Sadie exclaims.

"Just after seven. I couldn't sleep so I thought I may as well come in early. How are you? All good?"

"Yes, except for the queue at the baker's." Energy emanates from Sadie as she shrugs off her coat, unwinds a scarf from around her head, and attempts to flatten the blond curls that have sprung loose. "I didn't have time to dry my hair before leaving," she explains. She dumps her bag on the desk and I quickly slam my hand onto a pile of papers to prevent them from sliding to the floor. "But I did have time to get muffins!" Sadie adds triumphantly, digging into the depths of the bag.

"Great!" I say, smiling. I love Sadie's enthusiasm for life in general, the way she electrifies the atmosphere just by being. "Thank you."

In truth, I don't like any kind of muffin but I'd never tell Sadie that. She bought me one the first week she started working at Drop In and assumed—from my pretended enthusiasm, because I hadn't wanted to hurt her feelings by refusing it—that I love them, and she has bought muffins every Friday since. On Tuesdays, when it's my turn to treat, I buy croissants.

"Coffee?" Sadie asks.

"Let me get you one."

"By the way, Valerie isn't coming in this morning. One of her children is ill, so she's arranged for Annie to cover for her," Sadie chatters, walking back to the reception area and settling herself behind the desk. "She phoned here this morning and when I didn't pick up she called me on my cell phone."

"It's good of her to have arranged cover," I say, relieved to have an explanation for the mystery call. "I hope it's nothing too serious?"

Sadie shakes her head. "Just a cold, but her son has a fever so his day care won't take him."

Sadie and I are the only two paid members of the staff at Drop In. The rest of the team is made up of volunteers who work on a rota basis. It's important to me that my colleagues are happy to come to work so I do my best to create a good working environment. I also work hard to walk the fine line between keeping my distance and being approachable, both with my colleagues and with the regulars at the charity. What my colleagues know about me is that I spent most of my childhood in care and that I'm single. Only Sadie knows about Alex.

The morning passes quickly. I'm in the middle of sourcing other workshops that could be of interest to the charity when Sadie appears, carrying a huge bouquet of yellow roses.

"Flower delivery," she says cheerfully.

I can't help frowning at the blatant luxury of the bouquet. "Who are they from?" I ask.

"I don't know but there must be a card."

I take the flowers from Sadie and lower my nose into the satiny petals. "They actually smell," I say appreciatively. I peer into the bouquet. "I can't see a card, can you?"

Sadie leans over the desk, turning the bouquet this way and that, searching for the elusive card. She can't find one either, not even hidden deep among the flowers.

Sadie lowers her voice dramatically. "But you know who they're from."

I shake my head. "Alex wouldn't send flowers here, he'd send them to the house."

Sadie's eyes gleam. "Then you must have a secret admirer."

I resist a shiver that threatens my spine. Sadie disappears to find something to put the flowers in and I have to fight the urge to throw them into the bin. It will look strange if I do and there might not be anything sinister behind them. But what if there is?

"I'd really like to be able to thank the person who sent them," I say to Sadie, when she returns with a small bucket half-filled with water. "Would you mind phoning the florist and see if they have a name?"

Sadie nods. "They came from Le Jardin des Roses, farther down the street. I'll give them a ring."

While I wait for Sadie to get through, I carry the bucket to the main room and place it on one of the tables.

"From a local business," I say to the faces that have turned inquiringly in my direction. There's a visible uplifting of spirits; people smile and exclaim how beautiful the roses are and seeing their delight, I make a mental note to buy some flowering plants to brighten up the room.

"The person paid cash and didn't leave a name," Sadie says, coming to find me a couple of minutes later.

My disquiet deepens. "Did they say what they looked like?"

Sadie frowns at the question. "No—but then, I didn't ask. Do you want me to?"

Realizing how odd it must have sounded, I give Sadie a smile. "No, it's fine. Thanks, Sadie." And tell myself that nobody with a vengeance would send me such an extravagant bouquet of roses.

EXTRACT FROM NOTEBOOK 4

I felt sorry for you on the bus this morning, Nell. I think you thought the rather large man sitting next to you was me. But I was farther back, out of sight.

I've been following you for a while now, longer than you know. Months, not weeks. I remember the day it began. You came out of the building where you work and I was there, right in front of you. I could afford to take risks back then. Now I wait in the shadows. I may have learned how to make myself invisible, but I prefer to be careful.

That day, the day it began, I followed you all the way to the bus stop. As you passed the entrance to the underground station, you took a copy of the free newspaper and on the bus, once you'd read the main articles, you tackled the crossword, not the cryptic one, the easy one. I didn't think any less of you for it, you have to be of a certain mind-set to enjoy cryptic crosswords. It has nothing to do with intelligence. Although, when you got stuck on "volley of gunfire" in five letters, I was tempted to lean over—I was sitting behind you—and tell you the answer. I could have. You would have taken it well, I know that, and you would have thanked me for my help. I also know that as you thanked me, you would barely have given me a second glance, not from a lack of manners but because you avoid looking closely at people in case they look too closely back at you. Because you have secrets, Nell.

In the event, you finished the crossword in under ten minutes, then turned to the back page and completed the one there in equal time. I like that you try to improve your mind, rather than sitting with your earphones in, your head bent over your mobile, like others do.

Not that it changes anything. We won't be doing crosswords when I kill you.

ELLE

PAST

Tears pooled in my eyes as I stared at Bryony Sanders's pretty face, her blue eyes sparkling as she gazed at the camera. She had been named as the young woman found dead in the burned-out car near Wimbledon Common.

"It's her," I told Jaz, my voice trembling. "The young woman I saw getting into the car last Saturday."

Jaz came over and peered at my computer screen. "Are you sure?" he asked.

"Positive."

"I'm sorry, babe." He sat down next to me on the sofa and pulled me to him. "She looks so young."

"She was nineteen. I need to call the police." I stretched my hand out and scrolled to the end of the news bulletin. "There's a number here for witnesses to call. I told the responder that I thought the man who picked her up was local—what if she didn't pass that on to the police?" I gave a shiver. "I can't believe he might have murdered her. He seemed so nice."

"That's probably why she trusted him," Jaz said. "Shall I make you a cuppa while you phone them?"

"Yes, please."

My hands were shaking as I dialed the number and told the responder about my call the previous Saturday. Within the hour, a DC from the MIT unit arrived at the flat to take a detailed statement from me.

"Can you start from about five minutes before you heard the shout in the street?" DC Gail Moss asked. "Where were you, what you were doing?"

I closed my eyes in order to concentrate better. "I was here, in this room, reading a book."

"Was there anyone else in the house?"

"No, my boyfriend was out."

"Carry on."

"It was a lovely day so the window was open. I heard someone shout out and went to the window. I saw a young woman on the opposite pavement."

"What time was it?"

"Around 4:00 PM."

"Can you describe the woman you saw?"

I wanted to tell DC Moss that I'd already given the information to her colleagues when I'd called 101, the nonemergency police line. But I soon realized how much I'd omitted, and how much more I could remember when asked the right questions. I thought that the only thing I could remember about the car was that it was black, but when I was asked how many doors it had, I was able to say that it had had four, that there had been a silver rim around the windows and that it had no special markings. I also remembered that the black tote bag the woman had been carrying had had a purple logo on the bottom left-hand corner.

"Thank you, you've been very helpful," DC Moss said, stopping the recording. "Could you come down to the station and help create a likeness of the man you saw driving the car?"

"Sure. I think he might be local," I said, repeating what I'd said to the responder. "I saw him earlier that afternoon, on The Cut. I was coming out of the supermarket and I walked straight into him. I'd bought a jar of honey and it smashed on the pavement. He offered to help me clean it up." I paused. "He seemed nice."

"Which supermarket was that?"

I gave her the details and she nodded. "We'll look into it."

I thought I had a clear idea of what the man looked like but the reality of creating a likeness was more difficult than I'd imagined. Although the sketch artist was patient, I couldn't convey the man's features as accurately as I'd hoped. But I presumed that once it was in the public domain, someone would recognize who he was.

The following day, Bryony's mum, a widow from Boston, made an emotional appeal for help in catching her daughter's killer. I could barely watch as she explained that a year before, a few months before Bryony was due to leave for the UK, her husband—Bryony's father—had died after a long illness and that Bryony had hesitated about moving to London because she hadn't wanted to leave her mum alone. Mrs. Sanders hadn't wanted Bryony to give up her dream of studying at King's, and had persuaded her to go.

"First my husband, now my daughter," she wept. "I don't want anyone else to suffer as I am suffering. If you recognize this man, please, please contact the police."

I'd already looked at Bryony's social media. Under other circumstances, I'd never have looked at the Facebook account of someone who had died but I had a need to know as much as I could about the young woman whose path had so fleetingly crossed mine. There was nothing extraordinary about Bryony; she was just a regular nineteen-year-old, enjoying her time at university in the UK, missing her friends and her mum back home. But this evidence that she had barely started out on life somehow made it worse. She'd had everything to live for, and it had been taken away from her in the most terrible and violent manner. It affected me horribly; I couldn't stop thinking about Bryony, about how, with her heartbroken mother living in the US, she had no one to fight for her on British soil.

NELL

PRESENT

As I get ready in the office cloakroom for dinner with Alex, I think back to the day I met him at a party I almost hadn't gone to. Parties were a necessary evil as far as I was concerned and I'd been calculating when I could leave without causing offense when a man had appeared at my side holding two glasses of still-fizzing champagne.

"I couldn't help noticing that you don't have a drink," he'd said, offering me one of the glasses. "And also that, like me, you don't seem to be enjoying yourself as much as everyone else is."

I'd tensed at the trace of an American accent. In other circumstances, I would have found an excuse to smile and move away. But he was drop-dead gorgeous and I was horribly bored.

"I'm not really a party animal," I'd replied with a smile. I wasn't arrogant enough to have taken his gesture at anything other than face value—one person coming over to talk to another to ease the boredom of being somewhere neither wanted to be. In truth, I'd spotted him as soon as he'd walked into the room, mainly because he towered over most of the others there, and I'd been watching him surreptitiously ever since, attracted by his easy manner as he mingled with the other guests. "You're from the US?" I asked, hoping he would say that he wasn't.

"Partly. My father is American, my mother is French, and I was born and brought up in Paris. When I was ten years old, my parents separated and my father moved back to the US while I stayed in Paris with my sister and mother."

"And where do you live now? France or the US?"

"I have a flat in DC, where I spend most of my time."

It was probably just as well, I'd reflected. It would be easier to walk away if he lived abroad.

"What do you do?" I was aware that I was asking too many questions but I had an innate need to know everything about him. "Sorry, I don't mean to interrogate."

He smiled. "It's fine. I work as an independent advisor to US companies wanting to export to Europe." There was a pause. "I'm sorry, I haven't introduced myself. Alexandre—Alex—Stanton."

"Nell," I said. "Masters."

He raised his glass and looked at me with eyes that were a perfect match for the threads of gray just beginning to show in his dark hair. "Delighted to meet you, Nell Masters."

"Likewise." I waited until we'd both taken a sip of champagne. "Are you in London on holiday?"

"No, since Brexit, I've been spending a week here each month, working as a consultant for UK companies who export to France. It's become a lot more complicated since you left the EU." He paused. "What about you? Are you a journalist?"

It was a fair question. It was, after all, a media party.

"No, I'm only here for the contacts. I work for a charity in Brixton and I'm trying to raise its profile by persuading one of the mainstream newspapers to write an article about the work we do."

"And have you succeeded? In getting the article?"

I looked over to where Jane Stopes from *The Guardian* was chatting to a group of fellow journalists. "I think so."

"Good work. I'm only here because my sister Béatrice invited me along." He turned and indicated a beautifully chic woman with the same dark hair as Alex, who gave him a little wave. "She works for the French news channel BFM. And that's her husband, Victor."

I glanced at a dark-haired man with a close-cropped beard who was standing a few feet away, chatting to a group of people.

"Is he a journalist?" I asked.

"No, he works for the French Embassy here in London. Like me, he's only here because of my sister."

I'd never before wished for a man to ask me for my phone number but I began to wish it so much that when it came to saying goodbye, I found myself asking Alex for his.

"My main role is obtaining sponsorship and donations for the charity," I explained. "Would you be interested in meeting up at some point so that I can explain what we do? Perhaps one of the companies you give advice to would be interested in a sponsorship," I added, wanting to give weight to my request for his number.

"Sure." He took out a business card and handed it to me. "I look forward to hearing from you, Nell Masters," he said, and the formality of his words made me smile.

I'd made myself wait three days before calling him. My last brief relationship—by choice, I'd only ever had brief relationships—had ended a year before. I hadn't thought I'd missed having sex but all I could think of during those three days was what it would be like to go to bed with Alex.

"I thought you were never going to phone." The relief in Alex's voice when he answered my call made my stomach flip. "I'm going back to the US on Saturday and I was hoping to see you before I left."

We arranged to meet at a bar in Soho after work the following day and by the end of the evening, I knew he was different from any other man I'd met.

"Any significant others I should know about?" he asked lightly, at one point.

I shook my head. "No. A few short-term relationships but nothing serious," I said, wondering what he'd say if I admitted just how short term those relationships had been because, as soon as they'd begun to develop into anything meaningful, I'd walked away, repeating my internal mantra: *You don't deserve to be happy, you've ruined too many lives.* "How about you?"

"I was married, but I've been divorced for six years. I have a son, he's twenty years old. Unfortunately, I don't see him anymore." My heart went out to him at the sadness in his voice but it wasn't enough to keep my surprise to myself.

"Twenty?" I squeaked. I hadn't thought him to be over forty. "You have a son who's twenty years old?"

Alex laughed. "I was twenty-four when he was born, my wife was twenty-six. She was my first real love and I thought it would last forever. Sadly, it didn't. Parenthood turned us into the adults we were destined to be, which wasn't the same as the young people we'd been, and we grew apart."

I wanted to ask him why he didn't see his son but it was early days and I was more interested to hear about his significant others.

"And since then?" I asked.

Alex took a long drink of wine, as if he was psyching himself up, and I prepared myself mentally to hear something I wasn't going to like—that he'd been with someone until recently and they were sorting things out, or that they still saw each other from time to time because it was complicated and she, he, they, couldn't quite let go. When he went on to say that two years before, his girlfriend had died, the first emotion I felt was relief, that I wasn't going to have to compete with anyone, quickly followed by shame, that I could have found consolation in the fact that someone was dead.

"I'm sorry." Being human, I wanted to know more, whether it was illness or an accident that had robbed his girlfriend of her life but the stricken look on his face quickly silenced my questions. Besides, it was only our first real meeting and I didn't know if there would be a second. But there had been, and a third, and now, after denying myself the chance to love and be loved for so many years, all I want is a future with the man who'd walked unexpectedly into my life four months before.

ELLE

PAST

After the release of the artist's sketch, and the emotional appeal by Bryony's mum in the US, I waited for DC Moss to call and tell me that they'd found the person responsible for Bryony's murder. When a month had gone by without news, I called DC Moss. She said that although people had come forward with names, the police had been able to eliminate each one from their inquiries.

"Is that it, then?" I demanded. "Is whoever killed Bryony literally going to get away with murder?"

"I hope not." DC Moss's voice was somber. "For various reasons, it's a complex case."

My heart began beating faster. "I've just thought—if he's still out there, am I in danger? He saw me at the window, he knows where I live. He must know that it was me who helped create the artist's sketch."

"Not necessarily. The sketch could have come from anyone who thinks they saw Bryony in a car with a man. But be vigilant. If you feel uneasy, or see something that worries you, call me or dial 999."

Over the next few weeks I scanned the road before leaving the flat, making sure there wasn't anyone hanging around. But nothing out of the ordinary happened and I began to relax, until one Friday evening, three months later, when I was having drinks with Jaz and some of our friends in a pub on The Cut.

It was five months since I'd bumped into him outside the supermarket but I recognized his voice immediately. It came from behind me and as I turned my head toward it, I told myself that it wouldn't be the same man, just an American from the same region of the US with the same accent. His face was in profile and as I caught a glimpse of it, my reactive body jerk sent lager splashing onto my jeans. My friends howled with laughter, causing the man and his drinking buddies to look over to where we were sitting. His eyes didn't meet mine but seeing him face-on set my heart racing. I was a hundred percent sure he was the guy I'd bumped into outside the supermarket, the guy I'd seen driving the car that Bryony Sanders had gotten into. And not just because he was wearing a pale blue shirt under his navy jacket.

He and his buddies soon lost interest and returned to their conversation. I dug in my bag for a tissue and dabbed at my jeans, giving myself time. I wasn't sure if I should say something to Jaz and our friends. They knew how much Bryony's murder had affected me and would probably rugby tackle the man to the ground if I pointed him out to them. What if I was wrong? I dithered for a moment, then decided to let DC Moss deal with it.

I used my damp jeans as an excuse to leave the pub, telling Jaz I was going home to change and would be back soon. As I was leaving, the man broke away from his group of friends, calling to them to have a good weekend as he made his way to the door, shrugging on a beige raincoat as he went. Worried that he might recognize me, I hung back, giving him space, then followed him out, already scrolling my contacts for DC Moss's number. A recorded message asked me to hold. I looked along the road; the man was almost out of sight and, making a snap decision, I pulled the collar of my coat around my neck—it was a dreary November evening and it had been drizzling all day—and hurried after him.

I was still waiting for DC Moss to pick up when the man disappeared into Southwark tube station, slapped a card onto the reader and went through the barrier. I stopped where I was but when he disappeared down the escalator to the Jubilee line, I began to panic. If DC Moss didn't answer soon, I'd lose him forever. A few seconds later, as if in response to my fear, my call was cut off and when I tried to redial, I saw that I was out of battery.

It was one of those now-or-never moments. Taking out my credit card, I went through the barrier and ran to the escalator. I could see the man farther down, so I hurried after him and caught up with him on the next escalator, where I stood a dozen or so steps behind him before following him onto the westbound platform. A train had just come in; the man stepped onto it so I hurried to the next door along and hopped on.

I had taken the Jubilee line before but only as far as Baker Street. I studied the tube map and when I saw that the end station was Stanmore, I prayed that the man wasn't going all the way there as it would take the best part of an hour, and nobody knew where I was. I was aware that what I was doing was foolish and possibly dangerous but it was too late to turn back and I truly believed that Fate, or Providence, had placed the man in my path so that he wouldn't be able to get away with what he'd done.

I glanced surreptitiously at him. He was staring ahead so I couldn't scrutinize him as much as I'd have been able to if he'd had his head bent over his phone or a book. I made a leisurely sweep of the carriage, as if I was looking around and allowed my eyes to linger on him for a few seconds. If my phone had been working, I would have taken a photo to send to DC Moss. Physically, he looked as good as I remembered. His thick dark hair, neatly parted to one side, was just long enough to reach the collar of his raincoat and I would have bet a hundred pounds that under the casual suit and the telltale blue shirt was the body of a man who worked out several times a week. It was hard to believe that someone so wholesome could do anything bad but the fact was, he'd picked up a young woman in his car and that young woman was now dead. A shiver ran through me at the thought that I was potentially in close proximity to a murderer.

Just as I was beginning to reach the end of my comfort zone—we had already gone past Baker Street—the man stood up and moved to the doors. I glanced at the tube map; the next station was St. John's Wood. He got off and I followed him along the platform, then up the escalator and onto the street, where he turned right and stood at the crossroads, holding a free newspaper that he'd grabbed at the exit over his head to protect him from the rain. Once again, I hung back, using the time to take in my surroundings. I'd heard St. John's Wood was upmarket and I could see why. Tall trees, their branches reaching into the night sky, wide roads and ultrasmart low-rise luxury flats gave the area a feeling of opulence, to say nothing of the Maserati that cruised by, swiftly followed by an Aston Martin. Jaz, with his love of fast cars, would have been in his element.

The pedestrian light turned green and I crossed over the road behind the man, to a street where large detached houses replaced the blocks of luxury flats. He walked for about a hundred yards, then ran across the road, the newspaper still above his head, and disappeared through a black iron gate nestled into the left-hand side of a redbrick wall.

From where I stood on the other side of the street, I looked up at the house partially hidden by the wall, shielding my eyes from the rain with my hand. Spotting a set of larger, black-railed gates farther to the right, I moved along the pavement so that I could see through them. Two cars were parked side by side in the wide driveway in front of a double garage, one silver, the other black. My heart thumped; the car the man had been driving had been black. My eyes swooped to the beautiful white house to the left of the driveway. Its upper floor had four leaded windows equidistant from one another. A light came from the farthest window to the right but the other three were in darkness. On the ground floor, a large bow window curved outward from either side of the front door. Lamplight spilled from these rooms, casting a golden glow over the front lawn. Near the gate that the man had gone through, a monkey puzzle tree jutted above the wall, its prickly branches glistening with raindrops. Even in the dark, it was one of the most beautiful houses I'd seen.

Wanting to see if the black car had silver rims around the windows, I crossed over the road and approached the gates. My presence triggered a security light and as the garden lit up, I ducked out of sight and hurried to the tube station, repeating the name of the road and the number of the house so that I could give them to DC Moss.

Back at the flat, I plugged in my phone. There were several messages from Jaz asking where I was and I realized I'd been gone for nearly two hours. I ignored them and called DC Moss, who, this time, picked up.

"It's Elle Nugent," I said. "I've found him—the man who picked Bryony up in his car." My words came out in a rush. "He was in a pub on The Cut. I tried to phone you but I couldn't get through, then I ran out of battery, so I followed him. He lives in St. John's Wood, I've got the address."

"You should have called 999. If the man you saw was involved in Bryony's murder, you could have been in danger." DC Moss's reproach was gentle but it told me what I already knew, that I'd acted foolishly in following the man.

"He didn't see me, I'm sure of it," I said.

"That's good. Thank you for your vigilance but please don't make a habit of it."

"Will you let me know what happens?" I asked, once I'd given her the address.

"I'll call you if there are any developments."

And I'd had to be content with that.

NELL

PRESENT

I walk quickly to the restaurant where I'm meeting Alex, happy to be seeing him again. He's usually punctual but tonight he arrives five minutes after me.

I stand up as he approaches the table, dressed in his work clothes, shirt, jacket, no tie, and as always when I see him, my stomach flips.

"Sorry I'm late," he says. At over six feet tall, he towers over my small frame and the tension that has held my body taut since the morning seeps away. Whenever I'm with him, I have this feeling, this certitude, that nothing bad could ever happen.

"It's fine," I tell him. "I've only been here a few minutes."

"You look beautiful." He bends to kiss me. "How are you? Good day?"

"Not bad," I say, the feel of his mouth on mine making me wish we were going straight home.

A waiter comes over and we order drinks. While we wait for them to arrive, I ask him about his dinner last night. But always attentive, he's picked up on my "not bad" and wants to know why my day wasn't great. I'd like to tell him about the man on the bus but any discussion about someone possibly following me could lead to a conversation about my past. I deflect to the random bouquet of flowers that had turned up in the office.

"I had a delivery of yellow roses at work today."

"Oh good, you got them." Alex smiles at me across the table.

"You sent them?"

"Yes."

"But why?" Alex meets my eye and I see his puzzlement. "I mean, thank you, they're beautiful. I'm just wondering why you had them sent to my workplace rather than the house."

"I suppose I thought you might need cheering up while I'm away," he says lightly. "I know you'll spend most of your time working. If I'd sent them to your house, you'd hardly see them."

I nod, knowing he's right but also realizing that I'm going to have to explain more fully the exact nature of the charity I work for, how the people who use the services we provide could take offense at such a blatant show of wealth. "Thank you, it was lovely of you. It's just that there wasn't anything to tell me who they were from so I spent the whole day wondering." I pause. "Were you in the area then? They came from a local shop—did you go in and order them?"

"Yes, and I wrote a card. Maybe it fell out."

"Probably," I say, wondering what he was doing in Brixton.

He reaches for my hand across the table. "So, was it only trying to decide who your secret admirer was that spoiled your day?"

"Yes, only that. What about you, how was your day?"

He gives a smile. "Not bad."

"So why wasn't it great?"

"Because I got a call from my ex-wife about Stephane, our son. He was caught by the police with cannabis on him." He grimaces. "A bit too much cannabis."

"I'm sorry," I say carefully, because Alex rarely mentions his son. "What will happen to him?"

He reaches for his whiskey and takes a sip. "Best-case scenario, he'll be fined," he says, replacing his glass on the table. "Worst case, he'll be sent to prison."

"It won't come to that, surely, if it's his first offense?"

"I hope not."

"Where does he live?"

"In Paris, with my ex-wife."

"I remember you saying that your mother lives in Paris. Do your son and your wife see her?"

"My son doesn't but Delphine does. They always got on well."

"Delphine." It's the first time I've heard his ex-wife's name. But then, we've never talked about her because most of the time I forget he's been married and that he has a son. When I think about it, which I do, a lot, this is only the fourth time Alex and I have seen each other. The rest of the time, he's been in the US. It's made the week we spend together each month extra intense, where we focus on each other to the exclusion of anyone else except, occasionally, Alex's sister and her husband. But all that is changing as Alex will now be dividing his time equally between the US and the UK, two weeks there, two weeks here. A thrill of pleasure rushes through me at the thought of him being a more permanent fixture in my life, followed by the usual crushing guilt at feeling happy. *You've atoned enough*, I tell myself fiercely. *For fourteen years, you've punished yourself, denied yourself. Surely you deserve some happiness?* "It's a pretty name," I say, returning to the subject of Alex's ex-wife. "What's she like?"

He picks up his glass and swirls the ice cubes around. "She's very nice, reasonable and intelligent, except when it comes to Stephane. He's her weak spot. In her eyes, he can do no wrong."

"You said you don't see him. Can I ask why?"

"It's complicated. For a start, he blames me for the divorce."

"Were you to blame? I mean, did you meet someone else?"

"No, it was nothing like that." He places his glass back on the table without taking a drink, as if the mention of his son has spoiled his enjoyment of the evening. "Simply put, Delphine and I couldn't agree on parenting. From the start, she spoiled and indulged Stephane and to counteract, I was stricter with him. In his eyes, she became the good parent and I became the bad parent and boy, did he play us off against each other."

I give him a sympathetic smile. "That must have been tough. How old was he when you divorced?"

"Fourteen. Believe me, if I'd thought that staying together would be better for our son, I wouldn't have left. But the situation was untenable. There was never any backup from Delphine. She just couldn't say no to Stephane and he began pushing any boundary I set. He had no respect for either me or his mother and the arguments were draining for all of us. In the end, Delphine asked me to leave, saying that her life would be calmer without me in it and our son agreed." The pain in his voice is tangible. "I was working in the US most of the time anyway so I gave them the space they needed and stayed away, although I'm in regular contact with Delphine by phone and see her whenever I'm in Paris visiting my mother. But Stephane has always refused any contact with me." He pauses a moment. "A couple of years ago, I tried to renew my relationship with him because I thought that at eighteen years old, he might have grown up a bit. But he didn't want to see me. In his eyes, I abandoned him by divorcing his mother even though it was Delphine who asked for the divorce. She eventually met someone else and wanted to get married. Unfortunately, it didn't work out due, from what my mother told me, to Stephane, who wouldn't accept Delphine's new husband." He sighs. "He was an angry child, an angry teenager, and now he's an angry young man. My wife and I failed him horribly. We weren't mature enough to have a child, I guess." He gives me a smile. "Let's change the subject; I don't want to think about my son tonight. He makes me feel a failure."

"I'm glad you'll only be away for two weeks this time," I say.

He takes my hand, kisses it. "Even that's too long. But for now, I can't do otherwise."

"I don't expect you to. It's already enough you're cutting down the time you spend in the US. I know how hard you'll have to work when you're there to make up for it."

"It's worth it," he says, looking deep into my eyes. "You're worth it."

My insides turn to liquid. "Do we have to have dinner?"

"Not if you don't want to."

"Do you want to?"

He pushes his chair back, his eyes still on mine. "Not anymore."

He pays the bill while I get my coat.

"Shall we take a taxi?" he asks as we leave the restaurant. "It'll be quicker."

"No, let's walk. Anticipation, and all that," I tease.

He smiles. "I hope it's never greater than the event."

"No," I say, taking his hand. "Never."

The mews house where I live is situated at the far end of a little cul-de-sac in Paddington. The street is so narrow that it's impossible for a car to turn around, so delivery vans have to back down to deposit their load. Alex knows how it came to be mine and he knows I was brought up in care. But that's all he knows about my past. When we arrive, we go straight to bed and only get up to make a hasty bowl of pasta, which we eat sitting at the island in the kitchen, our barstools turned toward each other, our legs wedged together, our free hands caressing each other, until we can't bear it any longer and go back to bed.

I should sleep well, with Alex beside me. But once he's asleep, I find myself reaching for my laptop. Alex doesn't wake as I type a name into the search bar. Even that small act sets my heart racing and I take a breath to brace myself, then press "*enter*." Headline articles flash up on the screen and as I scroll down, other words kaleidoscope from the text—"stalker," "obsession," "murder attempt," "court case."

Feeling breathless, I slam my laptop shut.

EXTRACT FROM NOTEBOOK 4

I was waiting when you left the office tonight, Nell. I stood on the other side of the road and watched as you turned to lock the door behind you.

The first thing I noticed was that you'd swapped the usual sneakers you wear for work for a pair of heels. As you lifted your arms above your head to fix the strap of your workbag across your body, your navy raincoat lifted slightly and I caught a glimpse of red. And the savage hate I felt for you doubled, then tripled, because if there's one thing you don't deserve, it's to feel happy and confident.

I followed you all the way to the restaurant and watched through the window as you were led to your table, where you took your coat off and handed it to the waiter, revealing a smart red dress underneath. As you sat down, your back to the window, I was able to see that your hair was a little shorter than the last time I saw you, which meant that you'd been to the hairdresser. I like that about you, I like that you take care of your appearance, and that even when you're wearing jeans and sneakers, you somehow manage to look classy.

Not that it changes anything. It won't matter whether you're wearing a Chanel suit or a bin bag when I kill you.

ELLE

PAST

"You did what?" Jaz asked, incredulous.

"I followed him to his house in St. John's Wood," I repeated.

He shook his head as if to clear it. "Let me get this straight. When we were in the pub earlier, you saw the man who kidnapped and murdered that American girl and decided to follow him back to his house?"

"That's right."

The look on his face told me he was dithering between anger and relief. Relief won. He pulled me into his arms.

"Thank God you're safe. It was a bloody stupid thing to do, going on your own like that. You should have come back to get me, I would have gone with you."

"I tried to call DC Moss but she didn't pick up," I explained, my voice muffled in his chest. "If I hadn't followed him, I would have lost him. Anyway, she's got his address now so with a bit of luck, he'll be arrested soon."

He moved his arms to my shoulders and held me away from him. "Look, I know you think you're worldly-wise because of having to stand on your own two feet from an early age. But you can't just go running off after a murderer. What if he'd spotted you? He knows what you look like, you said he saw you at the window when you shouted down to him."

"I made sure he didn't see me." I reached up and ran my fingers through his long dark curls, loving the way he looked out for me. I'd been brought up in the care system after the death of my teenage mum when I was just a baby, and had spent large chunks of my childhood in a variety of foster families, some good and some not so good. When I moved in with Jaz, it was the first time in my nineteen years that I'd felt secure.

I was thirteen years old when I was told by the couple fostering me that I was to have a visitor. A woman had come to the house and had introduced herself as my great-aunt Rose. She was tiny in height but large in body and had a gentle voice and demeanor that immediately drew me to her. It was my great-aunt who told me I'd been taken into care at an early age because the man who'd fathered me had disappeared before I was born and my seventeen-year-old mother, abandoned by hyper-Catholic parents for being pregnant and unmarried, had drowned herself while in the care of social services, not long after my birth.

My great-aunt explained that she had wanted to adopt me but had been forbidden to do so by her stern and unyielding older sister and brother-in-law, with whom she lived and that, dependent on them for the roof over her head, she hadn't had the strength of character to stand up to them. I learned that my grandparents had been in their forties when they'd been blessed with my mum, the child they'd always wanted. But my mum had been a free spirit and strong-willed and when she'd reached her teens, she'd rejected the religious upbringing her parents had tried to impose on her and the relationship between the three of them had broken to the point where it couldn't be fixed.

"What was her name?" I'd asked. "My mum?"

"Elizabeth, after your grandmother. But she hadn't liked it and asked everyone to call her Elle, which her parents hated. It was why she called you Elle. She hoped you'd be like her and not like your grandmother."

Am I? I'd wanted to ask. *Am I like my mum?* "What was she like?" I asked instead.

My great-aunt had smiled. "A handful. Headstrong. But also kind and beautiful. She truly loved your father and the pain of him abandoning her was too much for her."

I didn't think I was beautiful but I hoped that I was kind. I knew that I was headstrong because I'd been told it, many times. "Is my father still alive?"

"I don't know. He took himself off to Canada when your mother told him she was pregnant."

My great-aunt explained that the only reason she'd been able to make contact with me was because her sister and brother-in-law, by then in their seventies, had recently died within months of each other. Over the next three years my great-aunt continued to visit me, turning up at whichever foster family I'd been placed in, or at the care home, to take me out for afternoon tea and to visit London, where she encouraged me to have an inquiring mind and to use both a knife and a fork when I ate. She also taught me how to read the tube map, telling me that I needed to know how to get around because one day, I would live in London.

"How do you know that I'll live in London?" I'd asked, mystified that she could know something about my future self.

My great-aunt had smiled. "Because one day, when I'm no longer here, my house will be yours. When my sister and brother-in-law died, I sold their house and bought myself a little mews house in Paddington. I'd always wanted to live in London and their passing meant I finally got to live the life that I wanted."

I hadn't wanted to think about my great-aunt dying. I'd grown to love her but when I begged to be allowed to live with her, my great-aunt calmly told me about the debilitating illness she'd been struck with and how her health would deteriorate rapidly, meaning she would be unable to look after me.

"But I can look after you," I'd pleaded. I was nearly sixteen by then and desperate to get away from my current foster family, who were loud and rowdy with an older son I didn't like.

My great-aunt had only smiled and afterward I wished I'd never mentioned it, as I never saw her again. When I inquired, I was told she was too ill to come and see me. When I asked if I could visit her, I was told that no one knew where she lived. It was only when I was older that I realized the authorities must have known my great-aunt's address, as she would have been vetted before being allowed to contact me three years earlier. It was my great-aunt who hadn't wanted me to know where she lived.

Despite this blow, remembering the promise my great-aunt had extracted from me on what had been her final visit, I had buckled down and worked hard at school. With the help of grants and part-time jobs, I'd gotten myself through university and I now worked in PR, a job which, if I was honest, bored me.

I'd met Jaz, the older brother of a friend, at a house party at the beginning of my second year at university. He was small and wiry with black hair and startling blue eyes, which spoke of his Irish ancestry. At five years older than me, he had his own flat and a good job and I couldn't believe he'd be interested in someone like me. But the three years we'd been together had been the happiest of my life.

"The car was in his driveway," I said to Jaz. "The one that he used to abduct Bryony. Right down to the silver rims around the windows."

Jaz shook his head. "There are probably thousands of black cars in London with silver rims around the windows."

I moved from his arms. "It was the same car, I know it was. You'll soon see that I'm right. In the next few days, he'll be arrested and charged with Bryony's murder."

"I hope you're right, babe. I really hope you're right."

NELL

PRESENT

Because Alex is leaving for the US on Monday, we decide to spend the weekend on our own rather than socializing as we sometimes do with Béatrice and Victor, Alex's sister and brother-in-law. We've had dinner with them a few times and at one of the dinners I met Béatrice's friend Inès, who works at the French Consulate. It was during the dinner with Inès that Béatrice announced she and Victor were expecting a baby in the spring. Alex was delighted for them, but in the seconds before he hugged them I saw a shadow cross his face and guessed he was thinking about Stephane, his son.

So far, we haven't socialized with my friends. Apart from Sadie, I only have three; Romy, Rob, and Marcus. I first met Romy, a beautiful Corsican girl with long dark hair and almost black eyes, two years ago at a Pilates class I no longer go to. Rob, Romy's partner, is a brawny Scot and former rugby player from Glasgow and Marcus is Rob's roommate from university. As well as friends, the three of them are partners in an advertising agency they set up together.

Although they know about Alex, I haven't introduced him to them yet. As far as they know, Alex and I have only had dinner together a few times. They don't know that for the last four months, on his trips to London, he's spent most of his nights at mine rather than at his hotel.

"You know that Marcus thinks Alex is a spy, right?" Romy had teased one day.

I'd turned from the worktop, where I was pouring chilled white wine into our glasses, and raised my eyebrows. "A spy? Wow. Why on earth would Marcus think that?"

"Because, according to Marcus, a consultant is a euphemism for a spy. And also because Alex spends most of his time in Washington and hangs out with people from the French Embassy when he's here."

"So who's he spying for?" I'd asked, playing along. "The French or the Americans?"

Romy had grinned. "Both probably."

"A double agent," I'd breathed. "In my book, that makes him sexier than he already is."

Romy had arched her perfect eyebrows. "I wouldn't know, given that I haven't met him yet."

"You will," I'd promised. "Next time he's here."

Remembering that conversation, and my promise to Romy, I feel doubly guilty at the lie I told her. She had invited me to join her, Rob, and Marcus for dinner this evening and to get out of going, I'd invented a work function I needed to go to. I hate lying but if I'd told Romy the truth, that Alex was here, she would have insisted—in her charming Corsican way that makes it difficult to refuse her anything—on joining us at some point. And selfishly, I want to keep him to myself a little longer.

We spend the rest of the weekend in the same way that we've spent other weekends—shopping in the local market and walks along the Thames interspersed with leisurely lunches, early nights, and late breakfasts, because we're still in that honeymoon phase of our relationship when our main preoccupation is spending as much time as possible in bed. On Sunday afternoon, as we stroll hand in hand in Hyde Park, a cold wind lifting our hair from our scalps and stinging our cheeks, me wearing his gloves because I left mine at home, a question that I didn't know I was going to ask bursts from my lips, triggered perhaps by the sound of an ambulance siren nearby.

"How did your girlfriend die?" The words are no sooner out of my mouth that I want to take them back. "I'm sorry," I say, holding Alex's hand tighter. "I don't mean to pry. You don't have to tell me."

"It's fine." Alex's voice is quiet. "You have a right to know. I should have told you, Béatrice said that I should but . . ." His voice trails off. "She was killed. Murdered, for want of a better word."

Shock nails my feet to the ground. I snatch my hand from his, leaving him holding an empty glove.

"I'm sorry, that was clumsy of me." He stands there, holding the useless glove, then turns to face me, his eyes dark with pain. "But if there's an easy way of saying it, I haven't found it. I should have told you, I know. But it's the last thing you want to tell someone, especially someone you care about. I suppose I thought it might drive you away."

To my horror, I burst into tears and the knowledge that I'm crying, not from sorrow but from fear, makes me cry even more. Alex, mortified that he's the cause of my distress, tries to console me by pulling me into his arms. But my tears turn to anger.

"You should have told me!" I cry, my hands on his chest, pushing him away.

It's like trying to push back a mountain. He waits until I drop my hands in defeat and pulls me back into his arms, holding me tight against him, murmuring soft words in French, reverting to the language he learned as a child from his mother, as he always does in times of deep emotion. His heart thuds its anguish beneath my cheek and my anger gone, I press myself tighter into the soft cashmere of his coat, wishing I could be absorbed into his body, because only then will I feel safe.

"Shall we go home?" he murmurs and I nod against his chest.

We don't speak as he guides me toward the park gates, or as we walk back to the house. We don't speak when he takes me upstairs, or while he undresses me and takes me to bed. It's only after, when we're wrapped in each other's arms, that he finally breaks the silence.

"Tell me what you want to know."

I don't know what I want to know. I don't know if I want to know anything at all.

"What happened?" I ask finally, moving my head back so that I can see his face.

"It was just a random, senseless killing. If there had been a reason, it might have been easier to bear. A jealous ex-boyfriend, that kind of thing. But there was nothing, just a burglary gone wrong. At least, that's what the police concluded because her flat had been ransacked and her jewelry taken." Alex pauses. "They think her attacker was high on drugs at the time, because of the damage he inflicted."

I don't know if he's referring to the damage inflicted on the flat or on his girlfriend but the bleakness of his voice breaks my heart. "I can't imagine what it must have been like."

"It was the worst time of my life," he says quietly. "I've never let myself get close to anyone since. Until I met you."

I draw his face toward mine and kiss him. "What was her name?"

"Ariane."

"Was she French?"

"Yes."

"Are they in prison? The person who killed her?"

There's the minutest of hesitations. "Yes."

"It was a random attack." I make it a statement rather than a question.

"Yes. She was out for the evening with friends and the police think she was followed home. They maintained from the outset that Ariane was targeted because of the way she looked—you know, well off. And because of where she lived, Belgravia." He smooths my hair. "Promise you'll keep yourself safe while I'm away."

"Of course I will."

It's an empty promise, I know. The wheels of time have already started turning.

ELLE

PAST

Over the next few days, I couldn't stop checking my news apps, expecting to hear that a man had been arrested, or at least taken in for questioning, in connection to Bryony's murder.

It was Jaz who first pricked my bubble of euphoria.

"I know you probably don't want to hear this but I don't think he's your man," he said, coming to find me in the bedroom one evening where I was watching a true crime series while he worked on his new app. "They just said on the news that the car found on Wimbledon Common was a hire car. Nobody would hire a car the same model as the one sitting in their drive and use it to kidnap and murder someone."

"Well, he must have," I said stubbornly.

"Then why hasn't he been arrested?"

"Maybe he has and we don't know about it yet."

But the lack of news frustrated me, so a week later I called DC Moss.

"Our inquiries are still ongoing," she told me. "These things take time."

I wanted to ask her how much time but instead I took my frustration out on my phone, throwing it onto the sofa in disgust.

"Even if he is the man you saw driving the car, it doesn't mean he murdered Bryony," Jaz pointed out.

His remark gave me a new angle to consider. What if Jaz was right? What if the man in the car had done exactly as he'd said he'd do and had chased after the moped with Bryony beside him? And then had dropped Bryony off at a tube station, or in the street, whether they'd been successful or not? But then Bryony had been murdered and when the man saw her photograph, he recognized her as the young woman he'd given a lift to and had panicked.

Had the police thought about that possibility? Had they considered that the man hadn't admitted to giving Bryony a lift because he was afraid of being arrested for a crime he hadn't committed? The man. I wished I knew his name. I hadn't asked DC Moss because she wouldn't have told me. But the more he remained an enigma, the more frustrated I became.

"I need to know who he is," I told Jaz.

He looked up from his laptop. "Who?"

"The man who picked up Bryony in his car," I said, careful not to call him the man who'd murdered Bryony.

"Why?"

"I don't know. I just need to know his name." I'd been pacing the floor but now I stopped in front of the old, battered desk where he was working. "If I go to his house, will you come with me? Help me find out who he is?"

"Whoa." Jaz looked alarmed. "You're going to speak to him?"

"No, nothing like that. Maybe his name will be on the letterbox or something."

Jaz leaned back in his chair and I knew from the look on his face that he was analyzing the situation. In the days following the discovery of Bryony's body, he'd been my rock. He'd held me tight in his arms when I wept that I should have done more to save Bryony, that I should have run faster and pulled her from the car, that I should have called 999 instead of 101. He'd comforted me when I told him of my fear that

Bryony was alive when the car had been set alight, something I hadn't dared ask DC Moss in case I was told I was right. I hoped that despite Jaz's obvious misgivings about going to the man's house, he wouldn't abandon me now.

"If you promise that's all you're going to do," he said. "Look for his name on the letterbox."

"I promise."

"When do you want to go?"

"Now. While he's still at work. Yes, I know, I'm presuming he works but it looked as if he was with work colleagues the day I saw him in the pub."

Jaz eyed me suspiciously. "Is that why you came home early?"

"Maybe."

The truth was, I hadn't been able to relax all week and had left the office at lunchtime, pleading the migraine I could feel coming on. I'd managed to stave it off by taking a couple of paracetamols and a long walk in the fresh air, but I knew it was due to the stress of waiting to hear back from DC Moss. I was on the cusp of something major, a breakthrough in my quest to find Bryony's killer. Being told by the police that their inquiries were still ongoing was a huge blow and I felt I would explode if I didn't do something.

Sighing, Jaz closed his laptop. "Okay."

I wound my arms around his neck. "Thank you, thank you. I love you, I hope you know that."

Less than an hour later, we were in St. John's Wood.

"Wow, I didn't know it was so swanky here," Jaz said, as we emerged from the underground station. "You'd feel safe here, even late at night."

"Maybe we'll live here one day," I said.

He smiled and took my hand in his. "Maybe we will."

We crossed over the road and walked for about a hundred meters.

"It's that one," I said to Jaz, keeping my voice low. "The house on the opposite side of the road with the monkey puzzle tree in the garden."

Jaz turned his head to look. "The one with the black car in the driveway?"

"Yes."

"If there's a car, the chances are that someone is home. We should leave."

But I was already crossing the road.

There wasn't a name on the letterbox but as I went back to Jaz, I turned to look back at the house and saw a face at an upstairs window. If the face had belonged to an adult, I might have thought twice. But the person was wearing a hoodie, so I guessed they were probably a teenager.

"You're not serious?" Jaz asked, when he realized what I was doing. He grabbed hold of my arm. "Come on, babe. You said you were just going to look."

"It'll be fine," I said, disentangling myself, and before he could say anything else I ran across the road.

I rang the bell, thinking about how I would play it if I was let in. After a short pause, there was a buzz and the gate clicked open. Slipping though, I walked up the path that led to the front door. It opened, but only part of the way, as if whoever was there was having second thoughts about having let me in. Through the gap I saw a teenage boy, tall and gangly, dark hair just visible under the hood of his sweatshirt.

"Hello, is your dad in?" I asked.

The boy shook his head. "He's still at work." He seemed to be around sixteen years of age.

"At work?" I pretended confusion. "He told me to meet him here." I took my phone from my bag and brought up a message. "This is his cell phone, isn't it?" I reeled off Jaz's number, which I knew by heart.

"Dunno." The boy pulled a phone from his pocket and scrolled down his list of contacts. "This is Dad's." He read out the number and I surreptitiously added it to my contacts.

"That's not what I have," I said, frowning. "Your dad is Andy Taylor, isn't he?" I added, plucking the name of one of my previous foster parents from the air.

"No, my dad's Brett Parker."

I deepened my frown. "I don't understand. This is number forty-two, isn't it?"

"Twenty-four."

I clapped a hand to my mouth in a parody of an apology. "Oh I'm sorry! I must have taken it down wrong. It's number forty-two I want. Sorry to have disturbed you."

The boy was already closing the door. "No worries."

I walked down the driveway and crossed over to where Jaz was waiting.

"For God's sake, Elle!"

"It's okay, I didn't see him, it was his son that I spoke to." I took his arm and steered him away, buzzing with excitement. "His name is Brett Parker, so I'm even more certain that it's him. How many British people do you know with the name Brett? It's typically American."

"I suppose," Jaz said.

"I just need to work out what to do next."

Jaz looked at me in alarm. "I thought you only wanted to know his name?"

"I did. But I'd be letting Bryony down, and her mum, if I didn't pursue it. I'm not saying Brett Parker murdered Bryony, but he's definitely the man who was driving the car that she got into. Everything fits, his voice, his name, even his car."

Jaz looked at me curiously. "Would you stand up in court and testify that it was him you saw driving the car?"

"Yes," I said firmly. "I would."

NELL

PRESENT

All too soon, Monday morning arrives.

"I'll be back in two weeks," Alex says, as we stand on the doorstep.

Crushed against his chest, his lips in my hair, I want to tell him that two weeks seems a lifetime away, that being on my own for thirteen dark nights is too awful to contemplate.

"Will you message me when you arrive in Washington?" I ask, trying not to cling to him.

"Sure I will."

Another kiss and he's gone. Gray clouds scudding in a heavy sky mirror my low mood and the thought of leaving the house and having to cope with the feeling of being followed seems too much to bear. I close the door on the weather and look down at my bathrobe, thinking how lovely it would be to not get dressed. I tell myself not to be feeble, that I can't possibly stay home, and wait until eight thirty, hoping the feeling will pass. But it doesn't, so I send a message to Sadie to tell her that I'll be working from home today, something I've never done before.

No problem, Sadie messages back. *Hope everything is okay.* And I marvel at how easy it was.

I have such a productive morning calling companies to talk about possible sponsorships—since the article about Drop In appeared in *The Guardian*, the offers of sponsorship have risen, as have the number of donations—without the distractions which normally interrupt my day that by the time Alex calls to tell me he's arrived in Washington, I'm ready to work from home again. But not tomorrow. Tomorrow, I need to go in.

"How was your day?" Alex asks.

"You're not going to believe this but I didn't go to the office, I worked from home," I say.

"Wow, that's a first. Perhaps you'll do it more often now."

"If I can. One day a week would be perfect. How was the flight? Did you manage to get some work done?"

"Not as much as I wanted because I had a snorer next to me. He must have taken something to knock himself out. He was pretty loud."

A WhatsApp message pops up on my screen, from Romy. I catch the words *How was your weekend? Did you enjoy your work function?* before it disappears and I immediately feel bad for having lied to my friend.

"I'm sorry, I need to go." Alex's voice comes down the line. "I'm having dinner with my dad tonight and it will be too late to phone when I get back so I'll call you tomorrow. Is that okay?"

"Of course. Love you."

"Love you too."

I cut the call, then bring up Romy's message. *Busy and not really*, I reply. *Let's catch up soon.* A thumbs-up emoji appears on my screen and I'm grateful to have a friend who allows me to call the shots, who understands it's what I need.

On any other day I wouldn't have agreed to go for a coffee with Romy after our Pilates class when she asked, because I'd chosen not to have friends. Friendships were complicated; they demanded an exchange of experiences and I wasn't ever going to share my past experiences with anyone. I could have invented a backstory but I didn't trust myself not to trip up on some minor detail and unravel the lie I'd created. If the truth then got out, any friends I did have would feel betrayed. It was simpler not to have friends.

It was the same with my neighbors. The houses on either side of mine were empty, bought as investments by purchasers who lived abroad, but others nearer to the top of the street were lived in. A letter had been pushed through my door not long after I moved in, asking if I wanted to participate in a street party that was being organized in our area. I hadn't replied and when the day came, I'd made sure to stay inside. If I crossed paths with any of my neighbors as I passed by their houses, I'd mumble a quick hello and hurry past in case they tried to engage me in a conversation I didn't want to have. Although it pained me that they might think me odd, I accepted it as my destiny.

But with the passing years, my solitary existence became harder to bear. The ache of loneliness ran deep inside me. When I saw members of my Pilates group, who often turned up in groups of three of four, hugging one another as they said goodbye and making plans to meet during the week, I'd look wistfully at them, acknowledging that what I missed most about not having friends was never receiving a simple platonic hug.

The coffee with Romy had lasted two hours and at the end of it I knew much about her life, whereas I had shared only a little about mine. Apart from mentioning that I'd spent my childhood in care, I'd stuck to my present life and had managed to pad it out enough to satisfy Romy's natural curiosity.

"How did you know?" I'd asked Romy as we stood to leave the café. "That I needed a friend?"

She smiled. "You always seemed as if you were on the outside, looking in, wishing you could be part of a group but not daring to make the first move." Tears had welled in my eyes. "Don't worry," Romy had said, giving me the hug that I craved. "We can change all that. Are you free this weekend? Rob and I recently moved into a new flat. It's ground floor with its own tiny patio, so we're having a housewarming."

I'd taken an involuntary step back, instinct kicking in. "I'm not sure. I'm not great in crowds," I explained, needing Romy to believe that I was shy, not fearful.

"It's ten people, max. Please come. If you feel uncomfortable, you can leave and we'll just do coffee in the future."

So I'd gone to the party and to my surprise, I'd had a good time. I'd immediately warmed to Rob—it was impossible not to—and the rest of their friends had been friendly, but not overly curious, and as the evening wore on, the tension that had accompanied me since I'd left the house earlier that day seeped from my bones. For the first time in years, I was in a social situation that wasn't to do with work and it felt good to chat to people without any strings attached. The party wasn't about funding, or persuading people into sponsorships, or asking for donations, it was just a group of people relaxing and having fun together. When it had come to leaving, Romy hadn't pressured me into meeting up again, she simply said that she'd see me at our Pilates class the following week. It had allowed me to inch my way into our friendship, like a nonswimmer testing the water before immersing themselves completely. It was a couple of months before I could allow myself to trust Romy, and to trust myself. I had nothing to fear; Romy was exactly who she said she was and I quickly realized that the same was true of Rob and Marcus. They had no hidden agenda.

If they had, I'd already be dead.

EXTRACT FROM NOTEBOOK 4

I remember the day when I allowed you to be aware of me for the first time, Nell. It was on a Tuesday, and you were on your way to the bus stop after work. I made sure to get close to you, not so close that you could feel my breath on the back of your neck but close enough that I could smell your perfume. Aware of me behind you, you momentarily checked your pace and our bodies almost collided.

I stepped around you and melted into the crowd and you probably wouldn't have thought any more about it had I not doubled back and walked behind you again. I could see from your body language that you knew I was there; your shoulders tensed and you began to quicken your pace, so I did too. I imagined your eyes darting from side to side, hoping I would pass you by and when I didn't, you quickly spun on your heels. But the slight hesitation before you turned gave you away and by the time you were facing where I had been only seconds before, I was no longer there.

The following day, I spent some time in a department store, smelling different perfumes until I found the one you had been wearing. It was

Acqua di Giòia Profumo by Armani. That's your perfume for the daytime. In the evening, you wear a different one. It must be bespoke because I've never been able to find it.

Not that it matters. We'll hardly be discussing our favorite perfumes when I kill you.

ELLE

PAST

I went back to St. John's Wood the following Saturday, this time without Jaz. He'd refused to come with me, asking me what I hoped to achieve by going back.

"I just want to see him up close," I said. "Make sure that he is the man I saw driving the car."

"I thought you were convinced that he was?"

"I am. But there's no harm in making doubly sure."

I arrived around ten in the morning and walked slowly past number twenty-four, keeping to the path on the opposite side of the road. Both cars were parked in the drive, so I guessed that both he and his wife were home.

The week before, when I'd spoken to Brett Parker's son, I'd been casually dressed in jeans and a puffer jacket, my blond-streaked hair loose around my shoulders. This time I wore a black coat and tan boots, and had tied my hair in a ponytail. There was always the possibility that I might bump into the son going in or out of the house and I didn't want him to recognize me.

There was no one around so I walked a little farther down the road and found a tree to shelter under, keeping one eye on my phone so that it would look as if I was waiting for someone, and the other on the house. Twenty minutes later, I got lucky. The silver car pulled out of the driveway and as it passed by, I saw a fair-haired woman at the wheel and the boy I'd spoken to in the passenger seat.

If I could have been sure that Brett Parker was alone inside number twenty-four, I might have gone to the gate and rung on the bell. But it was possible that he had other children with him and I didn't want to ask him about Bryony in front of them. Not wanting to draw attention to myself—I had loitered under the tree long enough—I walked to a bench helpfully placed on the corner of the Parkers' street and the famous Abbey Road, and sat down. I'd thought to bring a book with me and digging a large scarf from my tote, I wound it around my neck and settled in for what might be a long wait. An hour and a half later my patience was rewarded when the silver car came back along the road. Blowing on my frozen hands, I waited until it had pulled into the drive before walking back toward the house.

The boy and the woman were already out of the car and standing on the front step. The woman had her back to me as she unlocked the door and the boy stood behind her, his body turned to the side, a tennis racket in one hand and a sports bag in the other. He was too busy swinging his racket back and forth to take any notice of me as I walked past. I continued to the underground station, satisfied with what I'd achieved.

"Well?" Jaz asked, when I arrived back at the flat. "Did you see him?"

"No, but I saw his wife—I presume she's his wife—and the son. He had a tennis game this morning. Maybe it's a regular thing."

Jaz folded his arms. "And what are you going to do with that knowledge?"

"I'm going to go back next week and if his wife and son go out again, I'm going to ring on the bell."

"And say what?"

"I won't mention Bryony in case there are other children there. I'll pretend I'm lost or something. I just need to see him up close, make sure that it's him."

"Babe, you can't." Jaz was horrified. "If it is him, you could be putting yourself in danger. He saw you at the window, remember?"

He was so adamant I shouldn't go that I ended up promising him I wouldn't. But the nearer Saturday got, the more I knew I wouldn't be keeping my promise. I told Jaz I was going shopping and instead I went to St. John's Wood. I hated lying but the need to see Brett Parker up close ate away at me.

Every kid in the foster families I'd stayed with had had some sort of activity on Saturday mornings. I'd even had dance lessons myself for a while, so I was pretty sure that the son's tennis outings were a weekly occurrence. Remembering that his mum had left with him at around ten fifteen, I aimed to be waiting in the road around that time. I'd just arrived at the tree I'd sheltered under the previous Saturday when the black gates opened and a car—this time the black one—pulled out from the driveway with the boy in the passenger seat and Brett Parker driving.

I stared at his profile as he drove past. It melded perfectly with the one in my memory, of the man who had driven off that day in June, with Bryony Sanders beside him.

NELL

PRESENT

The next day, when I return to the office, I feel so energized by my day working from home that I buy muffins for everyone and eat a chocolate-chip one, usually my least favorite.

A crisis at the charity—one of our regulars, Tony, has been made homeless—means that Sadie and I end up working later than usual.

"How about we go for a drink?" she asks, when we're finally able to leave. "To celebrate having found somewhere for Tony to stay."

"Why not?" I say, acknowledging that if I want the two weeks without Alex to pass quickly, I need to fill the time. I've started online French lessons—it was one of my strongest subjects at school and I want to surprise Alex by being able to speak his mother tongue well—but even those aren't enough to keep me occupied.

"I might see if Simon can join us," Sadie says, shrugging on her jacket and knocking the coat stand over in the process. "Would that be all right?"

"Sure, it will be lovely to see him," I lie, reaching to catch the coat stand before it hits the floor.

I've only met Simon, Sadie's partner, twice but there's something about him that I can't quite put my finger on. It isn't just that he's quiet and barely says anything, more that I don't feel comfortable around him. But then, he's a dog handler with the police, so maybe it's my guilty conscience. If he were to run a search on me, would he be able to find out who I really am, despite my change of name? Does he already know?

I cross my fingers that some emergency will keep Simon at work but he's already at the wine bar by the time we arrive.

"Sadie tells me Alex is away again," he says, when he comes back from getting a round of drinks.

"Yes, for two weeks," I say, uncomfortable that he knows more about my life than Romy. But I can hardly ask Sadie not to speak to Simon about Alex. They've been living together for six months now, along with Kintyre, Simon's German shepherd police dog, and they suit each other. If Sadie was with someone who talked as much as she did, nobody would ever be able to get a word in.

I watch Simon surreptitiously as he and Sadie exchange news about their days. In contrast to Sadie's bubbly, blond-haired, blue-eyed looks, Simon has dark hair and eyes and a heavy, brooding manner, as if he carries the weight of the world on his shoulders. Still, it can't be much fun working for the police in the present climate. And he seems to genuinely care for Sadie, arranging little surprises, a trip to the theater or a weekend away in the country, to compensate for all the times he's called back to work at a moment's notice. "It's not easy being in a relationship with a police officer," he acknowledged the first time we met. "Sadie seems to take it in her stride, though."

"Well, if you ever need anything while Alex is away, don't hesitate," Simon says now.

I can't help feeling touched and over the course of the next hour I come to understand that Simon is quiet because he's shy. He openly admits it, explaining that a stutter he'd had as a child made him afraid to speak, a fear that's still there despite him no longer having a speech defect, thanks to therapy. "Although once I have a drink in me, I'm much more vocal. As you can hear," he adds wryly.

Sadie pulls a face when a phone call takes him back to work.

"I need to go and fetch Kintyre," he tells her.

"Give him a kiss from me." Sadie gives me a grin. "I swear I love that dog more than I love Simon," she says, making me laugh.

I have another drink with Sadie and walk with her to the tube station, where I know I'll be able to get a taxi home as it stands on the intersection of two traffic-heavy streets. As we're saying goodbye, the sensation of eyes on my back creeps slowly down my spine. I try to ignore it but it becomes unbearable and I whip round, startling Sadie.

"What's the matter?" she asks, her hand on her heart.

"I don't know. It feels as if there's someone there, watching us." The "us" is subconscious, my mind needing to make it less threatening, as if it's not just about me but about Sadie too. "Did you see anyone?"

Sadie shakes her head. "Can't say I noticed." She peers over my shoulder. "There's not really anyone around."

"Will you wait with me until I get a taxi?" I ask, unconvinced.

"Why don't you take the tube? You'll only have to change once from here, won't you?"

"I prefer to be dropped right at the door." I give Sadie a quick smile. "Call it laziness."

"I'd never call you lazy," Sadie protests. "A taxi it is, then. Look, there's one." She raises her hand and a black cab pulls up alongside us.

"Do you want to share it as far as Paddington?" I ask. "You can take the tube from there."

"Thanks, but I don't mind riding the underground." She gives me a hug. "See you tomorrow."

Twenty minutes later I'm standing on my doorstep, my key ready, while the taxi chugs patiently in the background. I unlock the door and step inside, switch on the hall light, then turn and give a grateful wave to the taxi driver, wondering what he must make of a grown woman asking him to back his vehicle down the street where she lives so that he can deposit her right outside her front door and then wait until she's safely inside before driving off. But at least I'm safe, not like Ariane.

Ariane. I try to push her from my mind. I don't want to start thinking about her again, I don't want to think about her being murdered. But as I slip off my shoes and hang my coat on the peg behind the door, Ariane refuses to go away. There are too many questions still unanswered. How was she murdered? Who found her? Alex? If it wasn't him, how had he discovered she'd been murdered? I don't know why it's important for me to know these things, it just is.

After the noise and bustle of the wine bar, the silence in the house weighs on me. I walk through the rooms, switching on lights. It isn't a big house; a kitchen and sitting room downstairs, a bedroom and bathroom upstairs. Satisfied that there's no one hiding behind a door, I get ready for bed and wait for Alex to phone.

"How has your day been?" he asks.

"Good," I say, perching on the edge of my bed. "I went for drinks after work with Sadie and Simon."

"Friends I haven't yet met," he reminds me.

"I barely know Simon, so he's not really a friend. And I like you being a secret for now."

"Hmm. So you like having secrets, do you?"

"It depends," I tease. "On what they are."

"Right." There's a pause. "Are there any I should know about?"

Aware of the serious tone in his voice, my heart misses a beat. What if he's had me investigated? I don't know why he would have but maybe it's something he does when he meets someone new. What if he knows, and is waiting for me to tell him the truth?

Panic surges at the thought that Alex might be testing me. "Not that I can think of," I say. "Why?"

He laughs. "I was joking." Fear drains from my body, leaving me weak. "So, if you've been going out and about, I take it you're not missing me too much?"

"I am, I can't wait for you to come back," I say, my heart still racing. "How was your dad? Did you have a good dinner with him?"

"Yes, and he'd like to meet the woman who makes me deaf to his conversation because my mind is on her." Alex gives a rueful laugh. "He found me very distracted, this time. He's made me promise to bring you with me on one of my trips."

"I'd love that."

We talk awhile longer. The five-hour time difference between Washington and London means that it's nearly midnight when we finally hang up. As I get into bed, there's a part of me that wishes Alex *had* had me investigated, because then I'd have been forced to tell him the truth.

ELLE

PAST

I got my chance to speak to Brett Parker the following Saturday. I purposely arrived later in St. John's Wood and as I approached the house, I saw that the silver car wasn't in the drive but that the black Range Rover was. Maybe he and his wife took it in turns to take their son to his tennis games.

I stood for a moment, looking at the house through the railings. It was mid-December and a huge Christmas tree was visible in the nearest bay window, pretty decorations dripping from its branches. It hadn't been there the previous week and a series of unwanted images came into my mind, of Brett Parker, his wife, and son choosing the Christmas tree together, arranging to have it delivered—it was so big there was no way they could have taken it home themselves, even on the roof of the Range Rover—and decorating it to the sound of Christmas music, a fire burning merrily in the fireplace I was sure that they had. As the imaginary scenes played in my head, a familiar longing came over me, to be part of a family, a real family.

I was psyching myself to ring on the intercom when I saw someone on the driveway. Brett Parker was standing behind his car, dressed casually in jeans and a jumper. His head was bent toward the ground and, engrossed in whatever it was he was doing, he was oblivious to me standing at the gate. As I watched, he opened the boot, threw something inside, then moved to the driver's door.

It was another now-or-never moment. "Mr. Parker!" I called.

He lifted his head and looked to where I stood. My heart began to race, and as I waited for him to recognize me I was glad there was a closed gate between us. But his blue eyes weren't hostile, just curious. "Yes?"

"Do you have a minute? It's about Bryony Sanders."

I saw the jolt of surprise on his face. "Bryony Sanders?" He stared at me, as if he was unsure what to say next and I wondered if he thought I was from the police and was realizing that to pretend he'd never heard of Bryony Sanders would be futile when he'd already been questioned about her. "I'm sorry, but who are you?" he asked, moving toward the gate.

"I'm an investigative journalist, working on behalf of Bryony's mother." The words came out of nowhere and I felt a flash of admiration at my quick thinking. I hadn't planned to say I was a journalist, I'd planned to tell him that I'd seen Bryony getting into his car on the day she was murdered but some instinct, self-preservation perhaps, had kicked in. He didn't seem to know that I was the person who had shouted to him from the window that day and I wanted to keep it that way.

"I've nothing to say to you." His voice was terse. "This is private property and I'd like you to leave."

"The pavement doesn't belong to you," I said boldly, refusing to be intimidated. "I've been contacted by the person who saw Bryony getting into your car and I have some questions I'd like to ask you."

He took a step nearer and as his eyes scanned my face, he gave the smallest of frowns.

"Whoever contacted you is mistaken. For your information, it has been established that I was elsewhere on whatever date it was that the young woman was murdered."

"Are your alibis your wife and your son?" I asked, my voice rising. "Because of course they would say you were with them if you asked them to."

His face darkened. "You don't know anything about my wife or my son, or about me, for that matter. If you don't leave right now, I'm calling the police." He took his phone from his pocket. "You have five seconds."

I hesitated, tempted to push him further. I thought he was probably bluffing about calling the police and even if he did, I'd be gone by the time they turned up. But I'd riled him, and that was enough for a first visit.

I moved away. "See you again, Mr. Parker."

NELL

PRESENT

Blinking, I look around my office. The lack of noise from the main room tells me that everyone has gone home.

I have a vague recollection of Sadie coming in and wishing me a good weekend, reminding me that it was seven thirty. But I'd been lost in my past and had barely answered. I glance at the time on my screen and jump up, almost knocking my chair over in my haste. It's gone eight o'clock, there will be fewer people around.

Taking my coat from the hook behind the door, I put it on and slide my laptop into my bag. Locking up the center is laborious. I roll down the shutter over my office window, switch off the light, leave my office, and lock the door. In the main room, I check that all the appliances have been switched off in the kitchen area—the kettle is still plugged in—and activate the steel shutter that comes down over the front window. Sadie has already locked and shuttered the door that leads to the courtyard, giving me one less thing to do.

I wait until the shutter is fully down, because sometimes it jams, then switch off the main light and leave. In the street, I turn to lock the door. It's the part I hate most, especially when it's dark, standing with my back to the road, not knowing if someone will come up behind me. On more than one occasion someone has begged me to let them in because they need access to a computer or want somewhere warm to sleep and I hate having to tell them to come back the next morning, or point them in the direction of the nearest shelter when they're clearly exhausted. But I know that if I relent once, I'll relent a thousand times.

I've also had someone, as I fumbled with the keys one evening, try to steal my bag. Now I wear it across my body on a long strap and hold it wedged to my chest while I lock the door. It hasn't happened since, but the worry has never left me, especially once night has fallen.

No one accosts me tonight. I walk quickly to the bus stop, my bag heavy with my laptop and two books that Sadie lent me. I hate the dark more than I hate the cold. I used to dream of living in a country close to the equator just to have year-round warmth, until I understood there would be no long summer evenings, that night would come in brutally early, snuffing out the day as if it were nothing more than a candle in the wind. At least in the Northern Hemisphere night comes in slowly, apologetically, as if it understands it isn't welcome and is warning us of its arrival.

Although I've managed to stop thinking about my life as Elle Nugent, Ariane, Alex's murdered ex-girlfriend, plays on my mind as I wait for my bus. I give an involuntary shiver, wondering if the murderer was waiting for Ariane when she arrived home after her evening out with her friends, or if he broke in while she was sleeping. I need to know these details so when I get home, once I've completed my evening ritual of checking for signs of an intruder, I retrieve my laptop from my bag and type "Ariane" into the search bar, followed by the words "murder," "Belgravia," and the year 2023. I don't have Ariane's surname but I hope that what I have is enough. After all, the murder of a beautiful—I have no doubt that Ariane was beautiful—young and wealthy woman in the heart of London is the sort of story the media love. But to my frustration, and surprise, nothing of any importance comes up. I try the same keywords, changing the year to 2024, then 2022, despite knowing that Ariane died in 2023. But the only article I find relates to the murder of a young Brazilian woman called Ariane in another part of the world.

My stomach knots as I stare at the screen. Alex wouldn't have lied to me about something so monumental, so there has to be another explanation as to why I can't find any mention of the murder.

When Alex calls for our daily catch-up, I can hardly curb my impatience.

"Can I ask you something?" I say, after we've exchanged news about our day.

"Sure."

"It's about Ariane."

Even from three and a half thousand miles away, I can sense his reluctance. "What else do you want to know?"

The "else" throws me. It makes me feel as if I've gone a step too far.

"I just wondered who found her," I say awkwardly.

There's a pause before Alex speaks. "I did. She was meant to call me at my hotel when she got home that night. When she didn't, I tried phoning her but each time my call went to voicemail. I phoned the friends she'd been with and they said that when they'd left the restaurant, Ariane had decided to walk back to her flat as it wasn't very far. So I went over. I had a key and let myself in." He stops, leaving my imagination to fill in the rest.

"I'm sorry." "Sorry" seems too small a word. I can't imagine what it must have been like to find his girlfriend not just dead, but murdered.

"Is that it, or is there anything else?"

How did she die? I want to ask, because although I know she was murdered, I don't know how. But I don't dare.

"No, that's it. I won't ask any more questions, I promise."

"It's fine." His voice is tight. "It's just that it brings it all back."

"Of course."

Desperate to get back on track, I ask him about his plans for the weekend. He's going to stay with his dad, he says, who lives forty miles or so outside Washington. We manage to keep our conversation going for another five minutes but there's a strange tension between us and when Alex says that he needs to leave for a meeting, I'm glad to have an excuse to hang up. Although his reluctance to talk about what happened is understandable, there's a weight in my chest at the knowledge that Alex had been the one to find Ariane. It shouldn't make a difference but somehow it does. It wasn't even a question that I'd wanted to ask. I'd wanted to ask him why I hadn't been able to find any mention of Ariane's murder in the media but the way he'd made me feel, as if I shouldn't be asking anything at all, had made me opt for something less probing.

I get ready for bed, knowing I won't be able to sleep. Something has shifted inside me. For the first time, I feel unsure about Alex, mortified that I've let myself get close to someone I've only known a few months. Where was the caution that had colored every single relationship I'd had in the last twelve years to the point where I had very few friends? Why I had I let myself fall in love so blindly with a stranger? Feeling cold, I get under the duvet and lie on my back, staring at the ceiling. There's a part of me that wants to break things off with Alex because how can I stay with a man that I no longer trust one hundred percent? But the thought of losing what we have, of being on my own again, hurts too much.

And I have no moral high ground to stand on when I'm keeping secrets from him. Maybe when he comes back, I'll say *Let's be completely honest with each other*. I'll begin by telling him that my real name is Elle Nugent. Perhaps he'll recognize it. Nearly fourteen years have passed since I gained notoriety on both sides of the pond but people tend to have long memories when it comes to scandals.

ELLE

PAST

I took a breath, then called the number Brett Parker's son had given me.

"Hello."

"Mr. Parker?"

"Yes?"

"I'd like to ask you what happened after Bryony Sanders got into your car. Did you manage to catch up with the man who stole her phone? Did you drop her off somewhere, at an underground station perhaps?"

His voice, full of anger, came down the line. "Who are you? And how did you get my number?"

"If you could give me a few minutes of your time—"

"I will do no such thing. If you call me again, I'll inform the police."

He cut the call before I could say anything else. It wasn't the result I'd wanted but his anger only served to reinforce my belief that he had something to hide. The unease I felt about posing as a journalist came back but I told myself that Brett Parker had no way of checking my credentials, given that he didn't know my name.

The sound of a key in the door told me Jaz was home so I pushed

Brett Parker from my mind. Jaz had no idea that I'd returned to St. John's Wood twice since our first visit together, and that I intended going back the following morning.

"Hi, babe," he said, coming to give me a kiss. "You're home early."

"I had a migraine so I left work at lunchtime." My face flushed at the lie. I had used a migraine as an excuse to come home and phone Brett Parker where I couldn't be overheard. I'd been feeling restless waiting for Saturday to come so that I could make my pilgrimage to St. John's Wood and had suddenly remembered that I had his telephone number. And once I'd remembered, it had itched away at me until I had to call him.

Jaz grimaced in sympathy. "I'll make dinner tonight."

"That would be great."

He disappeared into the kitchen. "If your migraine has gone by tomorrow morning, do you fancy going to Camden Market?" he called.

"Can we go in the afternoon?" I called back.

He stuck his head through the open door.

"Why? Have you got something planned in the morning?"

"I'm thinking of joining that new gym that opened up in Southwark last month," I invented. "I want to go and check it out."

He gave me a look, then smiled. "Okay."

I immediately felt bad about having gotten away with another lie. If I'd thought Jaz would support me in my quest to get Brett Parker to admit he'd picked up Bryony in his car, I would have been up front with him. But since the news that the burned-out car had been a hire car, he'd dismissed any notion of Brett Parker being involved, which I found hugely upsetting. In my eyes, he was basically saying that I'd got it wrong. But I knew that I hadn't.

Later that evening, while we were sitting together on the sofa watching a film, my phone rang. The call was from an unknown number.

"It'll be a cold caller," Jaz said glancing at my screen. "Don't answer it."

"It might be DC Moss," I said, unable to hide my excitement.

I caught his look of surprise as I snatched up my phone.

"Hello?"

"Is that Sara Stephens?" a male voice asked.

"No, it's Elle Nugent," I said, still convinced it was the police.

There was a pause, then the sound of the call being cut. My heart plummeted, realizing too late that it had been Brett Parker on the other end of the line.

I gave a little shrug. "Wrong number."

Aware of Jaz's eyes on my face, I held my breath. But he nodded and turned his attention back to the television and I was so relieved that he hadn't questioned me I told myself that I wouldn't go to St. John's Wood the following morning. I wouldn't be able to speak to Brett Parker anyway, as if he and his wife stuck to the same arrangement, he would be the one taking their son to his tennis game. Instead, I promised, I would go to Camden Market with Jaz and treat him to lunch there to make up for not having been honest with him. But the next morning, Jaz slept late and when he still wasn't awake by the time I'd had my shower, my good intentions evaporated. I scribbled a hurried note, reminding him that I was checking out the gym and left the flat quickly.

St. John's Wood was busier than I'd ever seen it. It was the last Saturday before Christmas and it seemed as if everyone was up early, either to travel to see loved ones or to do some last-minute shopping. The first thing I noticed when I walked past Brett Parker's house was that both cars were in the driveway, which surprised me, as I was later than usual. When, after another ten minutes there was still no sign of activity, it dawned on me that the schools had broken up for the holidays and that the family was having a lie-in.

I don't know how long it took me to realize that the house was empty. It had never occurred to me that the family might not stay in St. John's Wood for Christmas and I felt stupidly betrayed as I stared through the gate at the unlit Christmas tree standing forlornly in the window.

Deflated, I began a slow walk back to the station, pulling my coat tighter around me. It was six months since Bryony Sanders had been murdered, over a month since I'd seen Brett Parker in the pub, and the lack of progress frustrated me. I couldn't understand why he hadn't been arrested. The last time I'd spoken to DC Moss, she'd said that their inquiries were ongoing. How much longer did they need?

Remembering what Brett Parker had said about him being elsewhere on the date Bryony was murdered, panic took hold. I searched my memory for his exact words: *It has been established that I was elsewhere on whatever date it was that the young woman was murdered.* I hadn't thought about the significance of those words but now they come back to haunt me. Who had established that he was elsewhere? The police? What if they no longer considered him a suspect because he had given them an alibi that they had accepted?

I stamped my feet in childish frustration as I traipsed along, wondering where he and his family had gone for the holidays. Back to the US, probably. It didn't seem right that possibly the last person to see Bryony Sanders alive would be having a wonderful time, laughing and joking, eating and drinking with family and friends when Bryony's mum was condemned to spending the worst Christmas of her life, mourning both her husband and daughter.

The days until the Parker family returned stretched out in front of me. Jaz and I spent Christmas with his family but I found it hard to join in with the festivities, partly because my mind was on Bryony's mum, partly because I was filled with a nervous energy that wouldn't allow me to fully relax. I couldn't wait for the holidays to be over so that I could continue my campaign to discover the role Brett Parker had played in Bryony's disappearance. And to do that, I needed to find out more about him. While I'd been idly scrolling through a newspaper during the Christmas break, I'd found an article about a diplomat who hadn't been prosecuted for a crime he'd committed on UK soil because he had claimed diplomatic immunity, and a terrible thought had crossed my mind. What if Brett Parker had some sort of diplomatic status?

What if the police hadn't been able to arrest him even though they had enough evidence to do so? It would explain why there had been no news from DC Moss, why he hadn't even been made part of a lineup so that I—the only witness to what had happened—could identify him as the person who'd abducted Bryony Sanders. Devastated that he might be able to get away with a possible murder, I began to make plans for when he returned. I would find out where he worked and if it turned out that he worked for the American Embassy or somewhere else that would give him diplomatic immunity, I would make damn sure the press knew about it.

The more I thought about him having a carefree time in the US, the angrier I became. I was also angry that he'd tricked me into giving him my name by calling me from an unknown number. I should have thought to hide my caller ID the first time I'd phoned him. It was too late now, but as he knew who I was, I decided to give him a call. I knew he wouldn't pick up when he saw it was me calling but I left him a voicemail saying that I hoped he was having a wonderful Christmas and that I looked forward to speaking to him about Bryony Sanders on his return.

NELL

PRESENT

I wake the next morning after a frugal couple of hours' sleep, a lonely weekend looming over me like a dense, rain-filled cloud. My low mood is made worse by imagining Alex spending time with his father in his childhood home. It makes me wish I had a family to visit at weekends.

I spend an hour or so on my French lessons but by eleven o'clock I'm pacing the floor, searching for something to do. There's a food market on Saturday, a ten-minute walk away from the house and, although I'm not keen on shopping, I love cooking. On impulse, I message Romy, asking if she and Rob are free to come for dinner.

Are we finally going to meet Alex? Romy asks.

No, he's in Washington, playing at being a spy, I message back.

Not worth coming then. I wait a beat and another message appears. *Joke. Thanks, see you later!*

Now that I know Romy and Rob are free, I message Marcus and invite him to join us.

I wouldn't have felt comfortable having him over without Romy and Rob because Romy had never made a secret of her wish that Marcus and I would eventually get together. I'd been alarmed when Marcus had seemed to take her jokey hints seriously. When I mentioned that there was a film I wanted to see, and he suggested we go together, I told him that I'd already agreed to go with Sadie. When he told me about a restaurant he wanted to take me to, I pretended I'd misunderstood that it was meant to be just the two of us and had invited Romy and Rob along. Fortunately, now that I have Alex in my life, the problem of trying not to hurt Marcus's feelings has gone away.

Shrugging on my waterproof coat, I make my way to the market, my mood already brighter at the thought of seeing my friends this evening. As I pass the coffee shop on the corner, the smell of freshly roasted coffee beans reminds me that I haven't had breakfast. I go in; Aziz is behind the counter, slipping freshly baked croissants into the glass cabinet. The smell is wonderful.

Aziz gives me one of his huge smiles.

"Hey, Nell! I haven't see you for a while. Have you been on holiday?"

I climb onto a barstool at the counter. "I wish. Just busy."

"You shouldn't work so hard. It's not good for you."

"You work far harder than I do," I protest.

He grins. "I just pull cups of coffee."

"The best coffee in London. Talking of which, could I have a double espresso and one of those lovely croissants?"

Aziz shovels beans into the coffee grinder and presses the button. "How is Alex?" he shouts over the noise.

"He's good, in the US at the moment." I pause, checking myself. Maybe I shouldn't be telling people in my neighborhood that Alex is away and that I'm home alone. I have nothing to fear from Aziz but what if someone comes in and starts asking questions? Aziz would never gossip about me but what if it was subtly done, a US newspaper placed casually on the bar, leading to a conversation about the number of Americans living in London, leading to the mention of an American having more or less moved in nearby but who is away at the moment, which means his partner is by herself. I mentally scold myself for my massive overthink. "He'll be back soon," I say.

Aziz nods at this, and happy that the information has registered, I relax into my coffee and croissant.

When I get to the market, I try to ignore the pervading feeling of eyes on my back. At one point, when the intensity sharpens, I turn quickly and scan those behind me, hoping to catch whoever it is. Most people have their heads bent over a stall, looking at produce, or are engaged in conversation with the stallholder and those that aren't don't seem interested in me at all.

I haven't yet resorted to using a shopping caddy, the kind you pull along behind, but as I struggle home with a bag on each shoulder, I begin to wish that I had. I stop for a moment to adjust the bags and release strands of hair that have become caught in the straps, acknowledging that while fruit might be healthy, it's also heavy. And I still need to buy wine.

I spend the afternoon in the kitchen, listening to music while I prepare the meal for the evening. I love my house, I had loved it as soon as I saw it. Unlike the other houses in the street, the kitchen had been extended into what had been a small garden area by my great-aunt, who, I learned from the solicitor, had loved cooking more than she'd enjoyed gardening. The kitchen soon became my favorite place. Longer than it is wide, it has a small island that runs lengthwise down the middle, with two stools tucked underneath to make a breakfast bar. The sink is to the right of the island, the cooker to the left, and with no windows, the light comes from a glass light well set into its roof.

When my friends arrive, I move around the kitchen, sourcing drinks for everyone, beer for Rob, a gin and tonic for Romy, and a glass of wine for myself.

"Where's Marcus? I ask, handing Romy her gin and tonic.

"He's popped upstairs," Rob says, and I nod. Not having a bathroom downstairs is the one drawback of the house as it means guests have to go upstairs to pee.

"I'm here," Marcus says, walking into the room.

I give him a smile. "What can I get you to drink? Beer, gin, wine?"

"Damn," he says. "I meant to bring a bottle of champagne."

"Since when have you started drinking champagne?" I tease.

"I do, on special occasions. And tonight is a special occasion."

"I'm intrigued," I say. "But I'm afraid I only have wine."

He moves to the door. "I'll go and get a bottle. I won't be long."

"Are you sure wine won't do?" I call after him. But he's already gone.

I look questioningly at Romy. "Champagne?"

"I think he has some news he wants to share."

"Good news, obviously."

"For him, yes."

"That sounds ominous. He's not leaving the agency, is he?"

"No, nothing like that. More on a personal level."

"He has a girlfriend?"

Romy looks uncharacteristically uncomfortable. "I'm afraid you'll have to wait. It's not my news to tell."

While we wait for Marcus to come back, we carry plates and cutlery through to the sitting room. Apart from the lack of a bathroom downstairs, the other thing I regret is that there isn't enough room for more than two people to eat in the kitchen. I could have installed a dining table at the far end of the sitting room but decided it would be a waste of space when nobody seems to mind eating at the low but suitably large square table I invested in. The four footstools tucked underneath it act as impromptu chairs.

"Thanks for these," I say, looking at the bowls of olives, sun-dried tomatoes, and nuts that Romy and Rob brought. I pop an olive stuffed with anchovy into my mouth. "These are my favorites."

Marcus comes back and I manage to locate four champagne glasses, give them a wipe, and carry them through to the sitting room.

"So," Marcus says, untwisting the wire from around the cork. "We're having champagne because it was Rob's birthday last Saturday and you weren't able to celebrate it with us because you were at your work event." He puts the bottle down on the table and eases the cork out with a pop. Bubbles spill over the rim and I quickly push a glass in front of him, trying to hide my confusion at having missed Rob's birthday and guilt at Marcus's mention of my fictive work function.

"I'm so sorry, Rob," I say, my hand on my heart. "Romy didn't tell me it was your birthday."

Rob laughs. "Don't worry about it. Marcus is only teasing."

"You couldn't have come anyway, because of your work event," Romy says.

I frown, uncomfortable that Romy and Marcus have both emphasized the excuse I'd used so I could spend the evening with Alex.

"What?" I ask, catching the two of them exchanging an amused glance.

"It's just that we decided to go to L'Escargot instead of having dinner at Romy and Rob's," Marcus says.

"And?"

He pushes his navy-framed glasses, which enhances the deep blue of his eyes, further up his nose. "Well, as L'Escargot isn't far from here, I decided to make a quick detour to your house in case your work event had been canceled. I saw a light on downstairs, so I was going to ring on the bell and see if you could join us for dinner after all. But then I saw someone walk into your sitting room—and it wasn't you."

The three of them shake with laughter and I raise my hands in a "you've caught me" gesture. "Sorry," I say, contrite. "I should have told you the truth, that Alex was here. But I didn't want you to put pressure on me to bring him along—and before you start denying it, you know you would have!"

"We might have, just a bit," Romy agrees.

"If I promise to introduce you to him next time he's here, will you forgive me for not being truthful?" I ask, wondering if it will ever happen, now that are so many lies between me and Alex. Memories of last night and our near-argument when I asked about Ariane—because that was how it had felt—crowd my mind.

"Done!"

Romy grins across at me. "So, it's serious, you and Alex?"

"I don't know. It's complicated."

"In what way?"

"For a start, he spends half his time in the US."

"But he'll be back soon?"

"Yes, next weekend." Romy opens her mouth but I get there first. "And yes, you'll meet him, I promise."

As she whoops in response, I wonder what she'd say if I told her about his murdered girlfriend.

"Wait a moment," Romy says, holding her hand up. "That's not all we're celebrating, is it? Rob's birthday?" She gives Marcus a meaningful look. "Don't you have something you want to share with us?"

Marcus shrugs. "It's just that I've found a house I'm thinking of buying."

"Really? That's great," I say. "I didn't know you wanted to move."

"I've been thinking of it for a while now." He shoots Romy a look. "Sorry, I don't want to say much about it for the moment as it's not a done deal or anything. I don't want to jinx it."

"Fair enough," I say, giving him a smile. "But we can still drink to it." I raise my glass. "To your maybe house."

"To your maybe house," Romy and Rob echo.

There's a strange silence, which even Romy doesn't seem to know how to fill, and for the rest of the evening, I can't help but notice Marcus glancing my way on multiple occasions, as if he wants to tell me something but can't quite bring himself to. When he follows me through to the kitchen at one point, I immediately leave so that he doesn't have time to tell me whatever it is he has on his mind. I can't understand it; he knows I have Alex in my life, yet he still seems to believe that if he declares his interest in me, I'll drop Alex in favor of him. And that is never going to happen.

EXTRACT FROM NOTEBOOK 4

I enjoyed my weekend, Nell. It was fun following you around the market on Saturday. I always learn so much about you when you shop. Depending on what you buy, I know what you'll be doing that evening. If you stop at the local supermarket, it means you're not doing anything special, just cleaning your house or washing your hair. If you stop at the butcher's for steak, or the wine shop, it means that someone is coming for dinner.

This morning you bought an astonishing amount of fruit; apples, pears, oranges, grapes—green and black—kiwis, and some blackberries. I was glad you didn't buy strawberries, it's far better to wait until summer, when they're full of flavor. Although, if you knew that you wouldn't be alive next summer, you might have bought some.

You packed the fruit into two large canvas bags which you slung over your shoulders. Your next stop was the wine shop and I wondered how you were going to manage to carry that as well. You bought a bottle of white and two bottles of red—South African, a Pinotage, I think—and put it into another bag. Then you moved on to the bakery, where you bought a large loaf of crusty bread. Your last stop was the delicatessen. Although I hovered at the window, I couldn't see what you bought as there were too many people inside. But in view of the crusty bread, I imagine it was a pâté of some kind. And maybe some olives. You like olives.

You carried everything home, a bag on each shoulder and one in each hand. You were so laden I felt I should offer to carry the wine for you. Instead, I walked behind and watched your dark hair swing back and forth across your shoulders, thinking about all the fruit you had bought, wondering if you were going to make fruit salad or a pear and apple crumble, a particular favorite of mine.

Not that it matters. We'll hardly be exchanging our favorite recipes when I kill you.

ELLE

PAST

The holidays were over, school had started up again and, judging by the blaze of lights coming from the Parkers' house, the family was up and about. It was freezing; a soft frost covered the grass behind the black gates and I stamped my feet to keep warm as I waited under my usual tree.

From my vantage point, I saw the black gates swing open and held my breath, wondering which parent would be taxiing the son to his game. I peered into the car as it passed by; Mrs. Parker was driving. My eyes turned to the son sitting next to her and I saw that he was looking straight at me. For a brief moment, he held my gaze but I quickly bent my head toward my phone, avoiding his scrutiny. The car drove on without pausing and I breathed a sigh of relief.

I stood for a moment, trying to decide what to do. In all the times I'd stood watching the property, I'd never seen evidence of any other children, so hopefully Brett Parker was on his own in the house. I was about to cross over the road and ring on the bell when a movement at one of the upstairs windows caught my eye. I looked up; Brett Parker was standing there, staring right at me.

I lifted my head a little higher and stared back, rising to the challenge. I'd left him another voicemail, wishing him a Happy New Year and reiterating my wish to talk to him when he was back in the UK. Keeping his eyes locked on mine, he lifted his hand and showed me his phone and I felt a surge of excitement, thinking he was telling me that he was going to call me. But then he raised it to his ear and I could see he was talking to someone. It took me a moment to realize that he could be calling the police and, throwing him a disgusted look, I sauntered away as if it didn't bother me, only breaking into a run once I was sure I was out of his sight.

"How was the gym?" Jaz asked, when I arrived back at the flat forty-five minutes later.

"Fine." I gave him a kiss. "I'm going to have a quick shower and then we can go to Camden."

"Great."

I peeled off the gym clothes I'd thought to wear and got into the hottest shower I could bear, letting the heat warm my chilled bones. If Brett Parker thought he could intimidate me by threatening to call the police, he was wrong.

I was in the bedroom drying my hair when Jaz opened the door.

"Someone here to see you."

"Who?" I asked.

"DC Moss."

I ran a brush through my hair, hoping DC Moss had come to tell me that they'd finally arrested Brett Parker and went through to the sitting room where she was waiting with Jaz.

"Elle." DC Moss nodded at me.

"Hello." I looked at her hopefully.

"We've had a call from Brett Parker about a—journalist?—named Elle Nugent, who has apparently been harassing him, leaving messages on his cell phone and hanging around his house," she said, coming straight to the point. "Apparently you were there, earlier today."

My cheeks reddened under the stern gaze of her gray eyes. "Don't you think his refusal to talk to me is proof enough of his guilt?" I said, choosing to ignore her question behind the word "journalist." "He might not have murdered Bryony, but I know he was the man driving the car that day."

"When we questioned Mr. Parker back in November, he mentioned that on the day Bryony was abducted, a woman had bumped into him coming out of a supermarket on The Cut and had dropped a jar of honey on the ground. That woman was you. A few hours later, you saw a man driving the car that Bryony got into. He was also American, he also had dark hair and was wearing a blue shirt. But he was not Brett Parker."

I hid my shock at the news that Brett Parker had recognized me as the person who had bumped into him that morning. "So where was Brett Parker at four that afternoon?" I asked.

DC Moss sighed, unable to hide her exasperation. "You need to let it drop and let us do our work. I'm giving you a warning. Stay away from Brett Parker. Do not go and see him, do not try to contact him by phone. If I have to come back here, there will be serious consequences. Have I made myself clear?"

"Yes."

"Good."

Jaz closed the door behind her and turned, his arms folded across his chest. I waited for him to speak but he didn't and his silence was worse than anything he could have said.

"I'm sorry," I blurted out. "I'm sorry I lied to you."

He shook his head. "Not good enough, Elle."

"I didn't tell you because I knew you'd disapprove. You would have stopped me from going to his house—"

"Too right I would have. Hanging around where he lives, calling him. It's stalking."

I stared at him, shocked. "No, I'm collating information, trying to solve a crime that the police haven't solved. Have you any idea what it's like when you *know* something to be true and nobody else believes you, not even the person who says they love you?"

He shifted uncomfortably. "Okay, point taken."

"So you believe me? You believe me when I say that Brett Parker was behind the wheel of the car that Bryony got into? That's all I'm saying, Jaz, I'm saying that he picked her up, not that he murdered her."

He nodded. "But, Elle, you need to let the police do their job. That's what DC Moss said and if she said that, it's because their inquiries are still ongoing. Maybe she had to tell you that Brett Parker wasn't the man driving the car because she was worried that if she admitted he was, you'd go to the press. How can she trust you when you're behaving so erratically, pretending to be a journalist and all the rest of the stuff you've been doing? Promise me you'll stop. If Brett Parker is guilty, the police will get him, eventually."

I was about to tell him that they wouldn't get him if he'd claimed diplomatic immunity. But I didn't want to argue with Jaz. I'd come close to the wind by lying to him and I didn't want to anger him any more.

"I'm sorry I lied to you," I said again.

"Just don't do it again, okay?"

I nodded. He'd never been angry with me before and I wasn't sure how to move on. "Do you still want to have lunch in Camden or do you prefer to be on your own?" I asked, a tremor in my voice.

His face softened. "I don't want lunch but I don't want to be on my own." He moved toward me. "Any idea what we could do instead?"

We went to bed, made love, and all the while, I hated myself because I had lied to him again. There was no way I was going to be able to stop pursuing Brett Parker.

NELL

PRESENT

"I can't wait to see you again," Alex murmurs when he calls that night. "I miss you."

To my relief, the tension that had been there between us the previous day has gone. I'd messaged him during the afternoon to tell him I was having friends over for dinner and would call him once they'd left. *I'll call you*, he messaged back. *Enjoy your evening. Speak later xoxo.*

"I miss you too," I say, all thoughts of breaking up with him disappearing the minute I heard his voice.

I push earbuds into my ears so that I can carry on getting ready for bed while I talk. I've already brushed my teeth and I'm so tired after my sleepless night yesterday that I can't wait to slide between the sheets. I smooth cleanser onto my face. "Only another week to go. Will you be able to stay for two weeks, this time?"

"I thought I'd be able to but it's not going to be possible." He pauses, and I refrain from filling the silence by pleading with him to stay longer than his usual week. I know that if he could, he would. "But the next time I come over, I'll be able to stay two weeks, I promise."

The lid of the bin clangs as I throw the cotton wool inside. "We'd better make the most of the week that you are here, then," I say, reaching for the serum I apply religiously every night.

"Don't worry, we will." The promise in his voice makes me smile. "So, how was your evening?"

"It was lovely. It's been a while since I had friends over." I'm about to mention Marcus having a thing for me, then decide not to because I don't want to influence Alex's impression of Marcus before he's even met him.

"The friends I still haven't met," Alex says. "I'm beginning to think you're ashamed of me. Or is it just that they don't like Americans?"

I hear the laughter in his voice and smile. "They will love you, which is why I haven't been in a hurry to introduce you. Once they've met you they'll insist that we hang out together whenever you're here. But I've promised we'll see them when you're back."

"Great, but let's make it toward the end of the week. I don't want anyone monopolizing my precious time with you."

"Deal. What about you, what did you do today?"

"Caught up with some friends I haven't seen for a couple of years and talked about you nonstop." He laughs. "I'm so besotted I even showed them your photo."

My heart misses a beat—until I remember that I was blond back then and sixteen pounds heavier. But what if one of his friends *did* recognize me? Is that why Alex isn't saying anything now, why he's left a silence, so that I can fill the void with the truth? I force myself to relax; if I have been recognized, I'll tell the truth and accept the consequences.

I turn off the bathroom light. "I hope they approved." I keep my voice light as I move to the bedroom and climb into bed.

"They did, very much. By the way, I spoke to my sister earlier. She said she'd invite you over this week."

"That's nice of her. But wouldn't it be better to wait until you're back on Saturday so that we can go together?"

"She and Victor are away next weekend. It's up to you, of course. Shall I leave you to get some sleep? It must be one in the morning there."

"It is. Can we speak again tomorrow?"

"Sure we can. Make sure you lock up properly before you go to bed."

"I'm already in bed." I pause. "Why did you say that?"

"Why did I say what?"

"To make sure I locked up properly."

"I don't know." He sounds puzzled at my question. "Maybe because you had your friends over and it's on my mind that they left late, and I want to be sure you've locked up behind them? I know how you are about making sure the house is secure."

"I like to know that the windows and door are properly locked before I go to bed, that's all." I know I sound defensive but his remark, although well-intentioned, has thrown me. Now I'll have to go downstairs and check that I *did* lock up properly, because what if I didn't?

"I know, and it's good that you're security conscious," Alex says. "I'm sorry, have I upset you? It wasn't my intention. It was just a throwaway remark."

"I'm not upset, but I am tired. Let's speak tomorrow."

"Okay. I'll call you around seven your time. Good night, sleep well."

I suppress a sigh. It seems that every time Alex and I speak on the phone, one of us says something which throws the other off-balance. Yesterday it had been me asking him about Ariane, tonight it was him asking me if I'd locked up properly. When we're together, we never argue. It's the lack of visual signals, I realize. It's when we have to rely on our voices alone to communicate that there are misunderstandings.

I'm about to get out of bed to check the locks when I find myself pausing. I don't have Facebook but I do have WhatsApp—I'd felt obliged to register when I met Romy, so that we could message each other. It's how Alex and I communicate, by WhatsApp. Yet he has never called me using the video function. Why is that? And why is it always him who calls me? I have called him, I've tried to reach him on several occasions but my calls always go unanswered.

A frown knots my brow, wondering if it's something I should worry about, wondering if I should casually mention it when he calls tomorrow. *Hey, why do we never use the video function when we speak? And why is it always you who calls me?* But I'm not sure I'll say anything. Besides, sometimes when Alex calls, my hair's a mess, my eyebrows unplucked, and for now, I'm happy for him to see only the best of me. If we'd been in a relationship for longer, if we were living together, I wouldn't care. But we're still a relatively new couple and I'm happy to postpone the warts-and-all stage until further down the line.

But still. I look at the time on my phone. It's only five minutes since we hung up so I call Alex's number. He doesn't pick up but instead of cutting the call after a dozen or so rings, like I usually do, I wait. The call rings itself out so I close WhatsApp, find his number in my contacts and press "call." I wait for him to answer and when that call rings itself out too, I realize something else about Alex, which is that he doesn't have voicemail either.

ELLE

PAST

I wasn't stupid, I understood that I'd have to cool off for a bit. For three weeks I stopped going to St. John's Wood and I stopped leaving messages on Brett Parker's cell phone asking where he'd dropped Bryony off on the day she disappeared. But I was desperate to know if he worked for the diplomatic service.

I refused to believe it was a coincidence that I'd seen him in a pub just yards away from the restaurant where Bryony had had a part-time job. It had been a Friday night at around 6:00 PM and the people he'd been with had looked like colleagues, not friends, so I was pretty sure he worked in the area. I googled the address of the American Embassy and calculated that despite it being on the same side of the river as Southwark, it would take him a good forty-five minutes to walk there. It was a huge blow, because if he did work at the embassy, it was unlikely he and his colleagues would come all the way to Southwark for after-work drinks. But I told myself that the embassy might have other offices or that he could be working for a specialized US company which allowed employees to claim diplomatic immunity.

One Monday morning, at the beginning of February, I got up extra early, telling Jaz I needed to be in the office, and took the tube to St. John's Wood. It was 8:00 AM by the time I got there and I hoped I wasn't too late to catch Brett Parker on his way to work. I stood by the entrance to the underground station, my face partially covered by a woolen hat pulled down to my eyes and a scarf pulled up to my nose, scanning the street. I was lucky; less than fifteen minutes later, he came along the road wearing a navy overcoat and carrying a laptop case. He didn't see me as I followed him onto the tube, nor when I sat farther down the same carriage. He didn't see me when he got off at Southwark, nor when he stopped to buy a takeaway coffee, which he drank as he walked toward the Thames before disappearing into an office block. I waited until he was inside, then approached the main entrance. From the plaque on the door, I could see that it was home to a string of different companies, any of which could be a front for a US government agency. I wanted to follow him farther but when I looked through the huge windows, I knew I wouldn't be able to get through the security turnstiles. I watched while he fished a card from his pocket, placed it on the reader, then moved through the turnstile toward a bank of lifts, where he drained the last of his coffee and put the cup in a nearby bin.

I couldn't help feeling elated as I walked to my boring job on the other side of the Thames. I was sure that Brett Parker's and Bryony's paths had crossed, if only in the restaurant where she had worked. If they had known each other, even on a waitress-client basis, it made sense that Bryony hadn't seemed to hesitate before getting into his car.

When I arrived at the office, I found it impossible to concentrate on what I was meant to be doing. All I could think about was going back to the building where Brett Parker worked to see where he went during his lunch break.

I'd been to La Salsa, the restaurant where Bryony had worked, several times in the weeks following her murder. The first time I'd gone, Jaz had been with me but when he discovered its link to Bryony, he'd refused to go back, so I would go on my own and sit at a table for one. Once Bryony's workplace had become public knowledge, it had attracted a lot of voyeuristic customers but I'd never included myself in that category because I never asked the personnel about their ex-member of staff. Instead, I listened to other customers casually asking the waitress, almost as an afterthought while they were ordering their food, or paying the bill, if this was where the poor girl who'd been murdered had worked. And when they were told, sometimes tearfully, that yes, Bryony had worked there, I would listen to the customer's insincere commiserations before they went on to ask for more details—what she was like, how had her colleagues heard that she'd been murdered, how had it affected them, had the police told them anything else. Their questions were so invasive I guessed that some of them were journalists hoping for a scoop and it had sickened me. I told myself that I was there for the right reasons; I felt responsible for what had happened to Bryony so I had the right to know more about the young woman I'd failed to save.

For the next three weeks, I spent my lunch breaks casing the building where Brett Parker worked. If I thought I could get away with getting in to work late, I'd wait outside Southwark tube station and follow Brett Parker to his office. I pretended that I needed to be sure of his routine but I had enough self-awareness to know that "need" was a euphemism for obsession; the days when I didn't follow him were different from the days when I did, flat and without purpose.

I soon got to know the pattern of his days. Every morning, after arriving at Southwark tube station at around eight forty-five, he bought a takeaway coffee from the same coffee shop and drank it on the way to his office, arriving there at eight fifty. His lunchtime routine varied; sometimes he stayed in the office, sometimes he emerged to buy a sandwich. On Fridays, however, he had lunch with some of his colleagues, or maybe clients, at one of the restaurants on The Cut. But never La Salsa.

Then, one gray Friday in the middle of February, he came out of the building with two people I now recognized as his workmates, because he was often with them. As I followed thirty or so yards behind them, I wished I could catch up with them and tell his colleagues that he'd given a lift to Bryony Sanders on the day she'd been murdered. I was busy imagining the fallout when they disappeared into La Salsa. I waited a moment, then moved closer to the window. They had been shown to a table and were laughing and joking with the waitress as she handed them menus, and I wondered if they had laughed and joked with Bryony in the same way. And then, at that very moment, Brett Parker turned his head and looked toward the window where I was standing.

NELL

PRESENT

As soon as I leave the office on Monday evening, all my senses tell me I'm being followed. Hoping I'm imagining it, I cross over the road. But the feeling persists and I can't stop myself from quickening my pace, then breaking into a jog.

As I approach the bus stop, I pray for the bus to arrive so that I can jump straight on and when it doesn't, I push my way through the queue to the back of the shelter and try to calm my racing heart. A man arrives seconds later, as out of breath as I am, and I shrink down, making myself small but fixing him with my eyes so that I'll be able to see if he searches for me among the other passengers. He doesn't look my way but I'm not fooled; it's exactly what I'd expect him to do, to act as if he wasn't following me. He takes a phone from his pocket and keeps his eyes on the screen a little too intently. His age—late twenties, early thirties—adds to my unease. With the collar of his coat pulled up around his ears and his head bent over his phone, it's impossible to see his face. I register what I can: solid build, dark hair and lashes, straight nose, a glimpse of stubble, scruffily dressed. It could be him. I only caught glimpses of him in the past; he would be a stranger to me now.

He must be able to feel the intensity of my gaze on him but he doesn't look up and when my bus comes along and he doesn't follow me on, my anxiety deepens because, again, it's exactly what I'd expect him to do if he knew that I'd seen him. Abandon pursuit.

I arrive home, so unsettled by the experience that I roam the house for a while, unable to relax, double-checking that the windows are locked, annoyed that my day has been spoiled. I'd been having a great Monday until I left work. I'd done something I rarely do on workdays; after having a quick sandwich at my desk, I'd gone out for a coffee and a pastry, and it had been lovely to be away from the office for a while.

I force myself to make dinner and as I'm eating it my phone rings, piercing the silence with its shriek. It's lying next to me on the island but instead of reaching for it I physically recoil. I've only shared my cell phone number with Alex, Sadie, and Romy but there's no caller ID and my heart, which had started racing, plummets.

My mind flies to the man at the bus stop. I slide off the barstool, wanting to put more distance between me and my phone. Under normal circumstances, I wouldn't answer an unidentified call. But the simple act of being on my feet makes me defiant. *I will not be afraid, I refuse to be afraid,* I tell myself. Snatching up my phone, I accept the call and wait for the person to speak.

"Nell? It's Béatrice." Even before Béatrice identified herself, the sound of a woman's voice coming down the line made me weak with relief. "Alex gave me your number, I hope that's all right?"

"Of course." I swallow a shaky breath. "How are you—and Victor?"

"We're good, thank you. How are you? Did you have a good weekend?"

"Yes, I had some friends over on Saturday, which was lovely. But it was a bit awkward at times," I find myself adding.

"Oh, why was that?" Béatrice asks.

"It's just that one of my friends, Marcus, has made it clear that he likes me," I say, a part of me wondering why I'm telling her. But I don't have a female confidante apart from Romy and I can't really speak to her about Marcus. "It's really strange because he knows about Alex, yet he still seems to think I might be interested."

"I'd introduce him to Alex as soon as possible," Béatrice says. "When your friend sees how besotted the two of you are, he'll understand."

My cheeks flush with pleasure. "I hope you approve of our relationship?"

I sense her smile. "I do, one hundred percent. You're perfect for Alex. He's been so happy since he met you. It's funny, because I used to think he and Inès—you remember Inès, my friend who works for the French Consulate, you met her at ours? I always thought she and Alex might get together because she was wonderful after Ariane died. Alex stayed with us for several weeks, and Inès was the only person who could make him smile so I was always begging her to come round and cheer him up. I thought they might be falling for each other but then Inès met Maxime and that put paid to any thoughts I might have had about the two of them."

"When did she meet Maxime?" I ask.

"About eight months ago, I think. It was a couple of months before Alex met you but she didn't tell us about him until after Alex had told us about you. I think she didn't want to upset him in case he'd begun to have feelings for her."

"Did he? Have feelings for Inès? Sorry, it's probably none of my business," I add hastily.

Béatrice laughs. "Don't worry—I did ask him and he was shocked by my question. 'Absolutely not' was his answer. He said that he really liked her as a friend and enjoyed her company but that she wasn't his type at all. And now that he's met you, I can see why. You and Inès are chalk and cheese. Both lovely, but chalk and cheese."

"I really like her," I say. "She's good fun."

"That's good to know because I was calling to invite you over on Wednesday evening, if you're free and I'm going to invite Inès too. I thought it might break up the week for you, with Alex still being away."

I heave myself onto the barstool, my mind racing. If I'd remembered that Béatrice was going to invite me to dinner I might have made an excuse. But I'd forgotten and I'm unable to come up with anything fast enough.

"Thank you, that would be lovely," I say, knowing Alex will be pleased I've accepted his sister's invitation. "But are you sure you're not too tired?" I add, remembering that she's pregnant.

"No, not at all. I'm in what they call the golden period, that lovely time between three and six months. Come straight from work."

"Great—can I bring anything?"

"Just yourself." Béatrice's voice is warm. "See you Wednesday. Bye, Nell."

I stare at my phone, my anxiety levels rising. It isn't that I don't want to go to dinner with Béatrice and Victor, it's that I don't want to come home *after* the dinner. I'll take a taxi like I always do on the rare occasions I'm out at night. But it's one thing to check the house for an intruder at seven thirty in the evening and a completely different thing in the early hours of the morning. And dinner at Béatrice and Victor's always finishes after midnight.

I push my plate away, no longer hungry.

EXTRACT FROM NOTEBOOK 4

I haven't laughed so much in ages, Nell. You were in a complete panic on your way to the bus stop. I'm pleased that you're aware of me, that you seem to know when I'm following you. It makes everything so much more fun.

I didn't hang around while you waited for your bus, it was enough that I'd ruined your day. It had been going so well, not just for you but also for me. I was able to take an unexpectedly long lunch hour and I decided to make the most of it by going to your workplace to see if I could spot you through the window. The truth is, I miss you when I haven't seen you for a while.

I couldn't believe my luck when you came out of the building not long after I arrived. I followed you to a coffee shop and I presumed you were going to get a takeout. But once you had your order, you moved to a table by the window, so I crossed over to the tearoom on the other side of the street and ordered myself a coffee and a sandwich. It was crowded, but I managed to squeeze myself onto a little stool near the front of the shop, where I had an almost perfect view of you.

I couldn't work out what you were having with your coffee. It didn't look like a sandwich, it seemed to be either a croissant or a pain au chocolat and I wondered if you were partial to cinnamon buns, as I am.

Not that it matters. We'll hardly be discussing our favorite pastries when I kill you.

ELLE

PAST

I hurried into the supermarket a few doors down from La Salsa, hoping Brett Parker hadn't seen me at the window. I bought a carton of milk I didn't need and a loaf of bread I needed even less and swung by the flat to drop them off before heading back to work.

My phone rang as I was putting the milk in the fridge. It was DC Moss. I hesitated a moment, then took the call.

"Elle," she said. "Where are you?"

"At home," I told her. "It's my lunch break. Why?"

"I've just had a call from Brett Parker. Apparently, he saw you standing outside the restaurant where he was having lunch."

"When?" I asked, my mind racing.

"About ten minutes ago."

"He couldn't have," I said. "Ten minutes ago I was in a supermarket doing some shopping."

"Where were you doing your shopping?"

"On The Cut. There's a supermarket there, my local."

"I see."

"So I couldn't have been standing outside the restaurant where

Brett Parker was having lunch." I paused. "Unless he was in one of the restaurants on The Cut. And even then, he couldn't have seen me *standing* outside. He might have seen me walking past but that's all." I paused again. "But if he was in a restaurant on The Cut, wouldn't that be a bit strange? I mean, strange that he was in the area where Bryony worked? Unless he works in the area too?"

"Don't be smart." The detective's voice was weary. "You've been seen following him to work."

"If he does work somewhere nearby," I went on, ignoring what DC Moss had just said, "wouldn't there be the possibility that his and Bryony's paths might have crossed at one time or another?"

"Mr. Parker wants me to charge you with harassment." The detective's voice was steely. "So I'm going to give you a final warning. If you don't want to find yourself in court, stay away from him."

DC Moss hung up, leaving me reeling from the telling off I'd just had. A noise behind me made me spin around. Jaz was standing in the doorway.

"What are you doing here?" I said, leaping straight into attack mode. Things weren't going well between us. Every loving word, every kind gesture, increased the guilt I felt about lying to him. It was easier to put a barrier between us, a barrier of my own making.

"I took a day off," he said.

"You didn't tell me." I heard the accusatory tone in my voice and cringed inwardly.

"We need to talk."

He raised his arm and put it across the doorway, effectively blocking my way out. It was a subconscious gesture but it spoke volumes; I was going to have to stay and listen to what he had to say.

"I presume that was DC Moss on the phone." I didn't say anything. "I know what you've been doing, Elle. I know you've been hanging round the tube station in the mornings so that you can follow Brett Parker to the office, I know you've been following him during your lunch breaks."

"How do you know?" I demanded.

"I wanted to know what you were up to so I took a week off work."

I looked at him incredulously. "You've been spying on me?"

He gave a dry laugh. "I'm not the only one who's been following you. There's a young guy, he was with Brett Parker earlier today, he must be one of his colleagues. He was outside the coffee shop this morning, watching you watching his boss. He's probably been onto you for quite a while. I don't know why it took Brett Parker so long to call DC Moss." He shook his head. "I don't know who you are anymore." The sadness in his voice pierced my heart.

"Are you breaking up with me?" I couldn't hide the wobble in my voice.

"You're such a child, Elle." He moved from the doorway. "I'm going out."

Instead of heading back to the office, I slumped despondently on the sofa. The whole world seemed to be against me—Jaz, DC Moss, our friends, my work colleagues. I couldn't remember the last time I'd gone out with our group of friends. My obsession with Brett Parker meant that I was often distracted, barely joining in the conversation because my mind was elsewhere. It was uncomfortable for them and uncomfortable for me, so I now left Jaz to go on his own. Work wasn't much better. I'd already been asked by my boss to explain my erratic working schedule due to following Brett Parker during his lunch breaks. My colleagues knew I'd been badly affected by Bryony's murder and had been indulgent when I'd first started going AWOL during working hours, wrongly presuming I was having counseling. But they were becoming less tolerant and after DC Moss's latest warning, I accepted that I needed to stop trailing Brett Parker.

I comforted myself with what I'd managed to find out about him. I knew his name, his address, the office building where he worked. I knew where he bought his coffee each morning, I knew that he had a sandwich most days for lunch, except on Fridays, when he went for something to eat with his colleagues in a restaurant local to where he worked. There were still gaps in my knowledge; I still didn't know who he worked for, I didn't know what he did in his spare time, I didn't know what his relationship with his wife was like, or with his son. I didn't know how long he'd lived in the UK, if he was here forever or if he'd be going back to the US one day. And that made me consider something I hadn't considered before. If he *was* guilty of murdering Bryony Sanders, wouldn't he have gone straight back to the US once her body was discovered? If he was guilty, would he really have risked staying in the UK and being recognized by someone who'd seen him with Bryony? For the first time, a seed of doubt planted itself in my brain and I had to remind myself that I didn't know that he had killed Bryony, only that he'd picked her up outside Jaz's flat on the day she'd been murdered. And that was all I wanted him to admit to, because once he had, the police would ask him what happened after he had picked her up and even if he only admitted to dropping her off somewhere, it would be a step further toward finding her killer.

A sudden fury at Brett Parker came over me. His refusal to admit the part he'd played in Bryony's disappearance was ruining my life. Everyone thought I'd made a mistake in identifying him as the driver of the car that Bryony had climbed into and I was determined to prove them wrong.

NELL

PRESENT

"Well, look at you, all dolled up," Sadie says, looking up from her computer. "Where are you off to?"

"Alex's sister has invited me for dinner so I thought I should smarten up a bit," I explain, smoothing down the emerald green dress I'd just changed into. "Béatrice is very chic and so is her husband."

"The French always are," Sadie remarks.

"Hmm." I stuff my work clothes into my bag and release my hair from its clip so that it falls around my shoulders. "Are you sure you don't mind locking up tonight?"

"I don't mind at all. Simon is meeting me here. He isn't working tomorrow so we're going to the cinema and for something to eat."

"Nice. What are you going to see?"

Sadie's eyes are back on her computer screen. "We haven't decided yet but it will be some sort of action film otherwise we'll both fall asleep."

I laugh. "Well, have fun."

"Thanks, you too." Sadie, still engrossed, lifts her hand in a wave. "See you tomorrow."

I clutch the collar of my coat, keeping the wind off my neck as I hurry to the bus stop. The weather has turned cold and a light drizzle permeates the air. The glare from car headlights stuck in the usual evening traffic jam seem more intrusive than usual but it's because I'm on high alert. I'm about to make a journey I haven't made before and it's made me anxious.

Béatrice and Victor live in South Kensington, which means taking a different bus from a different stop. It would be quicker to take the underground but I can't bring myself to take the tube.

I arrive at the bus stop and scan the faces of the people in the queue, looking for the man I saw last Friday. I hadn't seen him on Monday, or yesterday, but if he's here now, at this different stop, it will prove that he's following me. There's no sign of him but it doesn't mean anything. It doesn't mean that he's not who I think he is.

A bus comes along and I take a quick step back as it slews rainwater onto the pavement before coming to a stop. It takes me nearly an hour to reach South Kensington but I know from previous dinners with Béatrice and Victor that they never eat until eight thirty. They might have lived in London for years and have adopted many British customs but French dining habits remain ingrained in their psyches.

Their flat is on the top floor of a beautiful Georgian building. The elevator is to the right of a black-and-white entrance hall, with a reception desk where I have to sign in. I don't like being in enclosed spaces so I take the carpeted staircase to the fourth floor and pause on the landing to catch my breath. Laughter rings out from the other side of the door on the left of the hallway, followed by chatter in French, and I guess that Inès has already arrived. I press the brass bell and the sound of heels clattering on the wooden floor is quickly followed by the heavy door being pulled open.

"Nell, lovely to see you," Béatrice exclaims, drawing me into the flat and kissing me on each cheek. "I'm so glad you could come."

"It's lovely of you to invite me." I dig into my bag and bring out a box of exquisitely wrapped chocolates. "I hope these are the ones you like."

"They are." She gives me a hug. "There was no need but thank you. I'm touched you remembered." Like Alex's, Béatrice's English is perfect. "Come through. Inès is here too and Victor is pouring champagne."

It doesn't take long for me to relax, and not only because of the glass of champagne that Victor has given me. He and Béatrice have the knack of making me feel that I'm already part of their inner circle despite only having known me for a few months. It's the same with Inès; she'd greeted me with a kiss on each cheek and seemed genuinely delighted to see me again, drawing me to the sofa and insisting that I sat next to her. They've switched to speaking English now that I've joined them and I'm amazed at the way they chat easily together in a language that isn't their own. I'm tempted to ask if they'd mind switching to French so that I can put what I've been learning into practice but I'm worried I'm not fluent enough yet to keep up. Besides, I want it to be a surprise for Alex.

I take another sip of champagne and sink into the sofa, marveling at how impossibly elegant the three of them are. Béatrice, slim in the way that French women often are, with narrow shoulders and equally narrow hips, is wearing a simple black sheath dress over her neat little bump. Her glossy dark hair is held back from her face with a thin velvet band and delicate pearls hang from her ears. Victor, slightly taller than Béatrice, is as stylish as his wife. Although he's wearing jeans, he's paired them with a blue-and-white striped shirt open at the neck and a navy jacket.

Inès, Béatrice's friend, is even more striking than Béatrice. Taller than all of us, her jet-black hair is cropped short at the back but left longer at the front, with a fringe that sweeps across her forehead, accentuating her perfectly oval face. Impossibly long lashes fan from her charcoal eyes, and her lips, with their prominent Cupid's bow, are painted a vibrant red. Crimson lipstick must be Inès's trademark as she had worn it the last time we met. Dressed in tailored black trousers, a crisp white shirt, and wearing four-inch heels, she looks as if she's stepped from the pages of a glossy magazine.

"Congratulations, Nell," Béatrice says, raising her glass of tomato juice in my direction. "I saw the article in *The Guardian* about Drop In. Alex told me it's worked wonders in terms of new sponsorships."

I smile. "Yes, it has. It's amazing how much publicity we got from that one article."

"I have contacts within the British press," Béatrice continues. "I'd be happy to try and get you another interview opportunity, maybe nearer Christmas when people feel guilty about the money they're about to spend on family and friends and look to relieve some of that guilt by helping those in need."

"Gosh, that would be wonderful! Thank you, Béatrice, I really appreciate the offer."

Inès offers me a bowl of olives. "So, are you missing Alex?" she teases.

"Yes, more than I thought I would," I say. "I mean, I lived on my own for ages and it didn't bother me. But now, when he's not around, everything seems a bit flat." I smile at Inès. "How did you all meet?" I ask. "Did you know Béatrice and Victor before coming to London?"

Inès shakes her head. "No, I met Béatrice when she beat me at tennis, here in London, not long after I arrived in 2021."

Béatrice laughs. "There's a tennis club in Hyde Park," she explains. "It's a great way to meet other expats and for networking. Inès and I hit it off straightaway and found we shared a love of skiing so I invited her to join us on our next trip to Verbier."

"They have this amazing group of friends who go skiing together every year," Inès says, reaching for her glass. "I thought I was a good skier until I met them. You should see Alex and Victor ski."

"Don't listen to her, Nell," Béatrice says. "Inès is a brilliant skier."

"So who's the best?" I ask, hoping to hear that it's Alex.

Béatrice looks over at her husband and smiles. "I think we all agree that Victor wins hands down in the skiing stakes."

"Only because I could ski before I could walk," Victor says, leaning forward and pouring more champagne into our glasses. "You know that sequence at the beginning of *Succession*, the flashbacks to when the children were young, and there's a very young child, no more than a toddler really, slaloming down a ski slope? Well, that was me—not literally, of course, but I was like that."

"Wow." I gaze at him in awe. "I've never been skiing."

"Then you must come with us in January."

"I couldn't. Even with a million lessons, I'd never be able to get up to your standard. I bet you all ski off-piste."

"Not anymore, not since Caitlin," Inès says. "We're so aware of the danger now."

"What do you mean?"

Inès's eyes fly to Béatrice's face, who gives an almost imperceptible shake of her head.

"Why don't we start dinner?" Victor suggests, pushing to his feet. "We can finish our drinks at the table."

"No, wait." I feel my cheeks reddening. "I'm sorry, I don't mean to be rude but I'm curious about what Inès said. Is there something I should know?"

Béatrice finds a smile. "I'm sorry, Nell, but if Alex hasn't mentioned it to you, it's not our place to do so."

"Mentioned what to me? I know about Ariane, if it's that." The silence tells me that it isn't about Ariane. I turn to Inès. "You said Caitlin. Who's Caitlin?"

Inès hesitates and after another glance at Béatrice, who nods, she takes a breath. "She was Alex's girlfriend."

"Before Ariane?"

"Yes."

"Okay." I take a moment, aware of being gripped by the same sensation that had taken hold of me when I first asked Alex about Ariane—that I'm about to find out something I'm not going to like. "So, what happened?"

Béatrice exchanges a glance with Victor, still standing behind the sofa. "I don't think Alex will mind us talking about it," she says. "It was in the news at the time, so it's not exactly a secret." She shifts on the sofa, angling her body toward me. "We were skiing off-piste and Caitlin became separated from us. It was our final ski of the day and we didn't know anything bad had happened until she failed to turn up where we'd all agreed to meet, outside a café near the bottom of the slope. It was getting dark so Alex went to look for her. When he couldn't find her, he called the emergency services." Béatrice pauses. "She was found the next day, at the bottom of a ravine. She wasn't as experienced as us and had lost her way and skied off the edge."

"Oh." I clutch my throat. "How absolutely awful. I can't imagine—it must have been terrible."

"It was. We all blamed ourselves." Béatrice's eyes, focused on the past, fill with sadness. "It was especially hard for Alex. He felt he should have stayed with her as she wasn't as strong a skier as us. But she'd seemed to be coping well and had told him to go on ahead."

"How long ago did it happen?"

"It will be four years in January. Alex was devastated. He had this tremendous guilt. It was only when he met Ariane that he began to smile again."

"And then she was murdered," I say, my voice hollow.

The silence that follows is acute.

"Shall we have dinner?" Victor says into the void. Béatrice and Inès get quickly to their feet and I follow slowly, horribly destabilized by the death of another of Alex's girlfriends.

there and if Fate had lured me there, it was because I was about to discover something about Brett Parker that would help me prove his connection to Bryony Sanders.

I was about to find somewhere to have a coffee when there was a flurry of movement from inside the restaurant. My view was broken for a few seconds by a stream of traffic but when it cleared, I saw Brett Parker and his family taking seats at a table in the window, with a view onto the street. Someone—a waiter—appeared at their table carrying a huge bottle of what looked like champagne. More cars passed and when I looked again, everyone was raising their glasses to the son. When he raised his glass in response, I understood that it was some kind of celebration for him. Maybe he had passed his driving test, or an exam. It was only when his mum slid a present across the table to him that I guessed it was his birthday—possibly his eighteenth, if he was drinking champagne.

The family scene mesmerized me. They looked so happy as they laughed together and whatever the gift was obviously pleased their son because he turned to each of his parents, sitting on either side of him, and gave them a hug. Fascinated, all thoughts of a coffee forgotten, I stepped into a doorway and watched through breaks in the traffic as they bent their heads over tall menus brought to them by the waiter. There were fewer cars around now; it was one o'clock, and most people were at home having Sunday lunch with their families. A wave of loneliness washed over me and I had to fight the urge to cross over the road, go into the restaurant and ask Brett Parker if I could join him and his family for lunch. I let my imagination run; Brett Parker would say "of course" and the waiter would bring a chair for me and I would sit down at the end of the table, flanked by Brett Parker and the man in the wheelchair, and they would ask me about myself and I'd tell them that I'd been brought up in care and had never had a proper family and they would explain that it was Damon's eighteenth birthday and that they were happy for me to join them and—

Feeling eyes on me, I snapped out of my trance. As the restaurant across the street came into focus, I saw that the son was leaning back in his chair, staring at me through the window. I shrank farther back into the doorway, my heart pounding, hoping he hadn't recognized me. His mum, sitting nearest the window, also had her head turned toward me and, fighting down a surge of panic, I scanned the seat on the other side of the son, expecting to see Brett Parker looking at me too. But his seat was empty, and I grabbed onto the possibility that he had gone to the bathroom. If he had, I'd have time to make my escape before his son and wife told him I was there.

I was about to leave when the door of the restaurant flew open and Brett Parker stormed onto the pavement. The fury on his face as he looked across the street at me galvanized me and I began to run. I heard him shout "You!" then, seconds later, a sound that would haunt me for the rest of my life—a screeching of tires, followed by an almighty thud and a piercing scream that came from a lady coming toward me, her eyes wide with horror as she looked into the road.

"Oh my God, oh my God." The woman looked as if she was about to pass out. "That poor man, oh my God."

Above the buzzing that had begun in my ears, I was aware of a clamor of voices as people spilled onto the street from surrounding restaurants and cafés. I could hear a woman wailing and people shouting for a doctor. Car doors slammed as people left their vehicles and ran to help. I didn't want to turn and look but I needed to be sure that it was a stranger who'd been hit by a car, not Brett Parker. It couldn't be Brett Parker, he would have stopped when he saw me moving away and would be calling DC Moss at this very minute and soon my phone would ring and it would be DC Moss telling me that I was going to be charged with harassment. I willed for it to happen, I wanted it to happen and while I waited for it to happen, I turned slowly, knowing that the terrible fear permeating every pore of my body would evaporate the minute I saw Brett Parker where I'd last seen him, standing outside the restaurant on the other side of the road. But he wasn't there.

My eyes scanned the crowd of people that had gathered on the pavement but he wasn't there either. A siren sounded, getting steadily louder, and as drivers got back into their abandoned cars and moved them out of the way, I saw Brett Parker's wife on her knees in the road, sobbing next to her husband's prone body. As I stood rooted to the spot, he momentarily lifted his head, then lay it back on the ground. A terrible fear gripped me.

"It was her!" I swung my head toward the voice and saw Damon Parker pointing at me from the other side of the street, his face contorted by grief and anger. "It's her fault! She's been following my dad!"

And as the people gathered there began to turn toward me, I ran.

NELL

PRESENT

I sit at the table in Béatrice and Victor's elegant apartment, wishing I could go home and call Alex to ask him why he didn't tell me that his girlfriend previous to Ariane had also died. But there are four courses to get through and once I accept that I won't be going anywhere for a while, I try to relax.

It isn't easy with questions clouding my mind, the uppermost of which is—what are the chances of two of Alex's girlfriends meeting death before their time? What about his partners or girlfriends previous to Caitlin and Ariane? Had any of them met with a fatal accident, had any of them been murdered? I know I'm being overdramatic but I can't help myself.

The others seem to understand that my thoughts are elsewhere. They chat easily together about what they've been up to since they last met up and about their plans for the weekend—Béatrice and Victor are flying to Bordeaux to visit his family, Inès is going to Paris to see Maxime, her boyfriend—and I'm grateful to Inès on more than one occasion for drawing me into the conversation when I've been silent too long.

It's a relief when Inès checks the time on her watch and exclaims that she needs to leave, as she has an early start the next day.

"I can't believe it's midnight!" she exclaims. "That's what happens when you have delicious food and great company. Nell, shall we take the underground together? I think we take the same line for part of it? I'm going to Notting Hill."

"Thank you, but I'm going to take a taxi home. It's been a long day," I add and Béatrice nods sympathetically.

"I'll get you an Uber," Victor offers, reaching for his phone.

"No thank you, it's fine." He seems surprised by my refusal so I hasten to find an excuse. "I'm going to walk for a while and then find a cab. I feel like some fresh air."

"Which way are you walking? Toward the tube station?" Inès asks, and not for the first time I wonder why it has to be so complicated.

"No, the other way."

Amused, Inès laughs. "Okay. Well, shall we at least go downstairs together?"

I smile. "As long as you don't mind taking the stairs. I don't like elevators."

It's another ten minutes before we've said our goodbyes to Béatrice and Victor and are standing in the street.

"I know you must be upset that Alex didn't tell you about Caitlin," Inès says, buttoning her black trench coat to the collar as she prepares to walk to the tube station. "But don't be too hard on him."

"He didn't tell me about Ariane either," I say. "He told me she'd died but he didn't tell me she'd been murdered, not until a couple of months later when I dared to ask what happened."

"I suppose it's not an easy thing to tell."

"No, I know." I wait as a group of people walk past, jostling one another on the pavement. "I'm sorry, I don't mean to sound angry."

"You don't sound angry, just upset. And you have a right to be." Inès puts a hand on my arm. "Béatrice will have already messaged Alex to tell him that you know about Caitlin, so you'll be able to talk it through when you next speak to him. Take care, Nell. Let's have lunch together soon."

"I'd like that," I say, surprising myself.

"Good."

We exchange phone numbers and I watch as she walks toward the tube station, waiting for her to be out of sight before I follow behind. When she turns and gives me a wave, I feel obliged to start walking in the opposite direction to give weight to the lie I told about wanting some fresh air. I feel stupid for pretending I wasn't going in the same direction as Inès but I was worried she would try to persuade me to take the tube and I'm too tired to think of a valid excuse as to why I can't.

I walk quickly toward the main road, hoping I won't have to wait too long for a taxi to come along. I couldn't tell Victor that I never take Ubers because I can't be a hundred percent certain that the car I'm getting into is legitimate, a throwback to Bryony Sanders climbing into a possible stranger's car. I'm in luck; within a few minutes, I'm sitting in the back of a black cab, glad that the evening is over.

I rarely chat to taxi drivers. But sometimes, if they've noticed me scrutinizing their reflection in the rearview mirror and think that I'm trying to catch their attention, it's necessary.

"Have you had a good evening, love?" my driver asks and I smile and tell him I've been at dinner with friends. He's in his sixties, I estimate, which reassures me.

We chat for a while and I use the story I reserve for taxi drivers, that I live with my husband and that we have two dogs instead of children.

"My husband is out with his friends tonight and I'm not sure he'll be back before me, so would you mind waiting until you see the lights in the house go on?" I ask, as he obligingly backs his cab down the narrow street. "Once, we got back to find a burglary in progress, so I'm a bit wary now."

The taxi driver looks aghast. "Quite right, love. Don't you worry, I'll make sure you're safe and sound inside before I leave."

"Thank you."

I let myself into the house and flip the light switch in the hall. The taxi stays where it is so I move to the living room, turn on the light there and wave through the window. The driver answers with a wave and once he's driven off, I hurriedly close the curtains, remembering what Marcus said about having seen Alex through the window. It's been bugging me ever since, not so much his comment about seeing Alex but the fact that he'd made a detour down my road in case my work function had been canceled. Why would he do that? Why would he even think that it might have been canceled?

I walk through the other rooms, turning on the lights, checking that the windows are secure, my feet heavy on the floor and then on the stairs, as if alerting anyone hiding that I'm unafraid. But the noise I'm making is for my benefit; the house is less silent, less scary with the sound of my stomping.

While I wait for Alex to phone, I wonder how he felt when Béatrice called to tell him that I knew about Caitlin. Relieved, upset, angry? I try to relax, but all I can think is that to lose one girlfriend in tragic circumstances is heartbreaking, but to lose two is suspicious.

EXTRACT FROM NOTEBOOK 4

I was waiting in the shadows when you came home tonight, Nell. It was dark, so I guessed you'd be feeling uneasy.

I don't know how you manage to persuade taxi drivers to drop you at the door but they always do, even if it means having to back the cab down or do a twelve-point turn to be able to drive back up the road. They never leave until you've turned on the light in the hall and have waved to them from the sitting-room window. I'm guessing you ask for them to wait until you're safe inside before driving off.

Safe. The word makes me smile. If you knew how unsafe you are, despite your bolted door and your security-locked windows, you'd probably curl into a ball and give up. I could kill you now if I wanted. But it amuses me to play a little more with you, up the fear factor, so that when it happens you'll be glad that the time has come. Because, in the same way that anticipation is often greater than the event, the fear of being murdered is often worse than its actual deliverance.

As always, you didn't just turn the light on in the hall and the sitting room, you turned on each and every light until the house was ablaze. That made me laugh, because I could have cut the electricity and gotten inside your house before you'd had time to reach for a flashlight, and I'd have been there, waiting for you in the dark.

Because that's how it will happen when I kill you.

ELLE

PAST

My memories of getting home from St. John's Wood that day were vague.

I remembered careering into people hurrying toward the scene of the accident as I ran away from it. I remembered someone grabbing my arm, telling me to slow down, someone else asking if I was all right as I rushed past them. It was only when I was sitting on the tube that I realized I was sobbing. A woman sitting across from me cast anxious glances my way and I avoided eye contact, not wanting to be asked if I needed help.

The next thing I remembered was fumbling with my keys, trying to open the door to Jaz's apartment and barely managing because I was shaking so much. And then, lying in bed, shaking with shock, weeping and praying that Brett Parker would be all right.

Sometime later, there was a buzz on the intercom and I knew instinctively that it was DC Moss. I didn't answer, and I imagined the DC trying other flats, and hoped no one would let her into the building. But someone must have, because shortly after there was a knock on the door.

"Elle, it's DC Moss. If you're there, can you let me in, please?"

The sound of her voice sent my stress levels soaring. I buried myself deeper in the bed.

"Elle, we need to talk."

I rammed my fingers into my ears to block out the sound of her voice, hoping that Jaz wouldn't arrive home from his weekend away and let her in. But he only returned later that night, long after DC Moss had left and when he opened the bedroom door, I pretended to be asleep, knowing he'd be wondering why I was sleeping in the bedroom when I'd been sleeping on the sofa for the last couple of months. He eventually closed the door, deciding to leave me where I was, and a part of me wanted to call him back and tell him what had happened. But I was afraid of what I might see on his face when I told him Brett Parker had been hit by a car because of me. All I could hope was that he hadn't been badly hurt.

I must have dropped off because I was brusquely awakened from an uneasy sleep by the slamming of the bedroom door against the wall as it was flung open. Disoriented, I emerged from under the covers. Jaz was standing in the doorway, looking as if he too had been pulled abruptly from sleep.

"Elle, what the hell is going on? There are people outside in the street, I think they're reporters. They've been ringing on the doorbell, didn't you hear them?"

"Reporters?" I looked at him dazedly. Through the open bedroom door I heard a clamor of voices from the road.

"Yes." Jaz ran his hand through his hair, a sign of his agitation. "They're shouting your name and something about Brett Parker. They're saying he's dead. Why are they telling you that he's dead?"

"Dead?" I stared at him wide-eyed. "Brett Parker is dead?"

"Yes, Elle, dead." He looked suddenly frightened. "What have you done, Elle? What the hell have you done?"

NELL

PRESENT

"Nell, is everything okay?" Sadie asks, putting her head around my office door. "Apart from the weather. Who would have thought that rain could be so unrelenting?" she adds with a grimace.

I check back in with difficulty. "Yes, everything's fine." I give Sadie a quick smile. "It was a late night."

"Was it fun?" Sadie pulls a chair out from under the desk and sits herself down, ready for a catch-up. "The dinner at Alex's sister's?"

"Yes, it was lovely. Too much to eat and drink but that was only my fault. What about you, did you find a film to keep you both awake?"

Sadie shakes her head, sending her curls bouncing. "Simon was held up at work, so date night was off. It's not the first time and it probably won't be the last." She sounds so unbothered that I decide Sadie is perfect for Simon. She seems to relish the drama involved in having a partner who is called to deal with an emergency or has to work late because something has come up.

"That's a shame," I say. "That you didn't get to go out, I mean."

Sadie leans forward. "So what did you eat? You said Béatrice is an amazing cook."

"Er . . . duck, yes, we had duck. And cheese. And other things too." My voice trails off.

Sadie tilts her head, appraising me. "You're not really in a mood for talking, are you?"

"Not really, no."

"Shall I leave you to get on with it?"

"Yes, thanks, Sadie."

I wait until Sadie has closed the door, then push my chair away from the desk, finally giving in to the crushing disappointment that had enveloped me when I woke this morning and realized that Alex hadn't called last night. I've tried to find excuses for him—despite what Inès said, Béatrice might not have messaged him to tell him they'd told me about Caitlin. But why hadn't he told me about Caitlin himself, when we had talked about our significant others? Even if Caitlin had been a relatively new girlfriend, wasn't the fact of her death enough for her to become significant?

These are the thoughts that plague me until I leave the office. I'd hoped that Alex would call me during the day but he hadn't, and I refuse to phone him. Besides, if I did, he probably wouldn't answer, which would upset me even more.

Sadie has already left so I go through the evening ritual of locking up, then activate the steel shutter over the front window, making sure it has fully closed before stepping into pouring rain. For a Thursday night the street is strangely deserted; the bad weather has sent people scurrying home. I curse under my breath. How had I not noticed it was raining? I have an umbrella in my bag but I can't juggle an umbrella, my bag, and the keys so I hunch further into my coat while I turn to lock the door. Rain spilling off the roof drips down the back of my neck, adding to my misery.

"Elle."

The word, softly spoken, comes from behind me. It strikes such terror in my heart that I freeze, the key still in the lock. My heart judders, stops, then surges ahead, palpitating wildly in my chest. I had always known he would come for me but now that the moment is here, I wonder how I could have been so blasé. Why hadn't I done more to protect myself? Was it because I'd subconsciously accepted the inevitable? Blood drums in my ears. *This is it, this is it, this is where it ends.* I tense my body and wait for the blow, the stab of a knife. I should scream—but I can't. Fear has trapped my breath in my throat.

I dig deep inside myself and find a small pocket of defiance. I refuse to die with my back to him. I will turn and face him, look him in the eye.

As I slide the key from the lock, something clicks in my mind. I can use the key as a weapon, gouge his eyes with it. Glad of the protective barrier of my bag across my chest, I spin around, my hand poised, the key at the ready.

I knew who I was going to find standing behind me. But it isn't him. Alex is there, an umbrella shielding him from the rain, his eyes wide with concern. Weak with relief, my knees buckle. But my relief soon turns to horror. He had called me Elle.

"Nell." He puts his free hand on my arm, gently lowering the key toward the ground. "I'm sorry, did I scare you?"

I don't let my face betray my terror. Instead, I let myself be pulled into a skewed one-armed embrace, my bag trapped awkwardly between us and silently accept the kisses he places in my hair. Above the sound of the rain splashing onto his umbrella, I listen to his tender explanation of how he has come to be here, how, following a message from Béatrice last night, he took the first available flight out of Washington, only to have it diverted back to Washington an hour later when a passenger on board became seriously ill. How they'd had to wait on the tarmac for the passenger to be taken off before they were finally loaded onto another flight.

"I was meant to arrive early this morning," he finishes. "I thought I'd be able to see you before you left for work. But I only got here at one o'clock and I didn't want to disturb you while you were working. I'm sorry."

I hear only half of his words. He had called me Elle. Or had he?

Had I imagined it, had my mind heard the word I've been expecting to hear ever since I became aware that someone was following me? I want to ask him *Did you call me Elle?* But either way, he would deny it.

My silence and the tension in my body reaches him. He moves back, searching my face. But I can't look at him. I can't let him in until I'm sure.

"Nell," he says again and this time there's anguish in his voice. "Please, will you let me explain? About Caitlin." He looks around. "Is there somewhere we can go?"

I find my voice. "No."

He nods, releases me. "As you wish. Will you be all right getting home?" The formal tone in his voice takes me by surprise. I hadn't meant for him to leave. What I'd meant was that I didn't know of anywhere nearby where we could go to discuss Caitlin. But perhaps it's for the best.

"Yes, I'll be fine," I say, still unable to meet his eyes.

"Here, take my umbrella."

"I have one in my bag."

"All right." He pauses. "When—if—you feel like talking, call me. Anytime, day or night."

Now I look at him. I raise my head, look straight into his eyes. They are darker than I've ever seen them.

"But whenever I call, you never pick up."

A shadow crosses his face. "I will," he says. "I promise."

He turns and walks away and the fear that he might never come back makes me want to run after him, wrap my arms tight around him and ask him never to leave me. I pray for him not to turn around, not to pause and look back at me because in that moment, I realize he is both my weakness and my strength and that I'd go to him in a heartbeat. But he doesn't pause, he doesn't look back, he walks steadily away from me, physically marking the emotional distance between us.

I walk to the bus stop, each step an effort, barely noticing the rain that quickly soaks my hair. I'm desperate to be home and I want to move faster but I'm still in shock. *Elle, Elle, Elle.* The name echoes in my brain. Either he said Nell, and my fear converted it to Elle, or he knows, and is playing with me.

On the bus I sit huddled against the window, my eyes closed, blocking out the world. I think about Alex, about how he must have felt when Béatrice told him that I knew about Caitlin, how he'd jumped on the first plane to London so that he could talk to me face-to-face. I imagine the frustration he must have felt when his flight was diverted, resulting in him arriving in London this afternoon instead of this morning and how he'd had to kill time while he waited for me to finish work. And then I wonder—why didn't he call and tell me he was coming?

The bus arrives at my stop, I get off, walk the short distance home. When I arrive, once I've turned on the light in the hall and locked the door behind me, the relief is overwhelming. I am home. I am safe.

I hang my coat behind the door, desperate for a hot shower. But first I need to check each room. As I start to move down the hallway, I come to an abrupt stop. I stand very still, waiting for the soul of the house to settle around me. And that's when I know.

Someone has been here, inside my house.

ELLE

PAST

I sat in the police station where I'd been taken for questioning. DC Moss and a PC had come to Jaz's flat to escort me through the crowd of reporters. It seemed that the death of an American expat, who'd worked for one of Silicon Valley's top IT companies was big news, especially as a young woman seemed to be involved in his death, and I had cowered from the microphones thrust under my bowed head and the questions fired at me.

"What is your involvement with Brett Parker, Elle?"

"Do you know that he's dead?"

"His son is saying that you hounded his dad to death, is that true, Elle?"

"Is it true that you masqueraded as a reporter to try and get access to him?"

"Is it true that you accused him of being involved in Bryony Sanders's murder?"

"How do they know?" I'd shouted down the phone to DC Moss when I called her to tell her there were reporters outside the flat. "Did you tell them my name, where I live?"

"No, of course not." DC Moss's voice had been calm.

"Then who? Someone must have!"

"Reporters have ways of finding out such things. I need you to come to the station, Elle. Brett Parker is dead and his wife and son are accusing you of manslaughter."

My teeth had been chattering so hard I could hardly speak. "It—it was an accident. He—he mustn't have looked when he was crossing the road."

"We'll talk about it at the station. We're on our way to fetch you."

She had cautioned me as soon as she'd arrived at the flat, charging me with involuntary manslaughter. The words rang through my brain in a never-ending loop—*involuntary manslaughter, involuntary manslaughter, involuntary manslaughter*. Sitting at the police station on a hard plastic chair with DC Moss and a PC sitting opposite, a tape recorder on the table between them, I couldn't stop shaking. I guessed that Brett Parker's wife, in the aftermath of the accident, had told the police that the reason her husband had run across the road without looking was because he was being harassed by a journalist looking into Bryony Sanders's death. Mrs. Parker must have given them my name and told them I'd been following her husband for months, and that seeing me watching them in the restaurant where they'd gone to celebrate their son's eighteenth birthday had incensed him so much that he'd gone to confront me.

Over the next few weeks, the story took on a momentum of its own. Maybe it was because I'd pretended to be a journalist that the press were particularly vicious toward me. When the police went on record to say that there was no proof at all to connect Brett Parker to the murder of Bryony Sanders and that they had told me that, I was vilified on both sides of the Atlantic. The persecution was relentless. Journalists camped in the street outside the flat. No longer able to go to work, I resigned from my job before they could sack me. Articles appeared in the British press portraying me as a stalker. The American press went further, calling me a murderer. Jaz, hounded by reporters whenever he left the flat, became more and more grim-faced. Coupled with the crushing guilt I felt over Brett Parker's death, I thought my life couldn't get any worse.

But it did.

NELL

PRESENT

I stand by the front door, a knife in my hand, waiting for Sadie and Simon to arrive. It's twenty minutes since I called them, so they'll be here soon.

I could have called Romy but I chose Sadie because I remembered her saying that she and Simon were having dinner tonight to replace the date night they should have had on Wednesday when Simon was unexpectedly called into work. And I need Simon here because he'll know how to check for signs of an intruder.

I hear their voices outside and hurry to the kitchen to replace the knife in the wooden block.

"Nell, it's us," Sadie calls. "Can you let us in?"

I'd already unlocked the door in case the intruder was still in the house and I needed to make a quick exit. I didn't think that he was but I'd armed myself with a knife anyway.

I open the door and move aside to let them in, reassured when I see that they've brought Kintyre with them.

"Thank you for coming," I say. "I'm sorry for dragging you away from your dinner."

"You didn't," Sadie says, giving me a hug. "We hadn't sat down, we were in the bar having drinks."

"Can you tell me what happened?" Simon asks, already in work mode. He takes off his coat and hangs it on the hook behind the door, then takes Kintyre's lead from Sadie. "Did you hear anything, see anyone?"

"No, nothing like that. I came in and I was about to check the rooms—" I stop, blushing. "It's something I do when Alex is away. I never used to but the house feels different when he isn't here."

"I know what you mean," Sadie says fervently. "I never minded living alone but now, when Simon is on night shift and I'm on my own in the flat, I jump at every sound."

I smile at her gratefully.

"What made you think someone had been in the house?" Simon asks. "Had something been moved, was there something missing?"

"No. It was just a feeling I had. I know someone has been here, I can sense it. I know that sounds lame but it's true."

"Then we need to find how they got in. Shall I take a look around?"

"Yes, please." I remember that Simon doesn't know the house. "There's just the kitchen and sitting room down here and a bedroom and bathroom upstairs."

"Let's start with the kitchen." He moves down the hall with Kintyre. "Before I go in, I want you to stand in the doorway and take a good look around. Do you notice anything unusual? Don't go all the way in yet."

I stand beside him and scan the room slowly, checking that everything is in its place. "It seems fine," I tell him.

"Okay. Now go farther in."

I move to the island and let my eyes roam the areas of the kitchen I hadn't been able to see from the doorway. Nothing has changed; it's exactly as I left it that morning.

Simon looks up at the light well. "Well, whoever it was didn't get in through there," he says. "Shall we check the rest of the house?"

"Why don't I put the kettle on while you do that?" Sadie says.

"Thanks." I point. "There's tea in the cupboard."

It's another ten minutes before I join Sadie in the kitchen.

"Well?" Sadie asks.

"Nothing. There's nothing out of place. At least, not that I can see." I give her a rueful grin. "You must think I'm mad."

"You're the most rational person I know," Sadie says, handing me a mug of tea. "If you say someone has been in your house, then someone has been in your house."

"Simon checked the windows from the inside and he's checking outside now to see where they got in. I've given him a flashlight."

"It's a shame Alex is away. When is he back?"

I take a sip of tea. "I'm not sure."

We fall into silence, our hands cupped around our mugs. But Sadie abhors silence and is soon chatting about ideas for more workshops at the charity. I let her words flow over me, grateful that she isn't expecting me to respond, and think about Alex. Why hadn't I phoned him as soon as I knew someone had been in the house? Shouldn't he have been my first port of call? He would have come straight over, he would have been glad to have a reason to see me after our awkward conversation outside my workplace less than an hour before. But I had called Sadie. What did that say about him, about me? About us as a couple?

Simon appears in the doorway, Kintyre at his heels.

"The windows are all fine," he says. "Not a scratch, nothing to indicate that any of them have been forced open. So if there was someone here, the only way they'd have been able to get in is through the front door."

"It's not possible that they got in through the front door," I say. "I'm the only one with a key."

"You don't have a spare?"

"No."

He comes over to the island and Sadie hands him a mug of tea. "Where do you keep your key?"

"In my bag, even when I'm here in the house. When I come in, I lock the door and put the key back in my handbag. That way I always know where it is." I fetch my bag from the hall, take my key from the zip pocket and hold it up.

"And nobody has ever asked to have a copy of the key made? Previous partners?" He pauses. "Present partners?"

"No. Are you sure there's no sign of forced entry?"

"Absolutely sure. Is there any way that someone could have taken your key without you knowing and had a copy made before putting it back in your bag?"

I take a moment to consider what he said. At work, I keep my bag under my desk. The only people who go into my office are Sadie and the other volunteers and I'm usually present. If I'm not, if I'm in the main room, they only go in to put something on my desk. I've never seen anyone hanging around in my office or hovering outside waiting for me to leave. And when I'm at home, my bag is either with me in the kitchen, or in the bedroom. The only visitors I have are Romy, Rob, and Marcus and when they're here, we have dinner, they leave and I use my key to lock the door behind them. There has never been an occasion when I haven't been able to find my key.

Simon and Sadie are both looking at me and I know they're wondering about Alex, it's as clear as if his name was written across their foreheads. It's true that he would have had plenty of opportunities to take my key from my bag. But he has never once left the house without me, which means he couldn't have had a copy made. And when we've gone out together, I lock the door when we leave and open it again when we come back, using the one and only key.

"No," I say firmly. "Nobody could have taken my key and had a copy made without me knowing."

"Then I'm sorry, Nell, it isn't possible that someone got in, not unless they know how to pick a lock. And your lock is one of the best. They would have to be extremely skilled to be able to pick it."

"But it would be possible?"

"Yes, if they were a criminal. But a criminal would only come into your house if they were going to steal something and you said that nothing is missing." Simon pauses. "Or unless they meant you harm. And that's not likely, unless they have a grudge against you." Another pause. "It might be something to consider, although I can't imagine that you have any enemies," he finishes with a smile.

I hide a shiver. "Not that I know of."

"What about someone breaking in hoping to steal something valuable then leaving again empty-handed when they see that there isn't anything they wanted?" Sadie asks.

"That's possible," Simon concedes.

"Can you tell if a lock has been picked?" I ask.

"I wouldn't be able to but a professional might. If you really think someone managed to get in, you should get the lock changed. And have a second one installed."

I nod. "I'll do that."

"Why don't you come and spend the night at ours?" Sadie suggests. "We have a spare bedroom. Then you can call a locksmith tomorrow."

"Thank you, but I'll be fine, especially now that Simon has checked the house and the windows." I look toward the stairs. "Would you excuse me a minute?"

I run upstairs, supposedly to use the bathroom. But I don't go to the bathroom, I go to the bedroom and check the wardrobe to make sure no one is hiding inside. I feel horribly foolish as I close the doors but when I was in the bedroom with Simon, he hadn't checked the wardrobe and I hadn't liked to ask.

I'm about to go downstairs when I stop, thinking about what Simon had said about someone potentially taking my key and having a copy made. The only people who've been in the house in the last couple of weeks are Romy, Rob, and Marcus, the night I invited them to dinner. My bag was in the bedroom that evening and they'd all come up to use the bathroom at some point, so they'd all had the opportunity to take my key. But I had used my key to lock the door behind them when they'd left.

Something niggles away at me, something to do with Marcus. And then I remember—he'd gone out, insisting he needed to buy champagne to celebrate Rob's birthday. He'd been upstairs before leaving the house, supposedly to use the bathroom. Had he taken my key from my bag and had a copy made while he was out buying champagne? My mind scans the shops in the area but I don't remember ever seeing a place to get keys cut. Anyway, Marcus wouldn't do such a thing.

"I'm really sorry to have dragged you here on a wild-goose chase," I say apologetically, when I return to the kitchen. "I'll make it up to you."

"Don't be silly," Sadie says. "That's what friends are for."

"I can't even offer you dinner, the fridge is practically empty. But I'm happy to order a takeaway, if you'd like to stay."

"Don't worry, we'll grab something to eat around here."

"Why don't you come with us?" Simon offers. "Take your mind off everything."

"That's lovely of you but I'm fine, honestly."

I move into the hall, suddenly eager for them to be gone. I give them a hug and thank them again for coming to my rescue.

"If there's anything at all, just call," Simon says. "I mean it. Even if it's the middle of the night."

"Thank you," I say, stooping to give Kintyre a pat.

"And please get your lock changed."

"Yes," I promise. "I will."

Another hug from Sadie and they're gone. I lock the door behind them and stand in the hall, at a loss at what to do next. Deflated, I sit down on the stairs. The silence wraps itself around me, not like a warm blanket but like a suffocating shroud, bringing with it a sense of impending doom.

ELLE

PAST

Gradually, the furor surrounding Brett Parker's death died down but with my court case pending—DC Moss had warned me I could be facing a prison sentence—I knew it was only a matter of time before it started up again.

Two months had passed but I still couldn't sleep and spent most of my time in a trancelike state, as if my mind couldn't compute what had happened. It terrified me that Brett Parker was dead—*dead, how could he be dead?*—because of me. I couldn't equate that my good intentions—trying to get justice for Bryony—had resulted in something so violent, so terminal. The stalker label the press had thrust upon me bewildered me; it wasn't true, how could it be? Stalkers were threatening, evil people, and I was neither of those things.

If I wasn't thinking about Brett Parker, I was thinking of his family. Because of me, his wife no longer had a husband. Because of me, his son no longer had a father. Although I'd tried to ignore any articles or news bulletins about him, it had somehow infiltrated my consciousness that the elderly man in the wheelchair was Brett Parker's father and that he had Parkinson's. Whenever I thought about the toll his death must have had on those close to him, my brain would shut down, as if it couldn't cope with the stark and painful truth that not only had I destroyed his life that day, but also the lives of several others.

I became a recluse, not daring to go out in case I was recognized.

"This has got to stop," Jaz said sternly one day. "You need to move on."

He had been brilliant since Brett Parker had died, never once reproaching me for what had happened, never asking that I leave. But now my heart lurched.

"You want me to go?"

"You can't hide yourself away forever."

I swallowed painfully. "Can I stay here until my case comes to court? There's nowhere really I can go. I'll make myself useful," I added, suddenly aware that I hadn't been pulling my weight either financially or chore-wise.

His face softened. Despite everything, he still cared about me, not as a partner but as a friend. "If you do the cleaning and the cooking, you can stay until your court case." He paused. "You can also do the shopping."

"The shopping?"

He held my gaze. "Yes. That's my offer, take it or leave it."

I knew that the real motive behind his last request was to get me out in the world again. So I began to venture out, hurrying along the pavements with my head down, shopping in supermarkets far from the flat rather than at our local, where I risked being recognized. Gradually, I began to feel more confident, until the day I was waiting to cross at a busy intersection, a laden shopping bag in each hand, when someone bumped into me from behind and sent me flying into the road. Out of the corner of my eye I saw a red bus approaching and the sudden screech of brakes and cries of alarm brought Brett Parker's death back in startling clarity. Accepting that karma was at play—a life for a life—I made no effort to save myself, just closed my eyes and waited for the bus to hit me. But hands had grabbed at me and pulled me onto the pavement, hauling me upright.

The doors of the bus swished open. "Stupid woman!" the driver yelled. "Be more careful next time!"

"Someone knocked me," I stuttered, as shock set in.

A taxi behind the bus sounded its horn, a sign to the driver to stop blocking the road. Others joined in and the ensuing cacophony made me clap my hands over my ears, unable to cope with the sensory overload after the fright I'd just had. The bus moved off, squashing a carton of tomato puree that had fallen from my bag under its wheels, staining the road bloodred.

"Are you okay, love?" a woman asked, as the people around me began to cross the road, jostling me and almost sweeping me along with them.

I lowered my hands, blinking back tears of fright. "I—I think so."

"Let me help you." The woman bent down and began retrieving what she could of my shopping while a new wave of people waiting to cross muttered under their breaths.

"It's fine, I don't want it."

"Don't be silly. I'm afraid your eggs and the milk are gone and the tomato puree, but the rest seems fine." The woman handed me the hastily repacked bags and as the pedestrian light turned to green, she gripped my elbow and propelled me across the road.

"Thank you," I mumbled.

"I never stand right at the edge of the pavement when I'm waiting to cross. Too many mad people around." The woman began to move off. "Take care of yourself."

Caught in a flow of people on the pavement, I moved back and slumped in a shop doorway. My heart felt as if it would burst from my chest and I desperately needed to catch my breath but the woman's words—*Too many mad people around*—made it impossible. Dark thoughts swirled in my mind. Had I been pushed into the road on purpose? Had someone recognized me? Because I hadn't been knocked into the road, I realized, I had definitely been pushed.

NELL

PRESENT

I seriously consider not going to work the next morning. I'm bone-weary after sitting on the stairs all night, the knife in my hand, too jittery to go to bed.

I'd thought of going to a hotel to save myself the misery of a sleepless night. But I couldn't stay away indefinitely so I decided to face my fears and stay home. I hadn't wanted to risk going to bed in case whoever had been in the house came back. At five in the morning I feltt safe enough to move to the sitting room and sleep for two hours on the sofa, reasoning that if whoever got into my house had to kill me, they'd have done it by then.

Sometime during the long night, as I sat on the stairs, I'd come to a decision about Alex. I couldn't be in a relationship with him, not when we were keeping so much from each other. I hadn't told him about my past, nor that I had a stalker, and he hadn't told me that another of his girlfriends had died. I didn't want to lose him but there were too many secrets between us for it to work. The only way to keep what we had was to be honest with each other and it didn't seem as if it was something either of us was prepared to do. But I had to try.

I make a plan; I would go to his hotel after work, without telling him, and see him there. He had mentioned its name once, Fifty-four Marlsborough. Or maybe that was the address.

Sadie is surprised to see me in the office.

"I thought you might have worked from home today, if you're getting the locks changed," she says.

"I'll look for a locksmith this morning and if they can come today, I'll go home this afternoon," I promise.

But my mind is too full of my surprise visit to Alex to think about looking for a locksmith. The day drags on, fatigue making each hour seem twice as long. I watch the time constantly and when it seems as if seven o'clock will never come, I ask Sadie if she'd mind locking up.

"Alex is here," I explain. "So it would be great if I could get off early."

"No problem." Sadie pauses. "When did he arrive?"

"Earlier."

"Have you told him? About last night? Is that why he's come back?"

I quickly weigh my options. Yesterday, I told Sadie that I didn't know when Alex was coming back despite him already being here.

"Yes," I say, cringing inwardly at another lie.

"Well, go on, get yourself out of here."

"I'll work another half an hour. Six thirty is fine."

"No way." Sadie points to the door. "You will leave right now!"

I can't help laughing. "Thanks, Sadie. I'll just get my bag from the office, if that's all right?"

"Yes, but don't take too long about it. You need to be gone, girl."

The rain of the last two days has been replaced by a brutal wind that instantly makes my eyes smart. I walk for five minutes, making sure I'm far enough away from Drop In before hailing a cab. I climb in thankfully, but guiltily. I can justify taking a taxi at night but not during the day. I make a mental note to buy another plant for the office to compensate.

The taxi driver doesn't seem to have heard of Fifty-four Marlsborough. He queries my pronunciation, asking if I mean Marlborough.

It takes him a while to find it on his GPS; I was right, he says, it is Marlsborough and it is somewhere in Knightsbridge.

Twenty-five minutes later, when we pull up in front of a few stone steps leading to a nondescript front door, I think we must have gone to the wrong place. But when I get out of the cab and climb the steps, a discreet gold plaque next to an ornate brass button bell tells me I'm exactly where I should be.

I'm about to ring the bell when it dawns on me that I don't actually know that Alex will be here. What if he decided, after I rejected him last night, to go back to the US? Or stay with Béatrice and Victor?

There's only one way to find out. I press on the bell and when the door is opened by a man dressed in a suit and tie, I presume that he's a guest on his way out and move aside to let him pass. Over his shoulder, I catch a glimpse of a beautiful crystal light suspended from the ornate ceiling.

"May I help you?" the man asks and realizing he must be the concierge, I quickly hide my surprise.

"I'm here to see Mr. Stanton," I say, as if I know that Alex is in and that he's expecting me.

"Of course." He opens the door wider. "You'll find him on the fifth floor. Please, come this way."

I had expected it to be more difficult, for the concierge to at least call Alex and check that it was all right for me to go up. His failure to do so makes me wonder if he's been primed by Alex to expect me. I hope not; I'd hate Alex to be so presumptuous as to be waiting—expecting me, even—to go to him. For a moment I feel wrong-footed and I'm tempted to wrong-foot Alex in turn by leaving. But the concierge is waiting, so I step inside.

There's no reception desk, just a marble entrance hall, and to the right, an elevator with a black door on either side. A further three doors stand on the opposite wall. I'm about to ask which one hides the staircase when the elevator catches my eye. Made of burnished wood, with glass windows and an ornate black wrought-iron cage, it's one of the most beautiful things I've seen. The concierge opens the gate, the inner doors slide open, and I find myself walking inside.

"Thank you," I say.

The concierge smiles. "You're welcome. Enjoy the ride."

He reaches inside the elevator and presses the button for the fifth floor. The inner doors close and I take a steadying breath. But this is an elevator unlike any other elevator. For a start, I can see out and as it glides silently upward, I have time to note that there is only one door on each floor.

The elevator comes to a smooth halt on the fifth. The inner doors move apart; I open the black wrought-iron gate and step onto a small landing with a single black door. There is nothing to tell me I'll find Alex behind it, no nameplate, no number, just a brass button bell, which I press.

It's a while before I hear footsteps, which are quickly followed by the hurried opening of the door.

"Sorry, Albert, I was in the—" Alex, still shrugging into a white bathrobe, stops in midsentence.

I had given a lot of thought to how our meeting would go. It went like this: I would turn up unexpectedly, taking Alex by surprise. He would invite me in and, my upper hand intact, I would take the lead. *Tell me,* I'd say. *Tell me about Caitlin. And when you've finished, tell me about your other girlfriends. I want to know everything there is to know. When you're done, I'll tell you about me. Then we'll decide if we have a future together.* I had never gotten further than that because I couldn't predict what Alex would tell me, but it was a start. And I have turned up unexpectedly, I have taken him by surprise. His shock isn't a pretense, any more than the relief on his face as he moves wordlessly away from the door, inviting me in.

But my upper hand is worthless. In the scenario I had created,

Alex had been fully clothed, not wearing a bathrobe, not fresh from the shower. And I had been cool and emotionless, not consumed by an aching, unbearable desire for him. Within seconds, I've untied his bathrobe. Another few seconds and my legs are clamped tight around him. A few seconds more and he is inside me.

EXTRACT FROM NOTEBOOK 4

I like your house, Nell. It's the sort of house I might choose for myself if ever I decide to live in your part of London. I don't mind that it's a terrace, with a house on either side. Neighbors rarely get to know one another and you are no exception. It's a shame, because if you chatted to the people in your street, you might be a bit more au fait with what is happening right under your nose.

I like that your house has been extended to make a bigger kitchen. There are no windows in your kitchen but I find the light well particularly useful. If I stood at a window and looked in at you, you would see me in an instant. But you rarely look up at the light well, so you don't see me watching you as you make dinner. I can spend hours up there on the roof.

If you've had friends over and there's wine left in the bottle, you'll have a glass while you chop and slice and finish it sitting at the island. Sometimes I look at the far end of the island and imagine cornering you there. It would be an easy kill because once you're there, there would be no way out. But I'm hoping that when the time comes, killing you will be a little more exciting.

How does it feel to know that you're going to die? In your heart, you must know that your death is imminent. Do you ever think about how it will happen, whether I'll use my hands to snuff the breath from you or a knife to bleed you dry? Which would you prefer, I wonder?

Not that it matters. We'll hardly be discussing ways to commit murder when I kill you.

ELLE

PAST

The morning after the incident where I'd almost been crushed by a bus, I looked out of the window and saw a man standing on the opposite pavement, at the very spot where Bryony had climbed into Brett Parker's car. Thinking him to be a reporter, a groan escaped my lips. Had someone discovered what had happened yesterday when I'd been pushed into the path of a bus and wanted to cause me more grief? But then he raised his head and as his eyes bore into mine, I realized I was looking at Brett Parker's son.

I pulled sharply back from the window, my breath catching in my throat. I didn't bother to wonder how he knew where I lived; any journalist would have been glad to share my address with him. My fingers were trembling as I found my phone and called DC Moss.

"Damon Parker is outside my flat!"

"Are you sure?"

"Yes." Because DC Moss was on the other end of the line, I found the courage to check the street. It was empty. "Oh, he's gone."

"Are you sure it was him?"

"Yes, positive."

"Well, if he comes back, let me know."

"But I need to go out," I said, shocked that DC Moss wasn't treating it more seriously. "What if he's hanging around somewhere? What if he follows me?"

"Why would he do that?"

"Someone tried to push me under a bus yesterday," I blurted out. "I think it was him."

"That's a serious allegation, Elle."

"It's true. I was pushed onto the road from behind. If someone hadn't pulled me back onto the pavement, I'd be dead."

"And you know for sure it was Damon Parker? You saw him?"

I couldn't lie. "No."

There was a meaningful pause. "You have my number. If you see him again, call me."

DC Moss hung up before I could say anything else.

I stood for a moment, wondering if I'd acted too hastily. What if Damon Parker only wanted to talk to me? What if he wanted to tell me not to blame myself for his dad's death, that it had been an accident, his dad's fault for running into the road without looking? A buzz on the intercom made me jump. My heart thumping, I edged closer to the window and angled my body so that I could see who was at the outside door. I recoiled in shock. Damon Parker was back.

The intercom buzzed again, and then again, and then again, each buzz accompanied by an angry shout—"Let me in! Let me in! Let me in!"

I redialed DC Moss's number.

"He's come back," I said, my voice shaking. "He's ringing on the intercom, I don't know what to do." The sound of the outside door being hit reached me. "He's thumping on the door! What if someone lets him into the building?"

"Make sure your door is locked." The DC's voice was urgent. "I'm sending someone over."

By the time they arrived, Damon Parker had gone.

"We've given him a warning," DC Moss told me when she called later that day.

"Is that it?" I asked.

"For now, yes. He understands that he isn't to go near you again."

But I couldn't relax. Whenever I left the flat, I felt I was being followed. At first, I put it down to paranoia; Damon Parker turning up at the flat had spooked me. But the feeling was so pervasive that I called DC Moss. The DC was sympathetic but she told me there was nothing she could do unless I actually had proof that he was following me.

"You've been through a lot, Elle," she said.

"I'm not imagining it," I said heatedly. "I'm not paranoid."

"If there is someone following you," DC Moss said carefully. "It doesn't follow that it's Damon Parker. There are journalists out there looking for a story while they wait for your case to come to court. A new angle, that sort of thing."

"I know how to spot a journalist," I said. "But it doesn't matter. I just wanted you to know because the day he pushes me under a bus again, I don't want you to turn around and ask me why I didn't tell you he was following me."

NELL

PRESENT

I lie in Alex's arms, as still as possible, not wanting to wake him. For the moment, the world is on hold. If I had to die now, like this, I wouldn't mind.

Alex stirs and I hold my breath, wanting the feeling of pure, undiluted peace to last. But he turns and kisses the top of my head, then my mouth and I try to wriggle under him, loving the feel of his body on mine, the way it covers me so completely.

But he resists. "We need to talk."

"We don't," I say, reaching for him. "Not yet."

"Nell." He smooths my hair, then cups my face between his hands and looks deep into my eyes so that I can't hide from him. "Why were you so scared yesterday, when I turned up outside your work?"

I want to look away but I can't. "You surprised me. I wasn't expecting you."

"All I did was say your name."

Which name? I want to ask. *Which name did you call me by?*

"I know," I say instead. "I don't like the dark. It makes me jumpy."

But he won't let it drop. "Who were you expecting, Nell?" he persists. "Who were you expecting to see when you turned and looked at me, holding the key like a weapon? You were terrified."

"I don't know. A thief, someone who was going to rob me."

The depth of his gaze is almost painful. "All right," he says, as if he knows he's not going to get any more out of me. "Would you like me to tell you about Caitlin? It's what I came to do."

"Yes. But why did you come? You could have told me about her over the phone."

"I wanted to tell you face-to-face. You deserve that much, at least."

"Then why didn't you message to tell me you were coming?"

"I was afraid you might tell me not to."

Is it really that simple, I wonder? I decide to believe that it is.

"Shall we go and sit where we'll be more comfortable?" Alex continues. "We can have a glass of wine. I'd asked Albert to bring me a bottle, I thought it was him at the door when you rang on the bell." He gives a rueful smile. "I needed to drown my sorrows."

I kiss him gently. "Not anymore."

"No, not anymore." He throws the covers off and swings his legs from the bed. "He'll have left it outside the door."

There's an en suite, so while he fetches the wine, I shower and put on the crisp white bathrobe I found neatly folded on a shelf. I cross the hallway to the room I had glimpsed when Alex had led me through to the bedroom, an eternity ago. An antique clock stands on a marble mantelpiece, its hands pointing to midnight. As if to confirm it, it begins to chime.

Alex comes into the room carrying a bottle of wine and two crystal glasses. He's swapped his bathrobe for jeans and a white shirt and his hair is noticeably damp.

"There's another bathroom," he says, in answer to the question in my eyes.

"Of course there is," I tease. "And I presume behind that door there's another bedroom."

He gives a little shrug and I roll my eyes. "When you said you stayed in a hotel, I imagined you had one room." I wave my hand around the apartment. "You must find my house a bit of a comedown after this."

"I love your house," he says, placing the glasses on a low table. "It's perfect. I hope you're hungry, I've ordered food."

"Ravenous."

"Good." He uncorks the bottle and pours deep burgundy wine into our glasses. "Come, let's sit."

We move to the sofa and Alex sits down. I'm about to sit next to him but instead I move to an armchair, so that I'm opposite him. I want to be able to see his face.

He leans forward, his elbows on his knees, his hands clasped together.

"I hadn't known Caitlin for very long when I invited her to join us on the skiing trip," he says quietly. "I met her in August and the ski trip was in January, so five months."

That's about the same length of time that you've known me, I want to say. *If anything happened to me, and future girlfriends ask about your previous girlfriends, wouldn't I make it on to your list of significant others?*

"She said she was a good skier, that she'd been skiing every year since she was a child and it wasn't a lie, she skied well. Just not as well as the rest of us. It wasn't a problem; I was happy to hold back and ski with her and sometimes the others did too. Then, on the last day, for what would be our last chance to ski, she told me to go on with the others. We'd started out as a group and were near the top of the mountain and the others were itching to go down fast. We were off-piste and I'd already said I'd ski down with Caitlin, as I always did. But Caitlin insisted I went. I can still see her practically pushing me after them. 'Go,' she said. 'Enjoy yourself. I'll follow at my own pace.' So I went, and boy, was I happy to be able to ski as fast as I wanted. I remember thinking that it was my reward for having stayed with Caitlin for the whole of the trip." He pauses. "I was also thinking that I wouldn't continue the relationship once we got back home. She was far more invested in it than I was and I didn't see her as a long-term partner." His voice drops to almost a whisper. "You can't believe how much I regretted that thought, how much I still regret it."

I don't add to his pain by mouthing useless platitudes. I reach for his hand.

"Why didn't you mention her when I asked about your significant others?"

"Because I'd already told you about Ariane."

"You told me she'd died," I remind him. "Not that she'd been murdered."

"Even so. 'My last girlfriend died and my girlfriend before that also died.' Can you imagine how it would have sounded? I already knew that I wanted to see you again and I thought you wouldn't want anything more to do with me if I told you about Caitlin in the same breath as Ariane." His eyes find mine. "Be honest, Nell. Would you have agreed to see me again if I'd told you that my last two girlfriends had died?"

"When were you going to tell me about Caitlin?" I ask, avoiding his question.

"I don't know." He sighs, rubs his eyes. "It feels as if Ariane is still coming between us, although I'm not quite sure why. I know I didn't explain the manner of her death when I first told you about her, I should have. But again, I didn't want to lose you."

I put myself in his position and imagine what it would be like to have a boyfriend who'd been murdered and another who'd met with a fatal accident. And I accept that, like Alex, I'd be wary about sharing that information, not only with someone I'd begun to care about, but with anyone.

"It's fine," I say. "I understand."

Tension whooshes out of him. "Thank you," he says.

"But there are some things I'd like to know. About Ariane."

I feel him tense, a minimal clenching of his facial muscles that I might have missed if I hadn't been expecting it. He slips his hand from mine and reaches for his glass.

"Ask," he says.

"I googled her." I hesitate a moment, then plunge on. "I googled her murder."

Alex pauses, his glass halfway to his mouth. "Why did you do that?"

"Because I was curious and because when I asked about her, you made me feel as if I shouldn't be asking."

"I don't understand what more you want to know. Is it how she died, because I can tell you, although I had hoped to spare you." His voice develops an edge. "You want the details, I'll give them to you. She was stabbed thirty-two times, a frenzied attack, the police called it, and her throat had been slashed. Or maybe you want to know what the room looked like when I found her, how she was lying on the bed in a sea of blood, how the walls, the floor, everything, was splattered red? Or what it was like to see the woman I loved being zipped into a body bag? And before you ask, no, she hadn't been raped or sexually assaulted and that is at least some comfort. Is that what you want to know or is there something else?"

I've never heard anger in his voice before, I've never seen him shake as his fingers are shaking on the glass. Nausea rises in me, not only because of what he's just told me but also because I've caused him so much distress.

"No," I say, striving to keep my voice calm in an attempt to diffuse his anger. "That's not what I want to know. I'd like to know why nothing came up when I googled her murder."

A silence stretches between us. Then, his breath shudders from him, as if something is being exorcised from deep within him.

"Forgive me." He places his glass on the table and rubs his chin. "You didn't deserve that."

I reach out, take hold of his hand again. "It's okay."

"I'll tell you as much as I can. Ariane had a specialized job. I only knew that after she died, when I was told that her murder wouldn't be officially recognized. As far as I knew, she worked at BNP Paribas but I found out after that she was working for the DGSE. That's the French equivalent of MI6."

My heart thuds. "She was a spy?"

"I presume she worked in intelligence so if that's the definition of a spy, yes, she was a spy. I told you that the person who murdered her had been caught, but to be honest, I don't know that and it's something I'll never know. When you asked, I had to make a choice and I preferred to tell you he was behind bars."

"What about her family? If her murder wasn't officially recognized . . ." My voice trails off.

"She didn't have any family. At least, that's what she told me. After, I wondered if it was true. But nobody contacted me after she died, so I presume it was."

"Thank you," I say. "For being honest about Ariane." I pause. "Marcus—my friend—thinks *you're* a spy."

"Why does he think that?"

"Because you're a consultant. He says it's a euphemism for a spy."

A ghost of a smile appears on his lips. "I'm not a spy."

Even if he was, it's what he would say. "Why do you never answer your phone when I call?" I ask.

Alex sighs. "The nature of my work doesn't always allow me to. I work with so many different time zones it's hard to keep up. Mine isn't a regular nine-to-five job and, like a lot of people, I have two phones, one personal and one for business. When I'm working, I turn off my personal phone."

It's plausible, I think.

A ring on the doorbell interrupts us.

"That'll be Albert with the food," Alex says. "Not that I'm hungry anymore."

He's exhausted, his face ashen, and although my heart breaks for him, I sense his relief at the interruption. He leaves to open the door and I hear him talking to Albert, followed by the sound of a trolley being wheeled into the apartment. Alex pushes it through to where I'm sitting and I leap to my feet and begin lifting lids from the platters.

"Oh!" I breathe, staring at a beautiful mousse in the shape of a fish, with scales of smoked salmon and an olive green caper for an eye. Under another lid, I find beef carpaccio nestling in a bed of parsley-scented oil. There are two salads and a bowl of piping hot French fries. "It almost looks too beautiful to eat."

Alex smiles. "Go ahead," he says. "Eat."

"You too," I say.

But he only picks at his food and when we go to bed, I hold him tight until he falls into a restless sleep. I'm relieved he's told me the truth about Ariane and Caitlin but my conscience needles away at me. If I'm to keep to the pact I made with myself, tomorrow it will be my turn to come clean about the past.

ELLE

PAST

Once again, I became afraid to go out. Before, because of the journalists, now because of Damon Parker. It was karma; I had followed Brett Parker, now his son was following me. Whenever I needed to cross a busy street, anxiety would set in and I'd hang back from the edge of the pavement until the pedestrian light turned green.

One morning, an appointment with my solicitor took me to Southwark underground station. He had already explained that it would have to be proved that on the day Brett Parker died, I had known I was committing an unlawful act by following him, which I had. The only thing in my favor was that I'd never been issued with a restraining order by the police; I had only been warned verbally to stay away from him. Although my solicitor was going to use my years in the care system to underline that I'd never had a constant adult in my life to advise me, and that following Brett Parker had come from a misplaced desire to get justice for Bryony Sanders, there were no real mitigating circumstances and I had already resigned myself to spending some time in prison.

As I headed down the escalator to the Jubilee line, I cringed at the memory of all the times I'd taken the tube to St. John's Wood. I had so many regrets about the way I'd behaved. I'd been naïve about the effects my actions could have on Brett Parker's family. I had been so obsessed with him that I couldn't see past him, I couldn't see that his wife and son would also be affected by my exploits. Yet no matter how guilty I felt for his death, no matter how much I regretted becoming involved, I still believed that he'd been behind the wheel of the car that day. A year on, nobody had been arrested in connection with Bryony's death. It still frustrated me Brett Parker had never admitted what I knew to be true, because if he had, someone might not have gotten away with her murder.

It was nine in the morning as I made my way onto the platform and although it wasn't the height of rush hour, it was still busy. As I moved down the platform, the sound of an approaching train caused people to move forward and, guessing it would be crowded, I decided to hang back and wait for the next one. Suddenly, without warning, my arms were gripped from behind and pinned to my sides. Startled, I turned my head and saw to my horror that it was Damon Parker who had hold of me. My scream of terror pierced through the sound of the approaching train. But he was already propelling me forward, cutting through the passengers waiting for the train. I heard cries of *Hey! Watch out!* as he pushed them out of the way with the force of my body. I could see the edge of the platform looming, and knowing what was about to happen, I screamed even louder and dug my heels in, trying to push back. But a final shove sent me onto the track and the screaming intensified, not just from me but from the people on the platform. Hands stretched down to me; there were urgent shouts of *Quick, quick! Get up, get up!* But the screeching of the approaching train's brakes struck such terror into me that I couldn't move. My vision blurred and the sounds around me became muted, as if I was underwater, and I accepted that I was going to die. And then, a man was standing beside me.

"Don't look, don't look." His voice was distorted, his face white with shock and I thought I must be badly injured and was grateful I couldn't feel any pain. There was the scorched smell of brakes and out of the corner of my eye, I was aware of the train, which seemed to have come to a searing stop only feet away from me. Hands reached down and hauled me and the man onto the platform. Someone made me sit and wrapped a coat around me and a woman put her arms around my shoulders, telling me that I would be all right. I still couldn't hear properly and, mute with shock, I could only nod until my hearing suddenly righted itself and I was hit by a wave of sound that robbed me of the breath I had left; people crying helplessly, others asking *What happened, what happened?* in voices high with disbelief and other harsher voices, shouting at someone to keep down, lie still. And then two paramedics came pushing through the crowd and knelt beside me. There was a flurry of activity as they checked me over and told me they were taking me to hospital because of a head wound I'd sustained.

I didn't speak in the ambulance, nor at the hospital, unable to process the horror of what had happened. A nurse gave me something that made me drowsy and when I woke, DC Moss was standing by my bed.

"Hello, Elle." Her voice was gentle. "How are you feeling?"

Maybe it was because she was familiar, or because she was the only constant in my life at that point, that I was finally able to speak.

"It was Damon Parker." My voice, shaky with shock and emotion, was barely a whisper. "He tried to kill me."

"I know."

A tremor passed through my body. "I thought I was going to die."

"Fortunately, he was detained by members of the public who saw what he did and he's now in custody. He won't be coming anywhere near you again."

I shook my head, trying to make sense of what had happened. "I don't understand why the train didn't hit me, how it managed to stop. I could hear it coming." I closed my eyes. "I could smell it."

I sensed DC Moss hesitating. "It hit someone else first," she said.

"Someone else? Who?"

"When you fell onto the tracks, people farther down the platform tried to see what was happening. A man got too near the edge." She paused. "He was hit by the train."

I stared at her in horror. "Is he—is he—?" I couldn't go on.

"Yes, I'm afraid he died. It was instant."

"No." Tears spilled from my eyes. "I was meant to die, not him."

"You can't think like that," DC Moss told me.

But it was impossible for me to think otherwise.

NELL

PRESENT

"So what exactly is it you do?" Marcus asks, looking intently across the table at Alex.

There's something in his voice—not hostility, but more than simple curiosity—which causes the rest of us to fall silent.

As promised, I'd invited Romy, Rob, and Marcus over to meet Alex. Sadie and Simon are also present, Kintyre in tow, as I thought it better to get all the introductions out of the way at once. It's going well, although it's obvious—to me anyway—that Marcus hasn't warmed to Alex as much as the others have and I wish, for the hundredth time, that Romy hadn't been so obvious in her desire to see me and Marcus as a couple.

All eyes are on Alex as they wait for him to answer.

"If I told you, I'd have to kill you," he says. There's a pin-drop silence, because his voice, until then full of laughter, was—not menacing exactly, but not far off. I will him to smile, tell us he was joking. But he waits another beat before grinning across at Marcus.

"Sorry," he says. "It was too hard to resist."

Everyone laughs except Marcus, who gives a small smile.

"I'll leave you to explain your consultancy job to everyone while I get more wine," I say, giving Alex a kiss.

"Sure," he says easily.

It's eight days since I surprised Alex by turning up at his hotel and I've never been happier. Last Sunday, as we lay in bed in his apartment, he asked me if I could some take time off so that we could spend more time together.

"I switched weeks to come over so I'm here until next Sunday," he said.

I snuggled deeper into his arms. "I would love that. But I need to give Sadie at least a few days' notice and arrange for one of our volunteers to come in and help."

"Then how about Thursday and Friday? I can reschedule the meetings I have on those days." He propped himself up on an elbow and ran a finger down my cheek. "That way we'd have four days to ourselves. My flight back is in the evening."

"Not totally to ourselves," I said, pushing away the thought of him leaving. "I promised my friends that they'd get to meet you when you were next here."

"When are you thinking of inviting them?"

"Saturday evening?"

"Sounds good to me."

"But there's one condition."

"What's that?"

"That we stay here until Saturday afternoon." I stretched lazily in the bed. "I rather like living in luxury with Albert to bring us food whenever we want."

He laughed. "It's a deal."

So I went home that afternoon and packed a bag with enough clothes for the week, then returned to Alex's hotel. Being away from home for eight days had done me a world of good. Even though I'd worked Monday to Wednesday, it had been fun staying at the hotel.

And Thursday and Friday had been wonderful. Alex and I had played at being tourists, visiting art galleries and museums and riding on the London Eye.

I take a bottle of white from the fridge and a bottle of red from where it's standing on the side, wishing that Alex's quip had been directed at Rob, who would have taken it well, rather than at Marcus. Tucking the menu for a local takeaway under my arm, I return to the sitting room, stepping over Kintyre, lying in the doorway.

"Let me open that for you," Alex says, taking the wine from me.

"Thanks. Who's hungry?" I hand the menu to Romy and she takes out her phone to register everyone's orders. I place mine for a chicken biryani then sink onto the sofa between her and Sadie, letting their chatter wash over me. Alex refills my glass and hands it to me, our fingers caressing as they touch on the stem. The rush of pleasure I feel is marred by the knowledge that the following day is our last together for another two weeks.

"So, what do you think of my friends?" I ask, once everyone has left.

"I like them. Romy and Sadie are lovely, and Simon and Rob are great guys."

"And Marcus?"

"Marcus seems to have a bit of an agenda. I'm wondering if he has a thing for you."

"Romy used to hint about the two of us getting together and I ignored it. But I think Marcus took it seriously and it was something he was working up to."

"And then you met me."

"And then I met you," I say, putting my arms around him. I look up at him. "I wish you didn't have to leave. I love you being here."

He bends to kiss me. "You don't know how much I want to stay—which is why I'm working toward spending even more time here in future."

I move back, searching his face. "Really?"

"Yes. I've been giving it a lot of thought and what I'd like is to turn it around completely and spend a week in the US and three weeks here."

"Are you serious?"

He smiles. "Business in the UK has picked up to the extent where I could do with being here more often. Do you think you could put up with me for three weeks at a stretch?"

"You mean you'd stay here with me, twenty-four-seven? No Fifty-four Marlsborough?"

"No Fifty-four Marlsborough," he confirms.

The breath rushes out of me. "I would love it."

"I wouldn't be crowding you?"

"You could never crowd me. But what about you? This house is smaller than your hotel suite. Wouldn't you miss the space?"

"No. I love it here. It's my home away from home."

I move back and lean against the worktop. "Where do you actually consider your home?" I ask, curious to know. "France or the US?"

Alex folds his arms across his chest, contemplating my question. "It's a tough one," he acknowledges. "I would say France because it's where I lived as a child and where I was educated, where I spent my formative years, if you like. Whenever I go there to visit my mother, I feel as if I'm home. But I love the US and feel very comfortable there."

"I remember you telling me that you were ten when your parents divorced. Béatrice would have been even younger. That must have been hard."

"Béatrice was only four. But it wasn't as hard as it could have been. It wasn't an acrimonious divorce. My parents stayed on good terms and they were honest with us about their reasons for separating. No one else was involved. My mother didn't want to live in the US any longer because she missed Paris and her family, and my father couldn't leave the US because of his work. They explained to us that we would spend term time with my mother in Paris and go to the US during the school holidays and we were happy with that. Sometimes my mother came with us to the US or the four of us would go skiing and those were the times I liked best, when we were together again. So their eventual divorce didn't affect me as much as it could have. Although—" He paused a moment, reflecting. "It might be why I married so young. Maybe, deep down, I wanted stability."

"How is Stephane?"

"Worried about the charge against him, apparently. Delphine asked me to find him a lawyer, which I have. Maybe this whole experience will wake him up a bit. He's still young, only twenty, so he has time to change. I hope he does, not just for his sake but also for mine."

"What do you mean?"

His voice becomes bleak. "Just that I don't want to lose my son, after everything else I've lost. Sometimes I think I'm cursed."

"Don't say that."

"I'm sorry. But sometimes it really does feel that way."

I move to his side. "You're not cursed, you're just unlucky."

"Not anymore," he says. "Now that I have you."

Later, as I watch Alex sleeping, his chest softly rising and falling, his eyes sometimes moving behind his closed lids, I'm horribly aware that I still haven't told him who I am. There is still time; I could wake him now and tell him about my past. But things are so good between us that I'm scared to.

A tear of self-pity falls from my eye and onto Alex's shoulder. He doesn't wake as I blot it gently with my finger. I'd always known that I'd have to pay for what I'd done and I was prepared to, because I deserved to be punished. But I don't want to die, not now that I have Alex in my life.

ELLE

PAST

When my case eventually came to court, my near-fatal experience at the hands of Damon Parker turned out to be the mitigating circumstance that saved me from a prison sentence, and I was handed a suspended sentence instead. I didn't feel jubilant. Another man had lost his life because of me and I felt I deserved to go to prison.

So did the man's family. They, and the media, made much of the fact that if I hadn't wrongly accused Brett Parker in the first place, leading inadvertently to his death, his son wouldn't have come after me. And if his son hadn't come after me, their own much-loved father, brother, and son wouldn't have fallen under a tube train and lost his life. Physically, mentally, and emotionally, I was a wreck. I was still living at Jaz's, sleeping on the sofa, but every time I closed my eyes, all I could hear was the terrible screeching of the train as it hurtled toward me and the screams of the people as I lay on the track. I could smell its scorching brakes, taste it on my tongue. If I did sleep, I was haunted by nightmares. And my ordeal wasn't over; there was still Damon Parker's trial to be gotten through.

The court case itself—giving evidence, being questioned by the defense, then the prosecution—passed in a blur of anxiety and guilt. I was back in the media spotlight, portrayed as the woman who had very nearly gotten the comeuppance she deserved for having hounded an innocent man to his death. The only thing I remembered clearly was closing my eyes in relief when Damon Parker was given twenty years imprisonment for attempted murder, with a minimum term of twelve years to be served before being eligible for parole. I was safe.

"One day, I'll get you!"

My eyes snapped open. Damon Parker was leaning forward in the dock, looking right at me, hatred in his eyes. As prison guards surrounded him and hustled him away, he broke free and pointed a finger at me.

"When I get out, I will kill you!" he yelled, as I cowered on the bench.

In a twist of fate, the court case led to my great-aunt's solicitor being able to trace me. My great-aunt had died the year before, I learned, and had bequeathed her mews house to me, just as she'd said she would.

"You deserve it," Jaz said generously, when I told him.

I stared at him, shocked. "How can you say that? Two men have lost their lives because of me. I don't deserve anything except to go to prison. I've only gotten away with that because Damon Parker tried to kill me. The worst thing is, I understand why he wanted me dead. I might not know what it's like to have a father but I'm sure that if I had one, I'd want revenge if he'd been killed by someone."

Damon Parker haunted me, not just because of what he'd done but because of what he'd become. I was stunned at how he'd turned from being the seemingly nice boy who had laughed and joked with his dad as they'd walked to the restaurant together into a raging, violent, potential murderer in so short a time. I had done that to him and it added to my shame. I couldn't bear to think about Brett Parker's wife, with her husband dead and her son in prison. My crimes were enormous. An image of Mrs. Parker in court came to me, pleading for leniency for her son, telling the judge that he was a kind and thoughtful young man and had adored his father so much that his death had destroyed him.

"You didn't kill Brett Parker, Elle," Jaz said. "Ultimately, his death was down to him. He didn't look before he crossed the road. And you weren't to blame for the death of the man on the tube."

I shook my head vehemently. "I'm not accepting the house, it's not right. I'm going to tell the solicitor to sell it and give the proceeds to the family of the man who fell onto the track."

Jaz sighed. "Look, this house is your lifeline and you need to embrace it."

I turned away from him. "I'm not taking it."

He reached out and caught my arm. "Yes, Elle, you are. Everything that happened, it came from a good place. You were convinced it was Brett Parker driving the car and you wanted justice for Bryony."

"I still am convinced he was driving the car," I muttered.

But Jaz wouldn't go there. "Anyway," he added, poking me playfully in the ribs to lighten the conversation. "I need you gone. I need my space."

"I've already told the solicitor that I don't want the house."

Jaz raised his eyebrows. "What did he say?"

"That I should take time to think about it. But I've made up my mind. I don't want it."

It took me another week to accept that my great-aunt's house could be the glimmer of light at the end of what had been a very long tunnel. Jaz had been incredibly kind and I couldn't impose on him any longer. I didn't tell him about my change of heart because I was embarrassed at having gone back on my decision.

While I was with the solicitor, going through the paperwork in relation to my great-aunt's house, the weight of who I was, of what I become, made me break down.

"I wish I could disappear," I sobbed. "I wish I could stop being Elle Nugent and start my life over again. I can't go on like this, with everyone knowing what I did." I didn't tell him that Damon Parker's threat to kill me was also a huge part of my desire to disappear. DC Moss had explained that, with good behavior, Damon Parker could be released from prison in twelve years' time. The thought of having to live most of my life in fear made me not want to live at all.

The solicitor was kind and sympathetic to my distress, because he knew my story. He explained that if I really wanted to start afresh, I could do so under a new name. He offered to help me with establishing the necessary deed poll and suggested that I move quietly into my great-aunt's house without telling anyone of my plans. Taking his advice, I told Jaz I'd decided to move abroad. I'd never told him where my great-aunt's house was and as far as he knew, I had told the solicitor I didn't want it. Saying goodbye was hard for both of us but I could sense Jaz's relief that he'd finally be able to get on with his life.

"Take care of yourself," he said, holding me tight.

"You too." My voice was heavy with tears at what I had lost through my own fault. For a moment, I wanted to ask him if there was any way back for us. But he deserved better.

Two months after I moved into my great-aunt's house, the solicitor called to tell me that I was now Nell Masters. I had picked Masters at random and had chosen a first name that resembled my old one so that I'd get used to it more quickly. I wondered if I should tell DC Moss about my new identity in case Bryony's murder, which was still being investigated, was ever solved. But any update would be broadcast on the news channels and although I intended to avoid social media, I planned to keep up with current affairs and would know if any progress had been made.

It was hard but I eventually found some sort of peace. My aunt's house became my haven; once I'd closed the door behind me I felt safe. I loved living there but I couldn't shake the crushing guilt I felt at my good fortune. I reminded myself that my luck was only temporary. One day, Damon Parker would be released from prison and I had no doubt that when he was, he would come looking for me.

PART TWO

NELL

PRESENT

I close the door behind Alex, unable to watch him walk away. He understands; he feels the same desolation that I do at the thought of not seeing each other for another two weeks. *Will I even be alive in two weeks' time?* The thought comes from nowhere and makes me want to weep.

It's 7:00 PM, and I wish it was later so that I could go to bed instead of having to spend the rest of the evening alone. I can't remember why Alex is traveling back to the US tonight rather than tomorrow morning, because he usually leaves on a Monday. I'm not sure I even asked.

I walk despondently to the kitchen, dismayed that uneasiness at being alone in the house is already seeping into my veins. I pull open the fridge door, intentionally making the bottles jiggle in the rack, needing to make noise to break the suffocating silence. But not so much noise that I won't be able to hear someone breaking in, because with Alex here, I haven't gotten round to having the locks changed.

A need for carbs makes me close the fridge and open the cupboard instead. There's a packet of chocolate biscuits on the shelf, already open, and I dig inside, aware that I'm about to start comfort eating. But I'll do whatever it takes to get me through the rest of the evening, and the night. Tomorrow, I'll call a locksmith.

Munching on the biscuits, I switch on the kettle, make a mug of tea and carry it to the island, trying not to dwell on the fact that it will be the end of November before I see Alex again. It seems incredible that ten days ago, I was on the point of breaking up with him because I felt I couldn't trust him. Now, I'd trust him with my life.

I take out my phone, bring up the calendar, and look at the dates. Alex is due back on Saturday the twenty-ninth; if he stays for two weeks, he'll be here until the middle of December. He'll return to the US on Sunday the fourteenth, and spend Christmas with his father in Washington. And—I mentally cross my fingers—I'm hoping he'll invite me to join him and his father for Christmas.

It's wishful thinking, because we haven't discussed Christmas, or the New Year. But Alex had said that since his divorce, he spends every Christmas with his father, and hadn't he said his dad wanted to meet me? I smile at the idea of us spending our first Christmas together in the US. It would be perfect.

Something interrupts my daydream and I sit up straighter, holding my breath. Above the hum of the fridge, my ears detect a noise from somewhere inside the house, a sort of creak, or a squeak. I take my phone, slip it into my pocket, then slide from the barstool, my heart beating erratically, my whole body on alert. Keeping my eye on the kitchen door, I move quietly to the worktop and take a knife from the wooden block. I stand poised, my hand raised, ready to pounce if the door handle so much as moves.

Would you though? a voice in my head asks. *Would you really drive that knife into someone's heart the minute they come through that door, without waiting to see who it is? Because that's what you'd have to do. If you so much as hesitate, they'd get to you first. What if it's Alex? What if he does have a key and has come back because he left something behind, or because he's decided he can't bear to leave you? What if you kill him? You'd have a third death on your conscience.*

A tremor whips through my body. The knife trembles in my hand. *Shut up!* I scream silently to the voice. I direct my focus back to the door handle. It hasn't moved so if there is someone out there, I'll need to go and find them. I take a step toward the door, then another. The thought of someone waiting on the other side makes me falter. My mind spins, frantically weighing my options. I should call the police. But what would they do if I tell them I'm calling because I heard a noise in the house? They wouldn't come out for a noise, so to give it weight, I'd have to tell them that someone has been following me and if there *is* someone on the other side of the door, and they hear me calling the police, they'll be in here before the conversation has even begun.

I force myself forward, a step at a time, until I'm by the door. I put my hand on the handle, my body so tense I can no longer feel my limbs trembling. I turn the handle slowly and pull the door open a crack, blocking it with my foot to prevent it being slammed open from the other side. I peer into the hallway through the gap, glad that I left the hall light on when I closed the front door behind Alex.

The hallway is clear but from where I'm standing I can't see if anyone is crouching on the stairs. To the right, the sitting-room door is wide open, as if it's inviting me in. The room is in darkness and I wish I could remember if I'd left it that way. I don't remember turning off the light but maybe Alex did. Or it could be a trap.

Reasoning that I can't go upstairs without having checked downstairs first, I leave the kitchen, close the door quietly behind me, and move silently into the hallway, then pause in the sitting room doorway, listening. There's no sound so I reach out with my right hand, still clutching the knife, and flick the light switch on the wall. Keeping my arm raised in front of me, I step into the room. A quick scan tells me it's empty; the only place someone could be hiding is behind the sofa. I move toward it in a sideways step, keeping one eye on the open door. I reach the sofa and peer behind it; no one is hiding there and realizing that with the curtains still open, anyone walking past will be able to see me with the knife in my hand, I quickly drop my arm and pull them shut.

I leave the sitting room, closing the door behind me. Reassured that there's no one downstairs, I move to the stairs and listen again. There's no sound, no creak of a floorboard, so I go upstairs, my tread light on the wooden steps. Arriving on the landing, I hesitate, torn between the bathroom and the bedroom. The bathroom is nearest, so I choose that. I switch on the light. It's empty. Only the bedroom is left, the door ajar.

When I get out, I will kill you. The echo of Damon Parker's voice spurs me on. I take a breath, then slam the door back against the wall. The noise ricochets through the house; I leap into the room, ready to bring the knife down. The room is empty and as I pull the doors of the wardrobe open to check inside, I catch sight of myself in the mirror, knife in hand, and feel suddenly foolish. Sinking onto the bed, I take a shaky breath; I scared myself for nothing. But as I sit there, my skin begins to prickle, just as it did the day I called Sadie and Simon because I sensed that someone had been in the house.

My eyes move to the window. It's the old sash-cord type and my heart trips when I see that it's been pushed up a couple of inches. I go toward it, wondering if Alex opened it when he came up to fetch his bag. Or was I right about someone being in the house and they left through the window when they heard me coming up the stairs? I peer down at the road, calculating. The distance from window ledge to the pavement is twelve feet at most. If someone held on to the ledge and lowered their body to the ground, the drop once their legs were fully extended would be between six and seven feet. Not far enough to deter anyone from doing it, if they were fit and healthy. And if they could close the window behind them. Maybe that's why it's not completely closed; it would be difficult to hang on to the ledge with one hand while sliding the window down with the other. But how did they get in?

As I stand there thinking that I really need to get my locks changed, my phone pings, making me jump. I look at my phone slowly, apprehensive about who the message might be from. Relief floods through me when I see it's from Sadie.

Hope you're not feeling too down now that Alex has left, she writes.

Just a bit, I reply.

Don't forget Simon and I are here if you need anything. He asked me to remind you to get your locks changed.

I frown at the coincidence then tell myself it's understandable that Simon is concerned. Yesterday, when I'd had everyone over to meet Alex, I had cornered Simon and asked him not to say anything about me thinking that someone had been in the house. And he had agreed, providing that I went ahead and got the locks changed.

It's on my list of things to do tomorrow, I reply.

A thumbs-up emoji appears on my screen. Exhausted from all the emotion, I think about going straight to bed. But realizing that I won't feel safe sleeping in the bedroom, I tug my green throw from the bed and pull it down the stairs after me.

EXTRACT FROM NOTEBOOK 4

It's funny how, once we've grown up, we don't have the same fears that we have when we're young. We might fear we're going to be burgled or stalked or murdered, yet very few people check their homes for an intruder when they come in from work in the evenings. Whereas children often fear that a monster is lurking in their bedroom and will check behind the door and in the wardrobe and under the bed before going to sleep.

You, Nell, check behind the door and in the wardrobe but you never look under the bed. Which is just as well.

Your bed is antique and high off the ground, and you've thoughtfully covered it with a pale green throw which reaches to the floor on all sides. If you'd thought to look under it tonight, and had found me hiding there, it wouldn't have mattered because you'd have been dead before you'd had the chance to scream. But it never occurred to you that there might be a monster lurking under your bed; thanks to the window I'd thought to leave ajar, you presumed I'd already left.

I almost wished you had looked, because I would have enjoyed seeing the terror that would have coursed through you when you saw me waiting with my knife. When you began to pull the throw off the bed, my excitement surged again; now, you would surely see me. But you didn't turn around so you didn't notice I was there, so close I could have reached out and nicked your foot with my knife. For a moment I was tempted to, just to see your reaction. But you left the room, pulling the throw behind you, and I guessed that you were going to sleep downstairs. It was just as well because had you chosen to sleep in your bed, I'm not sure I could have resisted the urge to drive the knife up through the gap in the springs, through the mattress and into your body.

It's such a delicious thought that it might be how it happens when I kill you.

NELL

PRESENT

Alex calls. We've progressed to doing video calls and I can see at once that he's upset about something.

"Nell, I'm so sorry but I won't be back on Saturday after all. I need to go and see my mother in Paris before coming to London."

I swallow my disappointment. "Oh. Will you be there for the whole weekend?"

"All week, I'm afraid. I haven't seen her since the summer and there are some things we need to sort out."

I wait, wondering if he'll invite me to join him in Paris for a couple of days so that I can meet his mother. But he doesn't.

"Will you see your ex-wife while you're there?" I ask.

"Probably. My mother always invites Delphine over for dinner when I'm staying with her. Despite everything, we get on well."

"Right. Will you see Stephane too?"

"I would love to but I doubt it. He always refuses to meet with me."

"So when will you come to London?"

"Saturday week."

Another ten days away.

"And you'll be staying two weeks?"

"No, just a week. I have a flight booked to Washington the following Sunday."

My heart sinks.

"I'm sorry. I'll make it up to you, I promise."

"It's fine," I say.

But it isn't fine. It's been a tough ten days since Alex left. I've had the lock on the front door changed and a second one added. The locksmith also put sensors on the windows and a sturdy lock on my bedroom door. The following day, the feeling that I was being followed came back with a vengeance, so I began varying my routine, taking the bus from different bus stops and leaving at different times in the morning and evening to throw my stalker off. It was exhausting but it worked, until yesterday. I'd left the office at three, telling Sadie I'd work the rest of the day from home, and I'd immediately felt someone behind me, as if they'd been hiding somewhere nearby, waiting for me to leave. I'd jumped in the first taxi I could find, glad that I'd only have to suffer the terror of being followed for another few days, because then Alex would be back. Except that now, he isn't coming back on Saturday.

If it wasn't for my past, I would speak to the police. But, like Simon, they will ask me if I have any suspicions as to who might be following me and if I mention Damon Parker's name, I would have to tell them of my connection to him. And within less than twenty-four hours, someone in the police will have tipped off the media and everyone will know that I was once Elle Nugent. It seems a small price to pay for my life; yet I have no proof that Damon Parker is following me, no proof that anyone is following me. It is just a feeling, and I know what the police would make of that. Sometimes I tell myself that it *is* my imagination, that my mind created a stalker for me because it remembered that Damon Parker was due for release this summer and that he'd said he would kill me.

By the time Friday comes, the thought of another lonely weekend with nothing but French lessons to keep me occupied makes me even more depressed. Before Alex, I'd never found the weekends long but now I'm climbing the walls by Saturday lunchtime. Last weekend, Romy had come over for a couple of hours while Rob was playing rugby, which had relieved the monotony of spending two days on my own. But this weekend she and Rob are going to Scotland to visit his family. I think about calling Béatrice and Victor, then remember Inès saying that the two of us should meet for lunch sometime. I find my phone and call her.

"Hi, Inès, it's Nell."

"Nell! Lovely to hear from you! How are you?"

"I'm fine, thanks. I was wondering—when we saw each other at Béatrice and Victor's, you said we should get together for lunch. Are you free at all this weekend?"

"Let me think—how about tomorrow?"

My spirits lift. "That would be great."

"Why don't you come round to mine? My flatmate is away this weekend so we'd have the place to ourselves. Shall we say twelve?"

"Perfect. Thanks, Inès."

"I'll message you my address."

"Brilliant."

Relieved that I have something to fill the day, I push away from my desk, thinking about Alex arriving in Paris tomorrow to spend the week with his mother. I know he won't invite me to join them but it doesn't stop me wishing he would. I imagine him calling me once he's arrived and suggesting it. *Hey, Nell, why don't you jump on a train and come to Paris? I've told my mother about you and she'd like to meet you. Perhaps you can take a couple of days off work.* I'd take a train to Paris and he would meet me at Gare du Nord and after lunch together in a little bistro and a walk along the Seine, he'd take me to meet his mother and I'd speak French to her and Alex would be amazed at my prowess and—my phone rings, snapping me out of my daydream. It's one of our sponsors and I slip seamlessly into work mode.

I take a taxi home because I don't want to have to cope with the feeling of being followed. It's only seven thirty so I'm happy for the driver to drop me off at the top of the road. As I approach the house, a flash of white on the doorstep catches my eye and as I get nearer, I see a bouquet of flowers propped up against the door. My smile of pleasure quickly fades when I see that the lilies are already decaying.

I unlock the door, then pick up the bouquet, turning my head away from its pungent smell. All I can think is that the delivery was left with a neighbor earlier in the week and they forgot to give them to me until today. But if Alex had sent them, wouldn't he have asked if I'd received them?

I take the lilies through to the kitchen and once I've checked the house I look for the card that came with the bouquet. There isn't one and, remembering the time I received flowers from Alex at the office without a message to tell me who they were from, I frown at the coincidence of it happening twice. I check the doorstep in case the card fell out but there's nothing there. And there's no card to tell me which florist they're from, just an empty staple where it should have been.

I study the bouquet uneasily. What if they're not from Alex but from my stalker? What if there's a hidden meaning behind the decaying flowers? I take out my phone, google "lilies" and find that they're popular funeral flowers. A cramping fear settles in my bones—but also a surge of excitement, because if they are from my stalker, they're the proof I need that he exists. I think for a moment then take the lilies back to the doorstep and photograph them as I found them, propped up against the front door. Then I take them to the kitchen and cram them in the bin, ramming their heads into the rubbish and crushing their stalks with the lid.

NELL

PRESENT

The next day, I decide to walk to Inès's flat. It's one of those bright November days which tricks people into thinking that spring is already on its way and as I cut through Hyde Park, I feel an unusual sense of well-being.

Being the weekend, there are plenty of families around. As I walk along a path, a small hand slips into mine and looking down, I see a tiny girl walking along beside me. At that moment, aware of my eyes on her, she looks up and smiles—and then, realizing that I'm not her mother, she snatches her hand away, her face already puckering.

"Charlotte!" A young woman comes running up and takes the girl's hand before she can start crying. "It's all right, Mummy's here. Sorry," she says, turning to me with a smile. "We're dressed the same, so she must have thought you were me."

"So we are," I say, looking at our navy jeans and green wax jackets. "She's lovely," I add. But the little girl is already tugging her mum away.

Overwhelmed by an emotion I can't define, I find the nearest bench and sit down, strangely shaken by what just occurred. At first, I think it's because, if the mother hadn't seen what had happened, she could have accused me of trying to take her daughter. But there's something else, something deeper and as I turn it over in my mind, I realize that what has upset me was the feel of the child's hand in mine, her little fingers tightening as she gripped on to me. And out of nowhere, I'm filled with an intense longing to be a mother.

It is so visceral and hits me with such force that I double over in physical pain. Tears of panic fill my eyes. What if I've left it too late? What if I find I can't have children? What if I can't find anyone to have children with? The longing coursing through my veins is like nothing I've ever felt before.

I fumble in my bag for a tissue, not wanting passersby to see that I'm crying. But my tears turn to sobs, scaring me with their violence. A little boy looks curiously at me as he walks by and I hear him ask his mum why I'm so upset.

"Perhaps she's just feeling sad," his mum tells him, which makes me cry even more.

It's a while before I feel calm enough to carry on to Inès's. But as I hurry to make up for the time I lost, my eyes fill repeatedly at the memory of the little girl's hand slipping into mine, so that when I arrive at the building where Inès's flat is located, I have to take a few minutes to compose myself before taking the stairs to the fifth floor.

"Nell." Inès steps back from the door and welcomes me with a kiss on each cheek. She's wearing black jeans, a cream cashmere jumper, and beautiful black suede boots with the usual four-inch heel. And her crimson lipstick. "I forgot you don't like elevators," she adds, noticing how breathless I am.

"Especially tiny ones with no windows. But your flat is lovely, well worth the climb," I say, catching a glimpse of a striking black-and-white kitchen at one end of the hallway and a wall lined with books through an open doorway.

"Are you all right?" Inès asks, looking closely at me. "Have you got a cold?"

"Just the start of one," I say, realizing my eyes must still be red. "I hope I don't give it to you."

"Don't worry, I have a good immune system. Shall I give you a quick tour of the flat before we go up to the roof terrace?"

"You have a roof terrace?"

"Yes." Inès's eyes gleam. "And the best thing is, with this lovely sunshine, it will be warm enough to have a drink there."

"Sounds perfect," I say, managing a smile. My eyes fall on a pair of scruffy white sneakers pushed under a console table that hugs the wall in the hallway. "Don't tell me those are yours?"

Inès looks affronted. "God, no. I never wear sneakers, or slippers. Heels or bare feet for me." She bends and scoops them up. "They're Cécile's." She opens a nearby door and pops the sneakers inside. "I won't show you her room, in case she's set a trap and will know if I've been in."

"Really?"

Inès laughs. "I'm joking. But I wouldn't go in anyway, not without asking her first. She's a very private person and I respect that."

"Is she a friend? Or just a flatmate?"

"More of a flatmate. Now and again, we'll have a glass of wine together if we're both here at the same time. But I'm out a lot during the week seeing friends and I spend one weekend a month in Paris with Maxime, and when he comes here, two weeks later, we stay in a hotel. So Cécile and I aren't here in the flat together that much."

"How long have you known Maxime?" I ask as we move down the hallway, remembering too late that Béatrice told me they'd met a couple of months before Alex met me.

"Around eight months or so. We met on the Eurostar when I was going to Paris to see my mum. He'd been visiting London with a friend and I happened to have the seat opposite them. We got talking and by the time we arrived in Paris, I was in love. So, this is the kitchen and through here is the living room." Inès moves farther down the hallway and opens another door. "This is my bedroom. My bathroom is through there and Cécile has her own bathroom, so we don't have to share, which I would absolutely hate. Come on, let's go up to the terrace. I have blankets if you're cold and a bottle of Chablis waiting."

"My favorite wine," I say.

"I know. I remember you telling Victor."

Inès leads me to the end of the hallway where a door conceals a tiny staircase leading up to the terrace.

"Wow, this is lovely," I say, admiring the row of miniature trees in wooden tubs placed against the railing to act as an extra barrier and give the terrace a garden feel. There's also a wooden table, a bench, and two chairs piled with cushions and blankets for extra comfort.

"I often come up here at night, even in the winter," Inès says, reaching for the Chablis and opening it expertly with a fancy corkscrew. "It feels very otherworldly, not like London at all."

"I can imagine," I say. "This is such an amazing view."

The table has been set with two wineglasses and a platter of salmon blinis dotted with lemon and crème fraiche.

"So, did Alex explain about Caitlin?" Inès asks, once we're sitting with our faces turned toward the sun, a blanket across our knees and a glass of wine within easy reach. "Béatrice told me he flew over from the US the minute she told him that you knew about her."

"He did," I say. "He said that he hadn't told me about her because I'd only just found out about Ariane and he was worried it would scare me off if I learned that another of his girlfriends had died."

Inès turns her head toward me. "Would it? Have scared you off?"

"It might have, if I'd found out at the beginning of our relationship when I didn't know him very well. I might have wondered if he'd had something to do with either of the deaths."

Inès reaches for the plate of blinis and offers it to me. "You must have been pleased to see him last night."

"I wish," I say, taking one. "He's not coming to London until next weekend. He's gone to Paris to see his mother."

"Yes, I know, he left this morning with Béatrice. I thought you might have seen him last night, as he was in London."

I stare at her, the blini halfway to my mouth. "Alex was here? He couldn't have been. He said he was flying straight to Paris from Washington."

Inès frowns. "I called Béatrice yesterday to see how she was and she said she was waiting for Alex to arrive and that he was staying the night at hers so that they could take an early Eurostar to Paris this morning."

"But—" I put the blini down on the table, unable to eat it. "I don't understand. Why didn't he tell me? We could have met up." Seeing my disappointment, Inès looks at me sympathetically. I force a smile. "Sorry. It's been one of those weeks. It would have been nice to see him, if only for five minutes."

"I shouldn't have said anything."

"I'm glad you did. I just don't understand why he didn't tell me he was going to be in London."

"Maybe because he knew he wouldn't be able to see you?"

I make an effort. "You're right. That explains the flowers. I found a bouquet of lilies on the doorstep when I got home from work last night. There wasn't a card to tell me who they were from but they must have been from him. Apology flowers. Shame they were dead."

"Dead?"

"Yes."

"You should phone the florist and complain."

"I would, but there was no florist's card attached to the bouquet, only an empty staple."

Inès raises her eyebrows. "No card to tell you who they were from and no card to indicate which florist they came from? And the flowers were dead? You don't have any enemies, do you?"

My heart thuds. "Not that I know of." I give a shiver and Inès stands up.

"You're cold! Come on, let's go downstairs where it's warmer."

But I'm not cold. It was Damon Parker, walking over my grave.

NELL

PRESENT

"Did Alex tell you about Ariane's job?" Inès asks when lunch is over and we're having coffee in her sitting room.

"Yes. He told me she worked for the French equivalent of MI6."

Inès stretches her legs out in front of her. "None of us knew, not until after she died. We were good friends and I honestly believed she worked for BNP Paribas. We used to meet outside their offices in Marylebone, for God's sake! That's how good she was at hiding it." She pauses. "I know that Alex, and Béatrice and Victor, think that her murder was linked to her job. But I'm not so sure."

"What do you mean?"

She gives one of her Gallic shrugs. "Not long before she died, Ariane told me she thought someone was following her. If her role in the secret service was dangerous, the possibility of being followed would have been part of it and she wouldn't have been allowed to speak about it. Not only that, she used the word 'stalker,' which is another reason why I don't think her murder was connected to her job. So, my theory is that she wasn't a spy as such and that her role was more administrative. In other words, her murder was nothing to do with her job."

Stunned at the mention of Ariane having a stalker, I forget to breathe. I reach for my coffee and take a gulp, then immediately start coughing when it catches my throat, which has become dry with dread.

"Sorry," I splutter. Inès jumps up to fetch a glass of water while I pull a tissue from my pocket and wipe my eyes, which are smarting with tears. I want to pretend they're a result of my coughing fit but for the second time that day, I find myself breaking into sobs.

"Oh, Nell, I'm sorry." Inès puts down the glass and sits next to me, her hand on my arm. "Is it what I said about Ariane? Take no notice of me, no one agrees with me anyway. They're adamant that she was killed because of the job she was doing and they're probably right."

"It's not that," I lie, because I don't want to hear any more about Ariane having a stalker.

"What then?" Inès asks. "Is it Alex?"

"No," I say, because I don't want to talk about him either. And as I have to say something, or perhaps because it's still there in my mind and in my heart, I find myself telling her about the incident in the park and how I found myself longing to be a mother.

"It's normal for you to feel that way," Inès says, when I get to the end. "Especially around our age. It's our body clock ticking. I remember you saying that you're thirty-six. Well, I'm thirty-seven now and it hit me last year when Béatrice told me that she and Victor wanted to have a baby. She had never mentioned babies in the four years I'd known her but as soon as she said the word 'baby,' I was filled by this terrible desire to have one too. It became such an obsession that I told Maxime not long after I met him. I was honest and said that I wanted to have a baby within the next couple of years and that if children weren't in his plans, I preferred not to waste any more time with him, given my age."

I smile, glad to have the focus away from me. "You're still together so I'm guessing he agreed."

"He did. But we can't even think about starting a family until we're living together full-time, which is why he's asked to be transferred to London."

"That's wonderful. I'm so glad for you."

She smiles. "Thanks. You know, if you really feel that strongly about having a baby, you need to tell Alex."

"I can't, it's too soon. Not just in our relationship but also for me. It only hit me today so I need to sit with it for a while. Anyway, he already has a son."

"That doesn't mean he wouldn't want another child. If Ariane hadn't died, I'm sure they would have had children. They were going to get married."

I can't hide my surprise. "Really?"

"Yes, once they moved to the US."

"I didn't know they were going to live in the US."

"It was where most of Alex's clients were at that time and Ariane knew how much he loved living in Washington. She was keen to move there and after, once I knew she'd worked for the French secret service, I wondered if it was because she wanted to get as far away from her old job as possible." Inès pauses. "At one time, I thought she might have been killed *because* she was leaving."

"What do you mean?"

"Her feeling of being followed started while she was working her notice. I don't know—maybe you're not allowed to leave the French secret service if you know too many secrets?"

My mouth drops open. "What, you think they might have killed her? The French secret service?"

"It was just a theory."

"But if she only had an administrative role?"

"That's where my theory fell apart."

"Did she say how long she thought someone had been following her for?"

"A couple of months, I think she said. I told her to go to the police but she said she couldn't. I thought she meant that as she couldn't prove it, there wasn't any point in telling them. But after she died, I wondered if she'd meant she couldn't say anything to the police because of who she was working for."

I turn it over in my head for a moment. "Do you know if Ariane told Alex that she thought she had a stalker?"

"She hadn't when she spoke to me about it. She said she didn't want to worry him. Also, she was due to leave her job—the one she supposedly had with BNP Paribas—and move to Washington so maybe that was a factor in her decision not to say anything, given that she was only going to be in the UK for another few weeks."

"Did you tell Alex that Ariane thought she was being followed?"

"Yes, after she died."

"What did he say?"

"The same as Béatrice and Victor said when I mentioned it to them. That it went with the territory. Alex spoke to someone from the French secret service. They didn't tell him much but enough to convince him that she died in the line of duty. But come on, let's change the subject and talk about brighter things."

"Good idea." I hesitate a moment, then decide to go for it. "Could we speak French together, do you think? I've been learning it online and I'd love to put what I've learned into practice."

"You've been learning French?"

"Yes, as a surprise for Alex."

Inès puts her hands together. "He will be so happy!"

I smile at her enthusiasm. "I hope so."

We speak French for the next thirty minutes and Inès's compliments about my ability to hold a conversation gives my confidence an enormous boost. It's 8:00 PM by the time I leave; there are people around, so I walk for ten minutes, the sting of the cold on my cheeks reviving me after a little too much wine, then hail a taxi to take me the rest of the way home. The driver obligingly drops me in front of my door and I do my usual thing of asking him to wait until I'm safe inside. Then I do my other usual thing of checking the rooms for signs of an intruder. Thankfully, there are none and, feeling as safe as I possibly can, I go to bed.

EXTRACT FROM NOTEBOOK 4

I should have guessed you'd get your lock changed after I broke into your house a second time, Nell. And you had an extra one added, which made my life a little more difficult, but not much.

It wasn't a problem per se because once I knew what type of locks they were, it wouldn't take me long to learn how to pick them. Sometimes, when I think of all the skills I've had to learn as a means to an end, I feel a little in awe of myself.

I needed to get up close and spend a minute or two in front of the door to see what had been installed. I didn't want to be seen loitering on your doorstep because now that everything is nearing an end, I don't want to run the risk of being discovered before I can deliver my coup de grace. So I decided to pretend I was delivering a parcel, which would allow me to stand on the doorstep for a while.

I had an empty box in mind, because why go to the trouble of putting something inside when an empty box could signify a coffin? But I felt something a little more subtle was required and in the end, I settled for flowers, which I bought past their best and kept them a few days so that they'd be nicely decaying by the time you found them.

I was surprised how long it took me to choose the lilies. I spent quite a while wondering if you might prefer roses, or germini or even lisianthus before realizing that it didn't actually matter.

We'll hardly be discussing our favorite flowers when I kill you.

NELL

PRESENT

The day after my lunch with Inès, I feel as if I'm coming down with flu.

Yesterday had been a lot. First there was the realization that I wanted a child, then the revelation that Ariane had a stalker, followed by the news that Alex was in London on Friday evening and hadn't bothered to tell me. There were also the flowers I found on the doorstep. If Alex was in London on Friday, they could have been from him, he could have hand-delivered them. But why wouldn't he have left a note—and why would he have removed the florist's card? Yet they can't have been from him because even if they hadn't been very fresh when he bought them, they wouldn't have reached such a state of decay in the space of a few hours.

The news that Alex and Ariane were going to get married has also thrown me. Lying in bed, my mind whirs, calculating feverishly. Inès told me, when I asked, that Alex and Ariane had met in October 2022, nine months after Caitlin died, so they would only have known each other for nine months before Ariane was murdered in July 2023. They were going to get married once they were in the US and their decision to move to the US must have been made at least two months before Ariane died because Inès mentioned that she'd had to give three months' notice and there was still a month to run when she died. If they already knew two months before she died that they were going to get married, when had they first talked about it? After six months? Alex and I have known each other for six months now. Is it something we'll talk about soon? If we don't, does it mean that Alex doesn't feel the same way about me as he did about Ariane? And if we do, what will I say?

I've never allowed myself to think about marriage before. I'd always imagined a future where I would die alone, without friends, without family, and although it had frightened me, I'd accepted it because it was what I deserved. Terrible loneliness had made me accept having friends. But marriage? How could I even think of marriage, or having a child, after what I'd done?

Hoping that my overwhelming desire for a child was temporary, I head to Hyde Park to test myself. But as I stroll among families out for a morning walk, I find myself gazing wistfully at the parents with babies in slings, or in backpack-like harnesses strapped to their shoulders. Some parents are teaching their children to ride bikes, or roller-skate, but my eyes are drawn again and again to the mothers with babies. I sit down, trying to sort through my emotions, and a young woman comes and sits next to me on the bench, carrying a tiny bundle.

"I need to feed her," she says a little hesitantly, as if she's worried I might object.

I give her a smile. "Go ahead," I say, looking in wonder at the tiny face peeping out from its shawl. The mother unbuttons her coat, lifts her jumper, and puts the baby to her breast. As she begins to suck, her eyes now firmly fixed on her mother's face, there's a primal tugging at my own breasts.

"I'm sorry," I say, realizing I've been staring. "I'd never thought about having a child until recently and now all I want is to be pregnant."

The woman smiles. "The great thing is that nowadays, even if you don't have a partner, you can have a child."

"I do have a partner but I haven't told him that I want a baby. We've only been together a few months."

"Is he someone you'd like as a father for your child?"

"Yes, definitely."

"Then, it's better to be honest and tell him how you feel."

I nod, my eyes back on the baby. "What's her name?"

"Clementine."

"That's so pretty. How old is she?"

"Three months yesterday."

"Is she your first?"

The woman shakes her head. "You see the little girl over there on the bike? That's Violet, her sister."

I look over and see a little girl on a blue tricycle, a fair-haired man by her side, encouraging her as she pedals along. "How lovely to have two daughters," I say.

"There's also a big brother. He's on a playdate, so it's just the four of us today."

The four of us. My desire to be able to say those words is profound. My mind races, calculating. Do I have enough time left fertility-wise to have two children? Yes, if I have one next year when I'm thirty-seven and another before I'm forty. Women still produce eggs at forty, and forty isn't considered too old to have a child, not nowadays.

"I'd better get on," I say, worried I might snatch the baby out of its mother's arms, just to feel the warmth of its little body against mine.

"Good luck," the woman says. "I hope it works out for you."

I give her a smile. "Thanks."

On my way home, I check my phone to see if I have any more missed calls from Alex. He'd called twice yesterday evening but I hadn't picked up because I'm still annoyed that he didn't tell me he would be in London on Friday evening.

I spend the afternoon on the sofa, turning everything over in my mind, only moving to the kitchen at the end of the day when hunger sends me there. While I'm searching in the fridge for something to put in a sandwich, Alex video calls. This time, I pick up.

"Good, I'm glad I've managed to get you." Alex's voice is warm with relief. "I called you yesterday but you must have been busy."

"How is everything? How's your mother?"

"She's fine, happy that Béatrice is here too. We had some family business to sort out—I think I told you that my grandfather died in April? Our solicitor wanted to see us so I had to change my plans. I ended up flying to London on Friday evening and stayed over with Béatrice. We took the Eurostar to Paris yesterday."

"So you were in London on Friday?" I say, pretending surprise.

"Yes."

"Why didn't you tell me?"

"I did think about it. But I needed to talk to Béatrice ahead of our meeting with our solicitor yesterday, so I decided not to disturb you."

"Disturb me?"

"It was a very rushed visit. I didn't arrive at Béatrice's until ten o'clock."

"You could have spent the night here."

His brow furrows. "I could have. But as I said, I needed to talk to Béatrice before our meeting with the solicitor yesterday."

"You could have talked on the Eurostar."

"Not about family matters." There's an edge to his voice followed by an uncomfortable silence and, unable to hold his gaze, I look away. "I should go," he says. "Delphine and Stephane are due any minute and I don't want to be on the phone when they arrive."

I lift my head. "Stephane?"

"Yes. Delphine phoned my mother at lunchtime and said that Stephane wanted to come along tonight. My mother nearly had a heart attack. She asked Delphine if he knew that Béatrice and I would be there and she said that he did. Can you believe it, Nell? After near enough six years, I'm finally going to see him."

He looks so happy that I regret my petulance over his presence in London on Friday.

“That’s wonderful,” I say. “Will you let me know how it goes?”

“I’ll call you tonight, once they’ve gone. It might be late.”

“That’s fine. It’s an hour earlier here, remember. And I’m sorry about before. It was disappointment speaking.”

I find it hard to relax so I catch up on laundry and housework to fill the time until he calls. I know it isn’t a good idea to ask him during a video call about Ariane, about his and Ariane’s plans to move to the US and get married, but I doubt I’ll be able to hold back. It irks too much that I’ve learned these things from Inès, rather than Alex himself. His caginess about Ariane, about his exes in general, is a huge red flag and once again, I wonder how well I really know him.

He calls at midnight, just as I’ve settled into bed in my clean and tidy house.

“I hope you weren’t asleep?” he says.

“No, I kept myself busy getting the house up to scratch. How did it go with Stephane?”

“Better than I could have hoped for.” There’s real joy in his voice. “I can’t tell you what it was like to see him after so many years. He was a boy the last time I saw him, now he’s a young man.” He laughs. “He’s taller than me, something he was very pleased about. It was a bit awkward at first. I wasn’t sure how he would react and a part of me thought he might not turn up. But he did and although he didn’t hug me—I didn’t really expect him to—he did shake my hand. It was good that my mother and Béatrice were there because they hadn’t seen him for years either, so I let them do most of the talking. I was too worried I might say the wrong thing.”

“Did you find out why he had the sudden change of heart and agreed to see you all?”

“When he and Delphine were leaving, he thanked me for having found him a solicitor—Delphine didn’t want to use our family solicitor—which was amazing because he’s never thanked me for anything before.

I think being arrested and the possibility of a prison sentence was a huge shock to him and he's finally grown up. At least, I hope it's that. With Stephane, you never really know."

"Will you see him again before you leave?"

"I hope so. I didn't ask because I didn't want to push it. I prefer to let him come to me."

"I'm really happy for you," I say.

"I'm seeing Delphine tomorrow, we're meeting for lunch. I guess I'll find out more then. Anyway, how are you? Have you had a good weekend?"

No, I want to say, *because I discovered I want a child. And because my past is catching up with me fast.*

"Yes," I say instead. "I had lunch with Inès yesterday. She invited me over."

"That was nice of her. Did she show you her roof terrace?"

"Yes, it's amazing." I hesitate, then decide to go for it. "She told me that you and Ariane were going to move to the US."

There's a pause at my mention of Ariane. But he quickly adjusts. "That was our plan, yes. She told me she'd been thinking about leaving her job and she wanted to make a fresh start somewhere abroad, so I suggested we move to Washington because back then, that's where I spent most of my time. I thought she was bored working in finance but after she died and I discovered that she was actually working for the French secret service I wondered if it was because her job wasn't compatible with family life. We had talked about having children, you see."

My heart twists. "Right." I want to ask him if he'd still like to have children but what if he tells me that he doesn't?

"What else did you do?" he asks when I've been silent a little too long.

"Not much. Are you still planning to come here on Saturday?"

"Nothing will stop me. I should be with you around 7:00 PM."

"Great."

There's another awkward silence. "Nell, is everything all right?"

"Yes, why?"

"It's just that you don't seem that thrilled about seeing me again." He hides his disquiet with laughter but the furrow between his brows is back.

"I am. But there's something I need to talk to you about."

"Okay. Should I be worried?"

"No. There's just something I need to run by you."

"Can you run it by me now? I'm not sure I can stand the suspense."

"Everything's fine," I say. "It's late. Let's speak again tomorrow."

NELL

PRESENT

"Sadie, I know this might be a stupid question," I say, when I get to work the next morning. "There was a bouquet of lilies waiting for me on my doorstep when I got home on Friday and there was no note to say who they were from. Do you have any idea who might have sent them?"

"Um, a tall French-American?" she says.

"No, they weren't from him. We spoke on the phone over the weekend and he never mentioned sending me flowers. Anyway, I think they were hand-delivered."

"Maybe they're from a neighbor. Did you do something kind, like rescue a cat?"

"No. I don't really have neighbors, not ones that I know. The thing is, they were dead."

"The neighbors?" Sadie jokes.

"The flowers."

Sadie rearranges her face. "You could ask the florist. They might have a record of who ordered them."

"That's the problem. The florist's card was missing but there was a redundant staple where it should have been."

"Hmm. Unless that's where the message was."

"What do you mean?"

"Well, let's say they were from a secret admirer who hand-delivered them to your door with a note declaring their love for you. Maybe they got cold feet and removed it at the last minute."

"But if they were hand-delivered, the person would have known that the flowers were dead."

"True." Sadie hesitates. "I know Simon already asked you this and I don't want to spook you, but is there anyone who might have a grudge against you?"

"I can't think of anyone."

"Nobody from here, from the charity? I can't ever remember you arguing with anyone but did you ever refuse anyone access, or something like that?"

My mind leaps, wanting to believe more than anything that the mysterious bouquet is something work-related because then I'd be able to breathe again. But there have been very few negative incidents since I started working at Drop In and the fact that the flowers were dead tells me they are from Damon Parker, a warning that he is coming for me.

I don't waste time wondering how he discovered my new identity or where I live. I imagine him in prison, biding his time, living under the radar, waiting patiently for his twelve years to be up so that he'd finally be able to finish what he'd started all those years ago—what I'd started all those years ago. I curse my naivety. I'd known all along that he could be out after twelve years, so why hadn't I done more to protect myself from his eventual release? I could have sold my house, moved to another country, made it more difficult, if not impossible, for him to find me. Instead, I had stayed, because I felt that I deserved to die.

It's too late to regret not having told DC Moss about my change of identity, because she would have let me know that he was being released from prison. I doubt it's something I can find out by googling his name but I do it anyway, finally acknowledging that facing my demons is the only way forward. When the same headline articles flash up on the screen, along with my old name, Elle Nugent, and the words "stalker," "obsession," "murder attempt," "court case," I don't slam my laptop shut but force myself to carry on scrolling, absorbing the horror of everything I lived through. My eyes are caught by an article from when Damon Parker pushed me into the path of the approaching tube train. At the time, I hadn't read anything about what had happened, but as the details of my link to my attacker are laid out in stark detail—how I'd harassed his father in a case of mistaken identity to the point where he'd lost his life—it becomes obvious, from the tone of the article and from the subsequent comments, that most people felt I got what I deserved. Much was made of the fact that I'd stalked a man twice my age and I was shocked at how much my attempts to speak to Brett Parker, whether in person or by phone, had affected him, if his wife and son were to be believed. I also realized that in being too scared to speak to the media I had never given my side of the story, my motivation, which was that I truly believed Brett Parker had picked up Bryony Sanders in his car that day.

I make a plan. The first thing I need to do is find out where Damon Parker is and the only person who might be able to tell me is DC Moss. I still have the number she gave me all those years ago but I doubt it's still valid. She could have been assigned to a different police force in another part of the country, she might even have changed careers. But it's all I've got.

I call the number. A male voice answers and I explain that I'm trying to trace DC Moss.

"You mean Superintendent Moss," the officer corrects. "Can I ask who's calling?"

"Elle Nugent." The name sounds strange on my lips.

"And what is it you'd like to speak to the superintendent about?"

"Damon Parker."

There's no sign that the officer recognizes the name, just a promise that he'll pass the message on to his superior. I don't expect to hear anything for at least a few days so I'm surprised when the officer calls back within the hour, asking if I'm free to see Superintendent Moss the following morning.

I go and find Sadie to tell her I'll be working from home the next day, happy that I'm finally taking back control of my life. I think of all the years I've spent punishing myself for my past because I didn't feel I deserved to be happy. I'd devoted my life to working for charities, often for a minimum salary, and when I'd begun to earn more, I'd plowed some of it back into whichever charity I was working for at the time. Anything to atone, atone, atone. I only let Romy in because I craved just a little bit of a normal life, to be able to meet a friend for a drink, to not sit in the cinema or theater alone as I'd done for so many years. And I'd been content with that until I met Alex and realized I could have more. But now something burns inside me, something that makes me want to live, and that's my newfound desire to be a mother. It fills me up, makes me fierce. I will not, I cannot, allow Damon Parker to take that away from me. I will fight him with my bare hands if I have to.

I am done with atoning.

EXTRACT FROM NOTEBOOK 4

I wonder what you would do, Nell, if you knew where I spend most of my free time. If you took a little more interest in the area where you live, if you stopped and chatted to the neighbors, you might have discovered that the house opposite yours is for sale. Fortunately for me, the current owners, who live abroad—China, I believe—don't want a "For Sale" sign advertising that the property is empty so it's only by looking on estate agents' websites that someone can see there's a house for sale in the very street where you live.

I came across it by chance, when I happened to be wondering how much your house was worth. I was looking at similar properties in the area to get an idea of the value when I found it. I went there in the dead of night to see if it had a lock I could easily pick and I was inside within seconds. It was empty, no furniture, nothing. I groped my way upstairs and into the room at the front, from where I had a spectacular view of your house.

It's made my life so much easier.

When I'm there, in the house across the street, I make sure to stand well back from the windows, although the chances of anyone seeing me are slim. And because you always come out of your house with your head down, I could stand stark naked in the center of the window without fear of you seeing me.

Do you have any idea how much your house is worth, Nell? I think you'd be surprised if you knew. If I were in your shoes, about to die, I'd sell it and go on a wonderful holiday, or do something I'd always dreamed of doing. I wonder what you would choose to do, Nell, if you knew you would soon be dead?

Not that it matters. We'll hardly be discussing our bucket lists when I kill you.

NELL

PRESENT

The police officer opens a door and ushers me in. Superintendent Moss moves from behind her desk and extends her hand. "Elle, it's good to see you after all these years. I have to admit, I was worried when you disappeared."

Apart from a few gray streaks in her hair and faint lines around her eyes, DC Moss looks the same as she did fifteen years before, although the look of exasperation when she spoke to me back then has been replaced by a look of concern. "What happened. Where have you been all this time?"

"An unexpected windfall gave me the chance to make a new start," I say, still wary of revealing too much.

Superintendent Moss moves back behind her desk and indicates to me to sit down. Her office is small but tidy, a reflection of the detective's neat physique. There are no personal objects adorning the walls, just a silver photo frame on the desk. It's facing away from me so I'm unable to see what it holds.

"There were times after you disappeared that I feared you might be dead. Every time the body of a young woman was discovered, I was worried it might be you," Superintendent Moss says.

"I'm sorry," I say. "I should have told you what I intended to do."

"I don't blame you for not sharing. What happened to you was terrifying."

"I still can't take the tube."

"I'm not surprised. Did you change your name? You must have, because I searched for you."

"Yes. I didn't want to be Elle Nugent anymore."

"Understandable."

I shift on my seat. "I was left a house in London by my great-aunt. I was going to sell it and give the proceeds away but my solicitor persuaded me to keep it and suggested that I changed my identity so that I could start over. I'm now Nell Masters."

Superintendent Moss nods. "And how has it worked out for you, being Nell Masters?"

"Generally, it's worked out well. But it's been quite lonely."

"I can imagine." She appraises me for a moment. "You look well."

"Thank you."

"I imagine you didn't get in contact just to let me know that you're alive," the superintendent says with a smile. "Although I'm very glad you did."

"No. It's about Damon Parker."

"Ah."

"I always knew that he could be released after twelve years but I didn't worry about it too much at the beginning because twelve years seemed a long way off. And I thought that even if he was released, I'd be safe, that he wouldn't be able to find me because I'd changed my name. But he has. He's been following me and—well, I'm scared."

Superintendent Moss frowns. "Damon Parker has been following you?"

"Yes. And not only that, he knows where I live and broke into my house. I've changed the locks but—"

She raises her hand. "Elle—I'm sorry—Nell, let me stop you there. Damon Parker hasn't been released from prison. I can assure you that, for the moment, he's still inside."

A drumming starts in my ears. "Are you sure?"

"Yes." The superintendent pauses. "He's due for release but he hasn't been released yet." Another pause. "The reason I know he's still in prison is because we're reopening the Bryony Sanders case."

Reeling from the news that Damon Parker is still inside, I almost miss what the superintendent said. When it registers, my heart leaps.

"You're opening it up again? Has there been some development?"

"I'm not at liberty to say much. But yes, we're taking a look at it again." The steely look is back in her eyes, warning me not to ask more. Older and wiser, I don't insist. "Which is why it's fortuitous that you've contacted me. I'd begun putting feelers out for you, in case I needed to make you aware of any developments. We managed to locate Jason Borders but he couldn't tell us anything except that he thought you'd moved abroad." Seeing my puzzled look, she smiles. "Jaz, I believe you called him. Your boyfriend at the time."

"Oh gosh, of course. Jaz. I'd forgotten his name was Jason. You say you saw him—how is he?"

The superintendent smiles again. "Married, three kids."

"Wow. Well, good for him."

"Let's get back to why you're here. I'm concerned that you thought Damon Parker has been following you and has broken into your house. Can you tell me more?"

It feels good to unburden myself and when I get to the end, Superintendent Moss refers to the notes she'd taken while I'd been speaking.

"To recap, you've never actually seen the person following you, and your police officer friend couldn't find any signs of someone having gotten into your house? I'm not saying that you're mistaken," she says quickly, aware of the set of my face. "I just want to be sure of the facts."

"No, I've never seen the person who's following me. But I wasn't wrong about Damon Parker following me last time and I'm not wrong this time." I lean forward in my chair, needing her to believe me. "I know you said he's still inside but maybe he has someone working for him on the outside. Maybe he's asked them to find out where I live ahead of his release."

The superintendent seems unconvinced. "If there is someone following you, have you considered that Damon Parker might not be involved, that it might be someone else?"

"No, because I'm sure that he's behind it. Is there any way he might know about Bryony's case is being reopened? Could that be why he's trying to scare me? Because something new might be coming to light?"

I'm gratified to see Superintendent Moss thinking seriously about what I said.

"It's highly unlikely," she says, after a moment. "But not impossible." She gives a weary smile. "Prisoners often have ways of knowing things that we ourselves aren't yet aware of. Are you happy to let me have your address? So that we can keep an eye on things?"

"Of course."

"Meanwhile, I'll make some inquiries about Damon Parker's possible contacts on the outside. And if you ever feel you're in danger, call me immediately." She hands me a card. "This is my direct line. I answer it night and day."

"Thank you."

Superintendent Moss pushes to her feet. "I'll let you know if the developments in Bryony's case amount to anything. Take care, Nell."

"I will, thanks."

NELL

PRESENT

The news that Damon Parker is still in prison is a huge shock. But it doesn't mean that he isn't connected in some way to whoever is following me. In fact, when I think about it, it makes sense that he's using his last months in prison to find out where I am so that on his release he can come straight for me.

Despite what Superintendent Moss seemed to suggest, I don't want to believe that my stalker isn't anything to do with Damon Parker. The alternative is too frightening because if not him, then who?

I spend the next couple of days trying to focus on the good news, that the police are looking again into Bryony's murder. I don't know what Damon Parker and his mother, and Brett Parker himself, told the police about his movements on the day of Bryony's disappearance but whatever it was, it was enough to convince them that he wasn't the man who picked up Bryony Sanders in his car. But if the police were right and he wasn't involved in her murder, why hasn't her killer ever been found?

On Thursday evening, a ring at my doorbell sets my heart racing.

Friends never turn up at my door unannounced. My mind whirs, searching possibilities. Best-case scenario, it's Alex. Maybe, unable to wait until the weekend to hear what it is that I want to discuss with him, he's come from Paris without warning me, just as he did when he turned up outside my workspace after I found out about Caitlin. Worst-case scenario, it's my stalker.

There's another ring on the doorbell, followed by a shout "Nell! Are you there?" It's not Alex's voice but it's one that I know yet can't quite place. "It's Marcus! I'd like to speak to you."

Marcus. I slide off my barstool, relief washing over me. It's only Marcus. Then doubt sets in—what is he doing here? Are Romy and Rob with him? But he'd said "I" not "we."

I stand in the hall in paralyzing indecision. Marcus will know that I'm in because the lights are on. But I could be in the shower. I don't have to answer the door. If I ignore him, he'll leave. If it's important, he'll call me. Why didn't he call me anyway and tell me that he wanted to speak to me, instead of coming all the way to the house and risk me not being in? Something doesn't add up.

But—what if something terrible has happened and he needs to speak to me face-to-face? I've never seen Marcus without Romy and Rob by his side. What if something has happened to them?

"Nell!" Marcus calls again. "I really need to speak to you."

His evident agitation decides me. My heart in my mouth, I open the door. It takes me a while because of the new locks.

"Hi." Marcus lifts his hand in a little wave.

"Are Romy and Rob all right?" I ask.

"What? Yes, they're fine. Can I come in?"

I don't want to let him in but he's already moved forward so I have no choice but to open the door wider. He comes into the hall, his presence making it feel crowded.

"Is there somewhere we can talk?" he asks. "The kitchen, perhaps?"

He moves down the hall and I hesitate before closing the front door, aware that I've let a man I don't know very well into my house and that by shutting the door, I'm cutting off my only escape route, effectively sealing myself inside with him. I close the door anyway, because I can't leave it open, and follow him to the kitchen, feeling horribly vulnerable.

"Shall we sit?" he says, as if the house is his.

I'm about to be polite and ask him if he wants to take off his bulky wax jacket. But I stop myself, not wanting him to get too comfortable, or take it as invitation to stay. Increasingly uneasy, I pull out the barstool nearest to the worktop so that I can grab a knife from the block if I have to. A part of me laughs at myself. Marcus is harmless.

He sits down opposite me, then gets to his feet again.

"There's something I need to tell you," he says, his agitation back. "Romy wanted me to tell you weeks ago but I couldn't find the courage."

My heart sinks, fearing a declaration of love. "You'd better make it quick," I say, finding a smile to lessen the hurt I'm going to cause him. "Alex will be phoning me any minute now."

Alex's name seems to confuse him. He begins pacing up and down. "Oh," he says. "Right." He takes a deep breath. "Here goes."

"Could you sit down and tell me?" I ask, wanting him where I can see him.

"Yes, of course, sorry."

I wait for him to settle but my interruption has cost him his nerve. His mouth is clamped tightly shut.

"Alex will be here on Friday," I say into the silence, hoping that mentioning his name again will deflect Marcus from talking about how he feels about me.

His mouth unclamps. "I've bought the house opposite yours," he blurts out.

It's so far from what I was expecting him to say that I think I must have misunderstood.

"I'm sorry—what did you say?"

"I've bought the house opposite yours, over there." He waves a hand in the direction of the front of the house. His face, from being slightly ashen before he spoke, has turned bright red.

"But—why?"

"Because I've been wanting to move and I was looking for something a bit like yours and it came on the market so I just went for it."

I know I look appalled but I can't help it. I would have preferred a declaration of love because then I could have refused his advances. Here, I'm powerless. He's not asking if I mind if he buys the house right opposite mine, he's telling me that he's already done it.

I blink rapidly. "I don't know what to say."

"I realize it must be a bit of a shock," Marcus says, shifting on the barstool. "Romy said I should speak to you about it before I signed but I was worried you'd tell me you didn't want me living opposite you."

I don't! I want to say. It's not just dismay I feel but confusion. There must have been other properties he could have bought if he wanted to live in the area.

"I did look at other properties," he says, as if he's read my mind. "But I didn't want a flat and other houses were too expensive for me. I've always loved your house and I wanted an outdoor space and mine has a tiny garden out the back, so that clinched it for me, really."

His use of the word "mine" hammers home that it's a done deed. There is nothing I can say to change what has happened.

"I'm surprised you've chosen to move so far away from Romy and Rob," I say, a little savagely. "You've always been such a threesome."

He smiles. "It's one of the reasons I wanted to move. We work together and then I would always be bumping into them when I was out and about, and they'd invite me round because I'm on my own and well, I wanted to kind of remove that obligation from them."

"Alex is moving in with me," I say, underlining that, unlike him, I am not on my own. "In the New Year. He's going to be spending most of his time here."

Marcus gives a slow nod. "Right. By the way, that evening, Rob's birthday, when I saw Alex through your window, I didn't really come to see if your work event had been canceled. I was visiting the house for a second time with the estate agent." He pauses. "When I told Romy and

Rob that I'd made an offer, Romy said I should be up-front with you. I promised I would be, which is why I went and bought champagne when we came to yours for dinner. But I chickened out. There was always a chance that the sale wouldn't go through so I decided to wait until it was definite."

"And now it is," I say.

"Now it is," he echoes.

I get to my feet. "Right, thanks for telling me."

He looks surprised at my dismissal and I wonder if he was expecting me to take out a bottle of wine and celebrate with him.

"When will you be moving in?" I ask, as we move into the hall.

"Beginning of January, hopefully."

I open the front door. "Well, I guess I'll see you around."

"Definitely."

I close the door behind him, wait until I'm sure he's out of earshot, then burst into tears. A part of me, a very small part, wonders if I'm overreacting. Most people would be happy to have a friend living across the road. But I'm not most people and Marcus isn't a friend, he's a friend of a friend. I've never spent any time alone with him, nor do I want to. When I remember how his face had dropped when I'd mentioned that Alex would be moving in with me, my anger resurfaces. Had he really thought that we'd hang out together, sharing cozy suppers and film evenings?

A message comes in, from Romy.

I hear Marcus has told you his news.

I can't bring myself to reply. I'm angry with Romy for not giving me a heads-up. If I'd had advance warning, I could have tried to put Marcus off, told him that it wasn't a great place to live, that drug pushers lined the street at night and knife crime was a common occurrence. But I hadn't known the house was for sale.

I pour myself a glass of wine and spend a moment analyzing why I'm so against the idea. If Romy and Rob had bought the house, I'd have been delighted. And if a stranger had bought it, I wouldn't have cared. It's Marcus, I decide. There's something about him that I've never quite been able to put my finger on.

I put down my glass, go to the sitting room and part the curtains so that I can see the house across the road. It's in darkness, as are the houses on either side of it; only the next house along has a light on downstairs. A movement catches my peripheral vision and I swing my eyes back to the house opposite mine. There's someone there, I'm sure of it, standing as still as stone against the wall, as if they've been caught unawares and are trying to blend into the background. For a moment I want to rush to the front door and yell across the street at him. But I prefer to let Marcus think that I haven't noticed him lurking there—although lurking is probably a bit harsh. It is his house, after all, and after my total lack of enthusiasm it's not surprising he feels awkward being seen there. But I refuse to feel guilty.

By the time I've had a second glass of wine, I've found the perfect solution. Much as I'll be sad to leave the house left to me by my great-aunt, I'll sell it. I have the perfect excuse; with Alex moving in with me, we'll need more space. He'll probably need an office and if we have a baby, the house will definitely be too small. It would be better to move into something larger now, a home we choose together, a home that will be ours, rather than mine.

EXTRACT FROM NOTEBOOK 4

You're certainly full of surprises, Nell. When you didn't leave home at the usual time this morning, I thought you'd decided to work from home and I was annoyed I'd had a wasted journey.

I decided to hang around for a while, in case you'd overslept. It was just as well that I did because an hour later, your front door opened and there you were, all dressed up in a suede jacket and brown leather boots. I guessed you either had an important work meeting or weren't going to work at all and the bounce in your step as I followed behind you told me it was probably the latter. Imagine my surprise when, after a convoluted journey requiring three different buses, you disappeared into a police station.

Were you telling the police that you had a stalker? Or were you seeing them on an entirely different matter? The ultrasmart clothing told me that you wanted them to take you seriously. I reckon it was to do with your past. I know what you did, Nell, I know who you are, I've always known. If you'd really wanted to disappear, you shouldn't have stayed in the UK, you should have gone abroad, where it would have been harder to trace you.

Not that it matters. We'll hardly be discussing the mistakes you made when I kill you.

NELL

PRESENT

"Are you busy tonight?" Alex asks, when he calls me unexpectedly at work on Friday afternoon.

"Not as such, but I have some work to catch up on."

"That's a shame."

"Why?"

"Because I was hoping to see you tonight."

My heart lifts. "I thought you were only arriving tomorrow?"

"I was, but we had a long session with our solicitor yesterday and everything is pretty much tied up, so Béatrice and I thought we may as well leave. We're at Gare du Nord now; our train leaves in an hour. With a bit of luck, I should be with you in about four hours."

"That's wonderful," I say. "Shall I get dinner ready?"

"Only something simple, please. I never thought I'd say this but I've had enough of French cuisine for a while. Too much rich food in too short a time. If I had more self-discipline it would help but I just can't resist those desserts."

I laugh. "How does pasta and salad sound?"

"Perfect."

By the time I get home I only have an hour to get ready, make dinner, and remove the knife from under my pillow. Despite having new locks fitted, I feel safer sleeping with a weapon within reach.

Alex arrives and we hold each tightly in the narrow hallway.

"I've missed you so much," he murmurs.

"Not as much as I've missed you," I say, inhaling the scent of him.

He releases me and we move to the kitchen.

"What was it you wanted to speak to me about?" he asks, when we're sitting at the island, a glass of wine in front of us.

For a moment, I have trouble remembering. And then it comes back to me with visceral force.

"It can wait," I say, not wanting to spoil our first moments together in three weeks. It's not the right time to tell him that I want to be a mother.

"No." Alex takes my hands in his. "It sounded important and I've been imagining all sorts of things. I'd rather you told me now so that we can get it out of the way."

I remove my hands from his and release my hair from its clip, giving myself time to come up with something.

"Christmas," I say. "I wanted to talk to you about Christmas."

"Ah." He rubs his chin. "I wanted to talk to you about that too."

I smile. "Okay, you go first."

"I wanted so much to be able to spend Christmas with you," he says. "But—well, Stephane asked if we could spend it together. I think I told you that when I saw him on Wednesday, he said he wanted to make up for lost time? He's changed so much, Nell, it's like he's grown up overnight. Delphine told me he has a girlfriend so maybe that has something to do with it."

I somehow manage to swallow my crushing disappointment and replace it with a smile.

"So you'll be spending Christmas in Paris?"

"Yes. Unfortunately, my dad can't fly over as he has a hospital appointment he doesn't want to miss on the twenty-seventh. But Béatrice and Victor will be there. Delphine too," he adds.

"Of course."

"I'm sorry."

"Don't be. I'm happy for you, really."

"I'll be back to see the New Year in with you, I promise. I'll book a flight or train to London on the thirtieth. Unless you have plans for the New Year?"

"No, no plans at all."

"That's good, because I'd like to take you somewhere to make it up to you for not being with you at Christmas."

"You don't need to make it up to me."

He comes round to my side of the island, pulls me to my feet and takes me in his arms. "Yes, I do. Could you take ten days off, do you think?"

I can't remember the last time I took such a stretch of time off.

"Yes, I'm sure that will be possible. Where will we be going?"

"I want it to be a surprise." He moves back, searching my face. "Do you have someone you can spend Christmas with?"

"Romy and Rob are probably around," I say, already knowing that they're going to Romy's family in Corsica for Christmas. "Do you have photos?" I ask, not wanting to talk about Christmas anymore. "Of Stephane? I'd like to see him."

"Sure." He takes out his phone, locates his camera roll and shows me a group photo. Béatrice is there but my eyes are immediately drawn to the tall young man standing beside her. I feel that I've seen him before—and then realize it's because he's the image of Alex.

"Wow, even handsomer than his father," I tease. My eyes move to an elegant blond woman sitting on a sofa, Stephane's hand resting lightly on her shoulder. Next to her is an older woman, dressed in navy, a triple strand of pearls around her neck, legs crossed neatly at the ankle. "I'm guessing those two impossibly chic women are your mother and Delphine?"

"Correct." There's pride in Alex's voice. "They might look formidable but they are both very nice."

"I'm sure they are," I say, passing him back his phone. "Hopefully I'll get to meet them one day. And Stephane," I add casually.

"You will, I promise. I wish I could invite you for Christmas but—" He hesitates.

"You haven't told them about me yet," I finish for him.

"No, not yet." He looks embarrassed and I laugh.

"It's all right. It's early days," I say, moving to the cupboard and taking out some pasta, plus a jar of anchovies and some olives.

"I fully intended to tell my mum and Delphine about you when I got to Paris," he says, as I put a pan of water to boil. "Then Delphine phoned and said that Stephane wanted to join us for dinner that evening and I didn't want to rock the boat. But I know they'll be delighted when I do tell them. My mum is always saying that I need to settle down."

A thrill runs through me at his words. "Are we settling down, then?"

"I guess." He looks at me, checking if it's okay. "I mean, if I'm going to be moving in with you, that's a commitment, isn't it?"

"Yes," I say, smiling. "It is."

He takes our glasses and hands me mine. "To us," he says, raising his glass.

"To us," I repeat. I take a sip of wine. "I wanted to talk to you about that too."

"About what?"

"About you moving in with me."

About to take a drink, Alex pauses. "Please don't tell me you've changed your mind."

"No, not at all. But I've been wondering—as we've decided to commit to each other—maybe we should move, rent something bigger. A new start for both of us."

He looks dismayed. "But you love this house. I love this house. And this part of London is great."

"We don't have to move out of this area, just out of this road. It would be nice to have more space."

Alex frowns. "What's brought this on? I'm not against the idea per se but wouldn't it be better to wait a while?"

"Marcus has bought the house across the road."

"Marcus?" He looks puzzled. "Across the road from where?"

"From here." I point toward the hallway. "The house opposite mine."

Alex frowns. "Wow. Isn't that—well—a little weird?"

The hiss of boiling water tells me that the pan is ready for the pasta. I move to the cooker and slowly wind a bunch of spaghetti into the water. "I think so, yes."

"When did you find out?"

"He came over on Monday to tell me."

"So." Alex's brow wrinkles, working it out. "That evening, when you invited everyone over to meet me, he must have already known—maybe have already bought it?"

"He might have been waiting for the final signature, but yes, he'd practically bought it."

"How do you feel about it?"

I turn from the cooker. "Uncomfortable. If you weren't moving in with me, there wouldn't be much I could do about it. But with you moving in, we have the perfect excuse, because it *will* be a little cramped."

"I like cramped," he says, coming over and putting his arms around me. He nuzzles my neck. "We have ten minutes until the spaghetti is ready, don't we?"

"Thereabouts," I murmur, holding him tighter.

He begins unbuttoning my shirt. "Perfect."

NELL

PRESENT

"I meant to ask," I say, a while later over soggy pasta puttanesca. "And this isn't in any way to make you feel guilty, but did you send me flowers last week? Lilies."

Alex groans. "No, I didn't, and now I do feel guilty because of course I should have thought to send you flowers, especially after letting you down by going to Paris."

"No guilt required," I tell him. "They were dead."

"I hope you told the florist."

"I couldn't, because there wasn't a card. Anyway, I think they were delivered by hand. I found them on the doorstep."

He looks quizzically at me. "But that would mean whoever delivered them would have known they were dead."

"Yes."

"And you don't know who they were from?"

"No."

"Hm. Have you thought that they might have been from Marcus?"

I look at him, shocked. "Marcus wouldn't do something like that."

"He bought the house opposite you and only told you after the event," he reminds me.

"Yes, but that's just weird. The flowers are creepy."

"Is there a difference?"

I fall silent.

"Hey." Alex's voice brings me back to the present and I decide that while Alex is here I'm going to live in the moment. For the next ten days, I won't think about the future, about the weeks ahead when he's no longer with me. I won't think about Damon Parker coming after me. I won't think about the past, or mention babies. I'll ignore the longing, the need to know if having a child is something Alex might consider, until after Christmas, when the New Year is about to begin, when we're away on holiday together. I can see everything coming together in my mind, almost tangible, if I can just be patient.

"Sorry," I say, twirling my fork in my pasta. "I've been thinking about what we could do this weekend. Any preferences?"

"Plenty. And they don't involve going anywhere." He looks suddenly alarmed. "Please don't tell me you've invited friends over."

"I haven't. But I was thinking we should have Béatrice and Victor over while you're here."

"I'd really like that. I miss not being able to invite people over. Not having my own place means I have to take them to restaurants."

"You'll have your own place soon," I say.

"Our own place," he corrects. "Are you sure you want to move?"

"Quite sure," I say firmly. "Why don't you see if Béatrice and Victor are free on Sunday? If they are, I'd like to invite Inès along as well."

"Good idea."

He takes out his phone and sends a message to his sister. She replies almost immediately, saying that she was thinking of inviting us over but that she and Victor are delighted to come to mine. I message Inès and invite her, adding that if it's one of her weekends with Maxime, he's welcome to come along as well.

It's a weekend without and I'm already bored so I'd love to come, she replies.

Great, I message back. *And please don't say anything about me learning French. I don't want Alex to know just yet.*

She sends a thumbs-up emoji and I turn to Alex. "Perfect. They're all free."

"Thank you," he says. "For thinking of inviting Béatrice and Victor over. I can't wait for the four of us to be able to spend more time together."

"Me too," I say, giving him a kiss.

On Sunday, I go shopping early, leaving Alex to recover from his ever-present jet lag. I come back laden with bags and he's mortified that I've carried bottles of wine as well as kilos of fruit and vegetables.

"Why didn't you call me?" he exclaims, taking the bags from me. "I would have come and carried them for you."

I slip the last two bags from my shoulders. "I didn't want to disturb you. And they weren't that heavy. I've carried more."

"You're not doing another thing." He heaves the bags onto the worktop. "Sit down, while I do the cooking."

I watch him as he moves around the kitchen, opening cupboards, working out where things are until he turns and looks at me.

"What?" he asks when he sees me smiling.

"Nothing. Just loving seeing the domestic side of you," I say.

Béatrice and Victor arrive, followed soon after by Inès. They all profess to love my house, even though it's far less grand than their apartments. Alex tells them that he's going to be working in the UK for three weeks each month and I tell them of our plans to move to something bigger.

"I have some news too," Inès says, when we're having a pre-lunch drink. "Maxime's transfer to London has come through. From March first, he'll be living with me."

"That's wonderful!" Béatrice exclaims. She leans over and gives Inès a hug, her bump getting in the way. She settles back on the sofa with difficulty. "I'll be glad when this one arrives," she says, rubbing her stomach.

"Only a few more weeks," Victor says, smiling at her. "Then all hell will be let loose."

We all laugh and he turns to Inès. "I'm very pleased for you, even if it means we're going to lose our babysitter."

"Maxime and I will babysit for you anytime. Hopefully your beautiful child will inspire us to start our family sooner rather than later."

"I wouldn't count on that. When you see how we look after a few months of sleepless nights, you might change your minds," Victor says, making us all laugh again. He turns to Alex. "You've been there before—tell me, seriously, how was it?"

Alex scratches his head. "Wow, you're asking me something, it was such a long time ago." He thinks for a moment. "Scary, confusing, but also wonderful. That sums it up best, I think. But you and Béatrice are older than Delphine and I were and that will count for a lot."

"Would you go through it again, though?" Victor asks.

I get to my feet, uncomfortable at where the conversation is going. "I'll just clear these away," I say, gathering up the empty glasses.

"Let me help you," Inès says.

"Thanks."

We carry the glasses through to the kitchen and put them on the island.

"Did you need to escape?" she asks, giving me a sympathetic smile.

"It's just that I didn't want to hear Alex's answer, not in front of everyone. What if he'd said no?"

"Haven't you discussed it with him yet?"

"No, I'm waiting until we're on holiday. I don't know where we're going, he wants it to be a surprise."

"You really have no idea?"

"Well, I think I've kind of figured it out. Alex told me I need to bring clothes for both hot and cold weather so my guess is that we're going to Washington to see his father, as he won't be seeing him at

Christmas and then on to somewhere hot for a beach holiday. But I don't mind where we go, all I want is for us to spend some time together, just the two of us. What about you? Are you spending the holidays with Maxime?"

"Yes, we're celebrating Christmas on the twenty-fourth with my family and on the twenty-fifth with Maxime's. Luckily our families both live in Paris so it's easy to divide ourselves between the two." She gives me a smile. "Shall we meet for a drink, once Alex has gone back to the US? Have a little Christmas celebration of our own?"

"That would be lovely," I say.

NELL

PRESENT

"So, tell me more about Marcus," Alex says as he's packing his case to leave. "I feel I really need to get a handle on the guy."

"I don't know that much about him," I admit. "I only know him because he's friends with Romy and Rob."

"He works with them, right?"

"Yes, they're partners in an advertising agency."

"Don't they all live in the same area?"

I nod. "He lives a couple of streets away from them. Until he moves in across the road."

Alex raises his eyebrows. "I can't work out if the guy is just needy or creepy. Did he say when he's moving in?"

I hand him a pile of shirts. "January, he said."

"What does Romy think about it? Did she even know what he was up to or has it come like a bolt from the blue to her too?"

"No, she knew, so I feel a bit annoyed with her. She could have warned me. There was this whole scenario when they came for dinner a month or so ago. Marcus went off to buy champagne, saying he had news to share and when he came back, he made it about Rob's birthday the previous week. I could tell that Romy had been expecting him to say something else and he admitted on Monday that he'd promised Romy he'd tell me about buying the house. But, in his own words, he chickened out. So she already knew at that point."

"Have you talked to her about it?" he asks, closing his case.

"No. She's sent me a couple of messages but I haven't replied. I should have, I know, but I can't bring myself to. It's hanging over me, I hate it."

"Why don't you call her now? Get it over and done with. Don't pussyfoot around, like you British always do. Tell her how you feel."

"Hmm." I hate confrontation but I need to clear the air with Romy and the longer I leave it, the harder it's going to be. "Maybe you're right."

He stands, picks up his case. "Do you want privacy?"

"No. It's fine. Let's go downstairs, I'll phone her from the kitchen."

I call Romy, part of me hoping she won't pick up. But she does, immediately.

"Hey, Nell, I'm glad you called."

"I thought I should," I say, putting her on speakerphone so that Alex can hear.

"I know you're probably annoyed that I didn't tell you about Marcus but it wasn't my news to give and anyway, he asked me not to."

"Don't you think it's strange that he didn't want me to know he'd bought the house across the road?"

"Yes, but it was the same with us. We only knew he'd rented a flat in the same area after the fact."

"Didn't you find that weird?"

"No, we thought it was great. It made it easier work-wise too, especially back then when we were just starting out and couldn't afford office space. We used to work from ours."

"So why has he suddenly decided to move?"

"It's not a sudden decision. He's wanted to buy for a while and he's always said that if he ever bought something it would be in the Paddington area, as that's the station his train leaves from when he goes to see his family. At the moment, he has to cross half of London." She pauses. "I know you probably see it as an invasion of your privacy but it's not as if he's going to be popping over every evening for a drink. At least, not unless you invite him," she adds.

I look at Alex, a question in my eyes. He understands and nods.

"It's actually not going to be an issue," I tell Romy. "Alex will be spending most of his time in the UK from January so we've decided to look for something bigger as he'll be working from home some of the time and will need a study." Alex raises his eyebrows in mock surprise and I give him a smile and a shrug.

"You're going to move?" Romy can't keep the surprise from her voice. "But, Nell, you love your house. It's lovely."

"I know, but I'm sure we'll find somewhere equally lovely."

"Marcus is going to be upset."

"I don't see why."

"It's just the way he is. As I said, he wouldn't have invaded your privacy but I think he liked the idea of you being nearby."

"Ten feet away," I say.

"Is that why you've decided to move, because he's moving in? Because that's how he'll see it."

I want to tell her that I don't care how Marcus sees it.

"No," I say. "As soon as Alex mentioned spending more time here and moving in with me on a permanent basis, we realized the best way forward was having a flat or a house we'd chosen together. But we'll be neighbors with Marcus for a while as it will take a few months to find somewhere," I add, to soften the blow. "We're going to start looking in January."

"I'm really pleased for you, Nell, it's great that Alex is moving in with you. You'll be telling me you're pregnant next."

"Let's try and catch up before Christmas," I say, neatly avoiding what Romy just said.

"Good idea. I'll have a look at the calendar and get back to you."

NELL

PRESENT

Alex leaves and to distract myself from being on my own again until New Year's Eve, I focus on the plans we made while he was here. After spending Christmas week with his family in Paris, he'll arrive in London on the thirtieth. We'll see in the New Year together and the next day, we're leaving on holiday. My suspicion that we're going to Washington to see Alex's father, then flying on to a resort, seems correct, because when I asked if I would need a swimsuit, Alex said I should pack more than one. I'm already counting the days.

At one point during our time together, I found myself asking about Ariane and to my relief, Alex hadn't bristled at the mention of her name.

"Did your mother meet Ariane?" I'd asked.

"Yes, she did."

"And did she approve?"

He smiled. "Of course. Ariane was French."

"Oh." My heart had sunk. "Is that important to her, that you're with someone French?"

"Absolutely. She will totally disapprove of you." Catching the look of alarm on my face, he'd laughed. "I'm teasing. The only thing my mother cares about is that I'm happy." He'd taken me in his arms and swung me around the kitchen. "And I am. Very happy. Everything is coming together. Moving here, moving in with you is perfect timing. For a start, I'll be able to see Stephane more often."

I'd experienced a moment of doubt at his words, wondering if that was why he wanted to spend more time in London. But then I remembered he'd suggested it before Stephane had come back into his life.

Sadie comes into my office, her laptop open.

"How about this one?" she asks, plonking it down on the desk in front of me.

I look at the advert for a two-bed flat to rent in Westbourne Terrace, a couple of streets away from where I live now.

"Beautiful but expensive," I say.

"It has a roof terrace," she points out, because she knows how much I want one since seeing Inès's. "But you're right, it is expensive. You'd be better off buying something together."

"Maybe, except we're not at that stage yet."

She closes her laptop. "Is everything all right? You seem a little distracted lately."

"I'm fine, just not loving the run-up to Christmas. I could do without pushing through the crowds on the way home, and the bus takes twice as long because of all the traffic."

She gives me a sympathetic smile. "It must be hard to get into the Christmas spirit when Alex is going to be in France. But at least you'll be spending the New Year with him."

"Yes," I agree. "It's nice that I have that to look forward to."

I feel her looking at me more closely and I know it's because my voice was flat. The truth is, I'm not looking forward to the New Year as much as I was, because on top of everything else, there's something about Alex that's been playing on my mind.

"Why don't you work from home tomorrow?" Sadie says.

I stretch my arms above my head, easing the tension in my neck.

"Actually, that would be really nice. But I'm meeting Inès for a drink after work so I may as well come in."

"Where are you meeting her?"

"I don't know. We haven't arranged anything yet."

"Well, suggest meeting in the Paddington area and then you can work from home."

I tilt my head, looking up at her. "Have I ever told you that you're a genius, Sadie?"

"Not often enough," she says.

"Sure you don't mind?"

"Will I miss seeing your downcast face? No, not really."

I look at her guiltily. "Have I really been that bad?"

"No. But you do seem to have the cares of the world on your shoulders at the moment."

"I just find it hard when Alex is away."

"I know."

I reach for my phone. "I'll message Inès now."

"Good."

Would you be able to come to Paddington tomorrow evening? I type. *We could have a drink at one of the bars along the Grand Canal.*

Sounds good.

Great! Let's meet outside Costa in the station.

She sends me a thumbs-up emoji and I feel warm inside at having made another friend.

I spend much of the next day wondering if I should tell Inès my worries about Alex. It will mean confiding in her but I can't expect her to help me without some background information.

"I'm glad you suggested meeting up," I say that evening, as we walk to one of the barges moored along the canal. "There's something I want to ask you. It's about Ariane." I turn and glance at her face under the beautiful black Panama hat she's wearing. "If you don't mind, that is."

"Ask away," she says, blowing on her hands, because the temperature has dropped a notch or two. "I'll help if I can."

"Let's find somewhere to have a drink first."

The canal looks beautiful. The barges moored along its bank are decorated with Christmas lights and there's an air of general good cheer in the atmosphere. As we push our way to a tiny table at the back of the first barge that has space for us, it seems, from the smattering of conversations I hear, that most people have taken the following week off and are having a last drink with friends and colleagues before heading off on their holidays.

I wait until we're settled with our glasses of mulled wine and have wished each other a happy Christmas.

"It's about Ariane thinking she had a stalker," I begin.

"Nothing was proved," she reminds me.

"I know." I take a sip of wine. "It's just that I think I have one too."

She pauses, her glass halfway to her lips.

"A stalker?"

"Yes."

"But—since when?"

"A couple of months," I say, even though it's longer. "Sometimes, when I'm out and about, going to and from work, I feel that there's someone following me. I've never seen them but I know that they're there. They even got into my house before I changed the locks."

Inès looks alarmed. "Nell, this is serious. Have you told the police?"

"Yes."

She lets about a breath. "Good. When Ariane told me she thought she was being followed, I advised her to go to the police but she refused. What did they say? I hope they took you seriously."

"They did and I have a number to call if ever I feel in danger."

"That's good. But, Nell, you've worried me. Is it a jealous ex, do you think? They say that stalkers are usually known to the person they're stalking."

"I thought I knew who it was but now I'm no longer sure. I've been wondering about Marcus, but—"

"Marcus? The guy who bought the house across the street from yours?"

"Yes, that one," I say, remembering that Alex had mentioned it when Inès had come to lunch with Béatrice and Victor the previous week. "It just seems a bit of a creepy thing to do." I twirl the stem of the glass between my fingers. "But I can't help thinking that it might be something to do with Alex."

"Your stalker?"

"Yes. I know it's mad but it seems a little strange that both Ariane and I, two of his girlfriends, have thought that we're being followed while in a relationship with him. So, I wanted to ask you—do you know anything about his job?"

"His job?" She sits back in her chair. "He's a consultant, isn't he?"

"Marcus thinks he's a spy."

"A spy?" Inès's eyebrows shoot up. "Why does he think that?"

"I suppose because I was never very clear on what Alex does when Marcus first asked me. And there are a couple of things which make me wonder if he might be right, like Alex having two phones, one for business and one for personal calls, and always calling me rather than me call him. And then there's the fact that Ariane worked for the French secret service." I take a drink of wine. "I thought Béatrice might have said something to you?"

"About Alex being a spy?

"Or working for the secret service."

She shakes her head. "If he is, Béatrice would be in the dark as much as the rest of us because he wouldn't be allowed to tell anyone. But maybe that's where Ariane and Alex met. Maybe he works for the secret service too. He's a French national, so it's possible."

"So, what if Ariane's murder wasn't anything to do with her job but more about who she was in relation to Alex?" I say. "And what about Caitlin. What if her death *wasn't* an accident?"

"Nell, you're scaring me."

"I'm scaring myself."

"Have you spoken to Alex about any of this?"

"No, because when I told him about Marcus thinking he was a spy, he said that he wasn't a spy. But he would say that, wouldn't he, even if he was?"

"Probably," Inès says. "I don't know how it works if you're married or in a serious relationship with someone. It seems crazy that you'd have to hide the true nature of your work from them."

"I can't believe we're sitting here discussing the possibility of Alex being a spy," I say despondently.

"Honestly, Nell, I don't think he is. I don't think he's capable of living a lie. You'd have to be really devious to do that."

I drain my drink, her words making me uncomfortable. What if she knew that I've been doing exactly that, living a lie, lying not just to my friends, but also to Alex?

"You're right," I say.

"Your stalker is more likely to be Marcus. Maybe he's jealous of your relationship with Alex. Has he ever tried to take things further than friendship with you?"

"No." I hesitate. "He did try and ask me out a couple of times but I managed to deflect him. But nothing more."

"It doesn't mean he isn't your stalker."

"I know." I nod toward her empty glass. "Do you want another drink?"

"No thanks. I'm leaving early tomorrow morning and I still haven't packed. Come on, I'll walk you back to your house."

"There's no need," I protest.

"After what you've just told me, there's every need," she says.

EXTRACT FROM NOTEBOOK 4

Sometimes, when I go into the room I use as an office, I scare myself. I look at the walls, covered in hundreds of photographs, and wonder at what I've become. How is it possible that I've let my life be defined to such an extent by another human being? It is madness, I tell myself. I am mad. Then nostalgia will take hold and for a moment I'll mourn the good, decent, honest person I once was. Because I wasn't born evil, I just became it.

On the outside, no one would ever guess at the obsession that lies within me. I live a normal life. I have friends, I have a job. When I'm not following you, I'm at work. It's why I only follow you mornings, evenings, and at weekends. Once, when you tried to avoid me by changing your routine, I took some days off, citing urgent business. But then, realizing I'd worked out what you were doing, you chose to work from home for a while, which was a lot less fun for me.

Not that it matters. You'll be exactly where I want you to be when I kill you.

NELL

PRESENT

I sit bolt upright in my bed, my heart pounding. Something woke me.

Sliding the knife from under my pillow, I peel the bedcovers back and get quietly out of bed, suppressing a shiver when my feet touch the cold wooden floor. Moving to the window, I part the curtain slightly, hoping to see a light on in one of the houses farther up the street so that I won't feel alone. As I look out, my eyes are automatically drawn to the house across the street, the one Marcus has bought. I breathe in sharply; I can't see anyone but the prickling down my spine tells me that someone *is* there—and that they are looking right at me.

My instinct is to pull the curtains shut and call Superintendent Moss. But by the time the police arrive, they'll be gone. More than that, I'm tired of being afraid. So I push down the fear and stay where I am, my body perfectly still, my eyes focused on the same spot, holding their invisible gaze. Is it Marcus?

I'm not sure why I do it. Maybe it's because imagining that it's Marcus standing against the wall of his soon-to-be home, his eyes unblinking behind his blue-framed glasses, makes it less frightening than imagining it's a stranger. But for whatever reason, I find myself parting the curtains a little more, so that whoever it is can see me clearly, and I raise my arm, showing them the knife I'm holding in my hand, its long blade pointing downward. *I'm waiting for you*, I mouth silently. I wait a beat, then step back from the window, close the curtains, and sink onto the bed, my limbs trembling, not for fear but from exhilaration. I have shown whomever it is that I'm ready to fight, that I won't cower before them.

It only takes a few moments for doubt to creep in. What if it was Marcus? What will he think of me, threatening him with a knife? What if it was someone sent by Damon Parker, or someone connected to Alex, because it's still there in my mind that he might be a spy and that Ariane, and maybe Caitlin, were killed because of his job. What if I've antagonized them? What if they're crossing the street at this very moment?

Leaping from the bed, I go to my dressing table and push it in front of the door. If they get into the house—but surely my new locks will make it impossible?—and I hear them coming up the stairs, the barricade will buy me enough time to call Superintendent Moss.

I stay awake with the knife in my hand and only sleep when morning comes. By the time I wake, half the day has gone. Alex phones to tell me he's preparing to leave for Paris, and while we're speaking, all I can think is that if he is working for the French secret service, someone might be listening in.

"Only another week and we'll be together," he murmurs. "And when we come back from holiday, our new life together will begin."

NELL

PRESENT

I'm about to leave for work on Monday when an early morning call from the police changes my plans. An officer tells me that Superintendent Moss would like to see me before she leaves on her Christmas break and wants to know if I'm free at ten o'clock.

"Yes," I reply, my heart in my mouth, because I hadn't expected to hear anything for weeks. "Thank you."

I call Sadie.

"I've got an urgent appointment this morning," I explain, "so I won't be in until lunchtime."

"No problem," she says cheerfully.

"Why don't you take Christmas Eve off?" I say, guilty that I'm leaving her to hold the fort again.

"Don't be silly. Besides, Simon is on duty on Christmas Eve so we can't leave for my parents' until Christmas morning."

"I'll bring cake," I promise. "To have this afternoon."

Sadie tuts down the phone. "Stop with the guilt complex. It's annoying."

Another taxi takes me to the police station, adding to the guilt

I feel about the amount of money I'm spending on cab fares to give myself peace of mind.

"First of all, let's talk about Damon Parker," Superintendent Moss says, once I'm installed in her office, sitting across from her. "We made some inquiries and apart from his mother, nobody visits him in prison. He's due to be released next month and I doubt he would jeopardize his chances by getting someone to follow you."

The air leaves my lungs, leaving me physically winded.

"We'll talk about the implications of that in a moment," Superintendent Moss continues. "First, there's been a development in Bryony's case that I wanted you to be aware of before it gets into the public domain."

The sudden drain of blood from my brain at the superintendent's words makes me light-headed. This is it, this is what I've been waiting for all these years. In my excitement, I lean forward and grip the edge of the desk with my fingers. "I was right, wasn't I, about Brett Parker driving the car that day?"

Superintendent Moss frowns. "No." She looks at me curiously. "I didn't think you still believed that."

"I've never stopped believing it."

"That isn't what I wanted to tell you, Nell." The superintendent's voice is gentle and my stomach cramps with fear.

"What then?"

Superintendent Moss's voice lifts. "After all these years, we finally have Bryony's murderer."

My mind reels, searching for who it could be. Damon Parker, it has to be him. Damon Parker killed Bryony Sanders and his father covered up for him. But even in my desperation not to be completely, totally wrong about Brett Parker being involved in some way, I know the straws that I'm clutching at don't exist. Damon Parker's release from prison wouldn't be imminent if he'd been found guilty of Bryony's murder.

"A week or so ago," Superintendent Moss continues. "A lawyer contacted us and told us his client wanted to confess to the murder of Bryony Sanders."

"But—" I clutch at another straw. "How do you know that his client is telling the truth?"

"Because his story checks out. We've verified everything. He was a lecturer at King's, and Bryony was one of his students. She told him he reminded her of her dad—if you remember, she had lost her father six months earlier. She began to confide in him, about her mum and her worries at leaving her alone in the US. He presumed, with the arrogance that sort of man often has, that she was in love with him but as it turned out, she saw him as a replacement father figure and nothing more. That only became apparent to him when he took her back to his flat the day you saw her getting into his car outside your flat. He'd been waiting for her to come out of the restaurant where she worked so that he could 'bump into' her. He followed her for a couple of minutes in his car and witnessed her getting her phone snatched. It gave him the chance to come to her rescue and although he made a halfhearted attempt to go after the man on the moped, he had already formed a plan to take Bryony back to his flat, telling her he had a book he wanted to give her to help with her course work." She pauses. "In his flat, she rejected his advances, and he lost his temper and strangled her. He waited until the early hours then drove the car with her body in the boot to Wimbledon Common and set fire to it." She draws a paper from a file on her desk. "He was interviewed at the time, like her other lecturers and classmates at the university. Nobody mentioned his name in connection with Bryony so he didn't come up on our radar as someone who should be looked into further. According to our records, on the day Bryony was murdered, he spent the day alone at home marking exam papers, then met up with a friend for dinner in the evening. Probably because of his status—he was an eminent professor at King's—his story about marking exam papers was believed and the restaurant checked out. What we didn't know was that while he was having dinner, Bryony was lying dead in his flat."

"But what about the car?" I ask, desperately looking for something, anything, to tell me that the man might be lying. "Didn't you think at one point that it was a rental car? How come you weren't able to trace it back to him?"

"It seems we were wrong about that."

"It wasn't a rental car?"

"Not exactly. We did check his car when we were making our inquiries in the weeks following Bryony's murder, as we did with everyone we questioned. He had a flashy Toyota registered in his name. What we didn't know—what we failed to check—was that it was in for a service on the day that Bryony was murdered and the garage had given him a courtesy car for the weekend. When he turned up at the garage without it, he told them it had been stolen. The garage in question reported the theft to the police but the police failed to follow it up. They also failed to make any connection between the stolen courtesy car and the car we were trying to trace in connection with Bryony's murder."

Despair suffuses my body. "Why?" My voice rises. "Why confess now, after fourteen years? He must know that he's going to jail."

"He won't be going to jail. He's terminally ill. According to his doctor, he'll be lucky to make it to the New Year. Hence his confession. He has nothing to lose by confessing and everything to gain." She gives a grim smile. "Redemption. That's what most people who confess to a crime on their deathbed are after. Redemption."

"Do you have a photo of him?"

Superintendent Moss nods, opens the file on her desk, and slides a photo across to me. "This was taken a couple of years ago, before he became ill."

I almost don't want to look. I close my eyes a moment, praying that the man in the photograph is going to look something like Brett Parker, then open them. The photo is of a man I've never seen before, a man who looks nothing like Brett Parker did. I clap a hand over my mouth, horrified at the extent of my mistake.

Understanding my shock, Superintendent Moss slides another photo across.

"This is his photo from when he taught at King's," she says.

I stare at it, mentally tightening the jawline, darkening the hair a little. There's a resemblance to Brett Parker but it doesn't bring me any relief. Superintendent Moss was right all along; I had remembered Brett Parker's face from when I'd bumped into him outside the supermarket on the day of Bryony's murder and had confused him with the man driving the car.

"Is he at least American?" I ask hopelessly.

"No. But he did tell us that when he spoke to Bryony, he often adopted an American accent. It was a joke between them, apparently. That's why he sounded American when he called to her from the car." She pauses. "I need to warn you, Nell. The news about Bryony's killer being caught is going to be major headline news. Once the media gets hold of the story, they'll drag up everything to do with the case, and your name and your photo will be out there. Every journalist in the land will be looking for you and they won't stop until they find you."

Fear bubbles inside me. I think of Alex, of my friends, of what they will say when they find out what I did. "I'm going to lose everyone," I say, my voice hollow. "I deserve it. I've ruined so many lives."

I'm glad Superintendent Moss doesn't patronize me by denying it. "You might want to think about taking an extended holiday until the initial furor dies down," she says.

"It won't go away though, will it? The press will find me wherever I am. Sooner or later I'm going to have to face the music."

"If I could give you one piece of advice, it will be to tell those close to you before it breaks."

I nod. "Do you know when that will be?"

"The man's lawyer extracted a promise from us that we won't go public until he's dead." She seems annoyed at having to keep to that promise. "He's in a hospice, so it won't be long. A couple of weeks, a month at the outside, maybe."

It's more, much more, than I could have hoped for.

"Will you give me twenty-four hours' warning, before the news breaks?" I ask.

Superintendent Moss nods. "I can do that," she says. "Now, before you go, I'd like you to give me a list of friends, work colleagues, current partners." She leaves a question at the end of the sentence.

"I do have a partner," I say.

"Have you known him long?"

"Coming up to six months. He's American," I add. "French-American."

She sits back in her chair. "Right. Does he know about your past?"

"No."

"Where is he from in the US?"

"Washington, DC."

"Can I ask how old he is?"

"Forty-four."

She straightens up and opens her laptop. "I'd like you to tell me more about him, please."

"You don't think—" I pause.

"Every person you know is a suspect," she says. "Until I rule them out."

EXTRACT FROM NOTEBOOK 4

I have to say that you continue to surprise me, Nell. If I wasn't who I am, if I wasn't what I am, if I was just an ordinary person, I might have been frightened by the sight of you standing at the window the other night with a knife in your hand.

It delighted me that you knew I was there, though it would have been impossible for you to see me dressed as I was, head to toe in black with only a minimal slit in my balaclava for my eyes. It means you're so attuned to my presence that you can sense me, even when there're a couple of brick walls between us. And that makes it so much more interesting.

But still, I need to bring it to an end. I never intended it to go on for so long. I was waiting for you to be so frightened by the thought of me that you would crack. I wanted to see you disintegrate before I finally killed you. But that hasn't happened and although I hate to admit it, I kind of admire your ability to function when deep down, you must be terrified at what you know is coming, and sooner than you think.

Christmas is a time of happiness and goodwill to all men. But it's something I won't be considering when I kill you.

NELL

PRESENT

It's only when Sadie calls me on my cell phone that I remember I was meant to have gone into work after my meeting with Superintendent Moss.

"I wanted to make sure you were all right," she says. "As you said you'd be in at lunchtime."

"I'm so sorry, Sadie, I should have let you know." I search for something to tell her because to say I forgot won't cut it. "I didn't feel great, so I came home after my appointment. I meant to phone you but I fell asleep on the sofa."

The part about not feeling great is true, the rest is a lie. I can't imagine ever being able to sleep again, not with the weight of so much guilt on my shoulders.

"And now I've woken you," Sadie says, contrite. "It's just that when it got to three o'clock, I got worried. You sound dreadful—are you coming down with flu, do you think?"

"I don't know. Maybe."

"Well, no coming back to work until after your holiday. You need to be well enough to spend Christmas with Romy and Rob."

I'd forgotten that I'd told her that. "It doesn't matter if I can't," I say.

"You can't spend Christmas Day on your own!" She sounds so aghast I almost smile. "Look, I need to go but if you need anything, just shout."

My eyes blur. "I will. Thanks, Sadie."

When Alex calls in the evening to tell me he's arrived safely in Paris, I can barely speak to him. All I can think is that within a few weeks, I'll have lost everything that is dear to me, not just Alex, but my friends, my job, my house, because the only way to avoid the nightmare heading my way is to disappear again. This time, I'll go abroad, change my name again and live a quiet life without friends, as I did before. I'm too much of a coward to stay and face it.

I vaguely remember Superintendent Moss telling me that I shouldn't let the knowledge that I'd been wrong about Brett Parker define the rest of my life. But it's changed everything. Two lives were lost because I stubbornly refused to accept that I might be wrong, despite the police repeatedly telling me that Brett Parker wasn't involved in any way in Bryony's murder. I had never wavered from my belief that he was driving the car that Bryony had gotten into. I had even begun to think he was also responsible for her murder, because if it wasn't him, why had her murderer never been found? It had afforded me the luxury of being able to justify my actions. How did I ever think that I, a twenty-two-year-old girl, knew more than detectives with years of experience?

I spend the next few days in a daze, unable to sleep because Brett Parker haunts me. I can't stop thinking about how bewildered and angry he must have been when I insisted he'd picked Bryony up in his car that day. No matter how much I tried to dress it up by calling it "collating information," I see now that my actions were those of a stalker.

When Brett Parker isn't haunting me, his son, having spent the best years of his life in prison because of me, takes his place. I have never blamed him for wanting to kill me, I've always understood where he was coming from. But I always thought that one day, he would see that I was right about his father. Now, that will never happen.

Sadie keeps in touch, asking how I am, and because I don't want her to worry, I tell her I'm feeling a little better each day. I should have told her that I was feeling worse because on Christmas Eve she messages to say that she's on her way over. Alarmed, I message back.

I'm still full of cold. Please don't come, I don't want you to be ill for Christmas.

I wait, hoping I've managed to discourage her. My screen lights up.

That's exactly why I'm coming—Christmas!

Knowing that nothing I say will make her change her mind, I hastily change out of the pajamas I've been wearing since the morning and run a brush through my hair. A look in the mirror makes me reach for my makeup bag. There are dark circles under my eyes and my face looks pallid. By the time she rings on the doorbell, I'm a better version of what I was before.

"Oh my God, you look terrible!" she exclaims. "Have you been eating?"

"Well—" I begin.

She barges into the hallway, carrying two large bags. A delicious smell of roast chicken emanates from one of them. "Go and sit down!" she barks. "I'm going in the kitchen, I'll call you in a minute. And if you really want something to do while you're waiting, there are a couple of emails that need your attention. I forwarded them to you on the way over."

"Can't I just—"

"No!"

I do as I'm told and go and sit with my laptop in the living room. There are more than a couple of emails and I know from their dates that Sadie has been holding them back so I wouldn't be overloaded while I was ill. I also know that she's only giving them to me now to keep me away from the kitchen, when the sounds of pots and pans being taken from cupboards makes me wonder what she's preparing. Forty-five minutes later, I find out when she calls me through.

The trouble she's gone to makes me cry. There's a small Christmas tree on the island, complete with tiny lights, three prettily wrapped gifts at its foot. The island itself has been beautifully laid with red place mats, champagne, and wineglasses. A bottle of champagne waits in an ice bucket and there's an assortment of canapes on a china plate.

"It's beautiful," I say through my tears. "But I don't deserve it, I don't deserve any of it."

She rushes over and gives me a hug. "Of course you do! Why would you even say that?"

"Because of what I've done. I've done some terrible things, Sadie." I try to stop, because even in my distress I know I'm treading on dangerous ground, and that if I continue I might end up telling her everything. But I can't seem to stop myself. "I'm not the person you think I am. I've lied to you, to everyone, even to Alex." The mention of his name makes me cry harder.

Sadie doesn't say anything, just leads me to the island and makes me sit down. She takes the champagne from the ice bucket, unscrews the wire, and pops the cork. Her silence is so unusual that my tears stop. She hands me a sheet of paper towel and I dry my eyes and blow my nose while she fills our glasses with champagne. All I can think is that she's decided to ignore what I said.

"I know who you are, Nell," she says, handing me a glass of champagne.

"You don't," I say. "If you did, you wouldn't want anything to do with me."

"You're Elle Nugent," she says. "And it doesn't change anything." She clinks her glass against mine. "Happy Christmas, Nell."

I stare at her, wondering if I heard right. "You know? But—but how?"

"Simon," she says. "When he first met you, he thought he knew you from somewhere." She smiles. "It was your big eyes, apparently. But it was only because of the Bryony Sanders case being reopened that he realized who you were."

"Is he involved in the case?" I ask, still trying to get my head around the fact that she knows who I am and is still sitting in my house, about to have dinner with me.

"No. But a week or so ago, a photo of you from back then was circulated internally by someone high up in the force who was trying to find you, and Simon recognized you." She pauses. "He hasn't said that he knows where you are. He wanted me to speak to you first."

"It's all right, we found each other. Funnily enough, it was me who contacted her."

Sadie slides off the barstool. "If you want to talk about it, I'm here for you. If you don't want to, that's fine. But before we do anything, we're going to eat." She moves to the oven. "I hope you're hungry."

"I am," I say, realizing. "Is that roast chicken I can smell?"

"Chicken?" Sadie looks affronted. "It's Christmas, girl. I cooked a turkey at home, just a small one, and it's in a special bag, so it should still be nice and hot. In the oven, there's stuffing, pigs in blankets, roast parsnips and carrots, and roast potatoes." She ticks them off on her fingers. "And on the hob, sprouts, which I'm going to do with bacon and walnuts." She laughs at the look of my face. "Does that sound okay?"

More tears well in my eyes. "It sounds perfect."

"Before I have another drink, is it okay if I stay the night? Simon doesn't finish until six tomorrow morning. He'll go home for a sleep and pick me up here around ten to go to Mum's in time for Christmas dinner. Unless you need to leave earlier to go to Romy and Rob's?"

"Of course you can stay the night," I say, neatly avoiding her mention of Romy and Rob's. If I tell her that I'm not spending Christmas with them, she'll insist I join her and Simon at her mum's.

"Great," she says happily. "I brought my toothbrush and pj's, just in case. If we stay up until midnight, we can see Christmas in together."

I laugh at her enthusiasm, feeling lighter than I have in years. If Sadie can forgive me, maybe others can too.

Later, we take our heavy stomachs through to the sitting room and once we're settled on the sofa, I tell her everything, including being wrong about Brett Parker driving the car.

"I only found out on Monday," I say. "For all those years, I truly believed it was him even though the police told me I was mistaken. But I thought I knew better than them. I always thought—hoped—that one day I'd be proved right. To know I was wrong all along is devastating. It's why I didn't come to work. It wasn't flu that kept me way but the knowledge that I have no excuse for causing the death of two men."

"Two?"

"Yes. Brett Parker and the man who fell in front of the tube train which was meant to have killed me."

"That wasn't your fault!" Sadie protests. "That was an accident. A horrible one, but an accident."

"If Damon Parker hadn't been trying to kill me for stalking his father and ultimately causing his death, that man would still be alive. And what about Damon Parker? He was just a kid when he went to prison and he's spent his best years locked in a cell. I'll never be able to forgive myself."

"Then you'll have to learn to live with the guilt," she says pragmatically. "Although I think you've atoned enough. It hurts me to think of the lonely life you led for all those years, just to punish yourself."

"There's something else," I say, because now that I've told her about my past, I want to tell her everything. "You know when someone broke in here and you and Simon asked me if I had any enemies? I thought it was Damon Parker who'd broken in, because he was due to be released from prison this summer. I also thought it was him stalking me. But I just found out that he's still inside."

Sadie stares at me. "Stalking you? You have a stalker?"

"Yes."

"But—" She seems unusually lost for words. "Since when?"

"About six months, maybe longer."

"So that time we came over, it wasn't just a random break-in?"

"No."

"Have you told the police?"

"Yes. And I've got a number to phone if I'm worried."

"Worried? You must be terrified!"

"I'm more terrified now that I know it isn't Damon Parker stalking me. When I thought it was him, I just sort of accepted it, because he told me he would kill me when he got out of prison."

"Nell!" Sadie's eyes fill with tears. "I can't believe what you've been going through. Why didn't you tell me?"

"I couldn't. I haven't even told Alex. The police officer I told thinks there's a chance it's someone I know. I did think it might be Marcus, because he's bought the house across the road. But now I'm not so sure."

"What—Marcus has bought the house across the road?" Sadie looks affronted.

So I tell her about Marcus and when I've finished she asks if I have any more creepy friends.

"No, thank God," I tell her. "Apart from you and Simon, my only friends are Romy and Rob, Marcus, Alex's sister Béatrice and her husband Victor, and Inès. And Alex, of course. I trust each and every one of them implicitly. It's not possible that any of them have a secret agenda, is there?"

"I hope not," she says soberly.

And out of the blue, Alex's two dead ex-girlfriends come into my mind.

NELL

PRESENT

I wake the next morning, knowing that Sadie will be cross to find I slept in the living room after all. We'd argued for a while as to who should sleep on the sofa and in the end, we'd agreed to share the bed. But I'd found it hard to sleep, and Sadie was snoring, only lightly, but enough to keep me awake. So I came down here.

There's a message from Alex wishing me a happy Christmas and I take a couple of minutes to reply. It's already nine o'clock, so I throw my blanket off and go to the kitchen to get breakfast ready before Simon picks Sadie up at ten. The Christmas tree Sadie brought is still on the island, a reminder of our lovely celebration the previous evening. I turn to put on the light but nothing happens when I flick the switch and I mutter under my breath, because I know I don't have a spare bulb.

I fill the kettle with water and turn it on. There's no answering hiss, so I pull open the fridge. The light doesn't come on and I realize there must have been a power cut and that it's still ongoing. Desperate for a cup of tea, I think about heating water in the microwave then realize I can't use that either. Grumbling about the great start to Christmas Day, I take juice from the fridge. I'd planned to heat up some croissants from the freezer but with no oven to bake them in, crispbread and jam will have to do.

It's a huge relief that Sadie knows who I really am. She didn't seem fazed by what I did back then and before I fell asleep, I found myself wondering if it wasn't so bad after all—until I remembered that if it hadn't been for me, Brett Parker wouldn't have run across the road without looking, an innocent bystander wouldn't have fallen in front of a tube train, and a young man wouldn't have spent twelve years in prison. But I'd still been able to sleep easier and deeper than I have for a long time.

I set plates out on the table then stick my head into the hallway and call up to Sadie.

"Merry Christmas! Breakfast is ready!" There's no answering call so I give her another five minutes then run up the stairs and knock lightly on the door.

"Sadie, it's time to get up," I say, inching open the door. "Simon will be here soon." My fingers find the light switch but of course, it doesn't come on. "There's been a power cut," I say. "Shall I open the curtains?" I go into the room, then stop, because there's a strange smell in the air and at first, I think that Sadie must have had more to drink than I thought and has vomited in her sleep. Worried, I move nearer.

A scream rips from me and I back toward the door, my hand over my mouth. Stumbling down the stairs and then to the kitchen, I snatch my phone from the island and call 999.

"Ambulance," I tell the responder, my words tumbling over each other. "And the police. It's my friend, she—she's dead. There's a knife sticking out of her. She—she's been murdered."

EXTRACT FROM NOTEBOOK 4

You are meant to be dead, Nell. YOU ARE MEANT TO BE DEAD!!! And yet, you are still alive.

I arrived in the early hours of the morning to kill you, Nell. I'd waited at home until the clock struck midnight, then made myself wait until the streets had emptied of revelers celebrating the arrival of Christmas Day before making my way to the house across the street from yours. It was two in the morning by the time I arrived and I was in such a state of excitement that I had to force myself to calm down so that I could enjoy every minute of what I was about to do.

You didn't hear me as I let myself into the house and crept upstairs to your bedroom. From the little I could make out in the darkness, you were lying on your back, buried under the the covers and from the noise you were making, I guessed you'd had quite a bit to drink the previous evening, drowning your sorrows at being alone at Christmas. I hoped the alcohol hadn't numbed you too much as I wanted you to be able to feel the knife going into your body, I wanted you to know that the end had come and that you were dying.

I was standing over you, about to deliver my coup de grace, when I remembered the day I'd hidden under your bed and imagined driving the knife up through the mattress and into your body. If you hadn't been so dead to the world, I wouldn't have changed my original plan. But the regularity of your snores told me I didn't need to hurry so I stooped down and measured the blade of my knife against the depth of your mattress plus the depth of your body and realized that the image that had tortured me in such a delicious kind of way could become a reality. You didn't stir as I slid under the bed and got into position.

The blade of my knife was so long that I couldn't drive it straight up into your body so I had to do it at an angle. If I'd been standing above you, I would have aimed straight for your heart. It was impossible for me to gauge exactly where your heart was from under the bed but I knew enough about the anatomy of the body to know that my chances of piercing a vital organ was high and that even if I didn't, you would bleed to death anyway. So I found a gap in the springs and with my two hands on the hilt, I took a deep breath and, savoring the moment, drove the knife up through the mattress.

You gave a kind of moan and ceased snoring. By the time I'd slid out from under the bed, your breathing had become labored and your body was twitching under the covers. I left quietly and quickly, closing your bedroom door behind me and crept down the stairs. I waited in the hall a moment but there was no sound from your room, so I went back to the house across the street and waited for your body to be found. I knew it could take days, but I had a plan. Sometime in the afternoon, I would make an anonymous call to the police, pretending to be worried about a neighbor who hadn't turned up for Christmas lunch.

I must have dozed off because I was woken by a police car screeching down the street, its siren sounding and its blue lights flashing. I jumped to my feet; I didn't want to miss your body being brought out on a stretcher. I checked my phone and I was surprised to see it was only nine twenty in the morning. I hadn't expected your body to be found quite so soon but I thought you must have invited a friend to spend Christmas Day with you, and I smiled, imagining the fright they must have had when they'd found you dead.

I watched as two police officers approached the front door. It was opened from the inside and as they disappeared inside, I wondered what they would make of the tip of the knife protruding from your body, what they'd make of a killer who had lain under your bed and driven a long-bladed knife up through the mattress and into your flesh.

An ambulance arrived. It parked behind the police car and dispatched a couple of paramedics. A few minutes later, another police car turned up and parked behind the ambulance. Two police officers got out, a woman and a man. They followed the paramedics into the house and I couldn't help thinking that it was quite a turnout for you, Nell, especially once the forensic team arrived.

I had to wait a while before the door opened again. There was a flurry of movement on the doorstep and a woman appeared with a blanket over her shoulders and I thought it must be the friend who had found your body. I watched as she was led toward the ambulance by a paramedic, the two police officers following behind. The male got into the police car and began to back it up the road so that the ambulance could get out. The female officer said something to the woman and the woman turned her head and—

I thought I must be seeing things. IT COULDN'T BE YOU, NELL, IT WASN'T POSSIBLE, YOU WERE MEANT TO BE DEAD! I rammed my hand in my mouth and bit down on it to stop myself from screaming in frustration. How was it that you were still alive? I forced myself to remain calm. You could still die; the blanket covering you could have been hiding terrible injuries. But the fact that you were able to walk made it unlikely.

I couldn't work out what had gone wrong. I thought I must have miscalculated the depth of the mattress and the knife hadn't gone in deep enough to do the damage I'd expected it to. I couldn't understand why you had waited seven hours before calling an ambulance but supposed you hadn't realized you'd been stabbed until you woke up this morning and found a knife protruding from your body.

White-hot rage burned within me as I watched you being helped into the ambulance. The police officer climbed in after you and once the ambu-

lance had left, I knew I should leave too, before the police started their house-to-house inquiries. But I was in such a state at my failure to kill you that I needed to compose myself first. So I was still there when a private ambulance arrived and when the medics went into the house with a stretcher, I thought that one of the forensic team had been taken ill. And then they reappeared, carrying a body bag.

It took me a while to realize what must have happened. You had someone with you last night and I had killed them, not you. A black rage filled me and I took my knife and stabbed it into the wall over and over again, imagining it was you.

I don't like that someone died unnecessarily, Nell, and I'll make sure that you pay for it when I kill you.

NELL

PRESENT

"I don't want to leave you," Alex says.

"I need to do this," I say, turning away from him.

He catches my arm and pulls me into a hug. But I don't respond and eventually, he lets me go.

"I don't understand how you can stay here," he says, his face etched with frustration.

"It's only for one night. I need to do it, for Sadie. To say goodbye to her."

"But why here? Why not say goodbye to her somewhere else?"

"Because it has to be here," I say stubbornly.

Alex isn't the only person who can't understand how I can come back to the house where Sadie was murdered. Béatrice and Victor—who we've been staying with—and my friends all feel the same. But my story hasn't ended yet and when it does, I want it to end here, in this house, not with a knife in my back in the street. I want it to be on my terms. And more than that, I want to know who it is, this person who wants me dead.

In the aftermath of Sadie's death, I told Alex everything. He knows about my past, he knows I was once Elle Nugent and that two men died because of me. He remembered reading about the case at the time and he said he'd felt sorry for me, because I was so young. I don't know if that's true but he couldn't believe that I'd let what I did color the rest of my life.

"I don't care about any of it," he said. "Anyway, you're not that person anymore. You need to forgive yourself."

"Even if I could, I now have Sadie's death on my conscience." I wiped the never-ending stream of tears from my eyes. "I shouldn't have left her on her own, I should have stayed in bed next to her. I don't understand how I could have been so careless. I should have moved out of here the minute DC Moss told me that my stalker wasn't Damon Parker." I'd raised frightened eyes to him. "Who is it, Alex? Who is it that wants to kill me?"

He'd shaken his head. "I don't know. But it must be someone from your past, someone connected to the Parker family."

We'd been sitting together on the sofa in Béatrice and Victor's sitting room, his arms tight around me. I pulled away from him.

"Has it never entered your head that it could be to do with you?" My voice had taken on an edge and he looked at me in surprise.

"With me?"

"Yes, you!" His naivety appalled me. "Your last two girlfriends are dead and now someone has tried to kill me."

His jaw had clenched. "Caitlin's death was a terrible accident, and Ariane was killed because of the line of work she was in."

"You asked me why I didn't tell you I had a stalker. Why didn't you tell me Ariane had had a stalker? If you had, I might have told you about mine."

"I only knew that she thought she was being followed when Inès told me, after Ariane died. I didn't mention it to you because once I knew that she'd worked for the French secret service, I put it down to it being part of the territory, spies following spies. And don't forget, I was told that she'd died in the line of duty." He held my gaze. "Be honest,

Nell. If I *had* told you that Ariane thought she was being followed, would you really have told me that you too thought you had a stalker?"

I hadn't been able to lie. "No, I wouldn't have. I'm sorry, I'm not trying to shift any blame onto you. I'm just scared. The worst part is not knowing who it is."

He'd taken me in his arms. "From now on, I'll always be at your side. I'll never leave you, Nell."

And I'd clung to him and had allowed myself to feel safe. Yet here I am, sending him away.

"Let me stay," he pleads as we move into the hall.

"No," I say.

"If not me, then Victor. You shouldn't be alone."

"I want to be alone."

He can't keep his frustration in. "For God's sake, Nell, someone tried to kill you! What if they know you're alone here tonight? What if they come for you?"

I want to tell him that's exactly what I'm hoping.

"Please can you leave?" I say instead, his presence making me increasingly uncomfortable.

"I can't bear the thought that I won't see you again." I freeze at his words. Why would he assume that we won't see each other again unless he knows I'm going to die? "Because it's over, isn't it? You don't want to be with me anymore, do you?"

I steel my heart. "No," I say. "I'm sorry." The look on his face breaks my heart.

He nods. "Thank you for being honest. But before I leave, can I do one last thing for you?"

"What?"

"Can I give you some pointers on how to protect yourself? Will you at least allow me to do that?"

"Yes," I say, because if I don't give him something, he'll never leave.

"If they come for you, it will be in the dead of the night. So nap during the day. When you go up to bed, barricade yourself in the room and stay alert. If you hear them inside, call the police."

"What if they come earlier, when I'm still downstairs?" I ask.

"You'll know they've arrived because they'll cut the power supply, like before. If they're not already inside, you'll have time to get upstairs. Despite the new locks, they will get in, because this person is a professional. So, focus on getting to your bedroom where you can lock yourself in. Don't let fear muddle your thinking."

"What if I can't get to my bedroom?" I say. "What if they're already inside?"

"Scream. Use your voice. Take a deep breath and scream as loud and as long as you can. You'll have a couple of seconds before fear numbs you. Use them well."

"Yes, I'll do that," I say, to show him I'm still listening.

"If you can't get upstairs, don't let yourself be backed into the kitchen," Alex says.

"But what if there isn't anywhere else to go?"

"Then try and arm yourself with a weapon. You have knives on the workbench."

"Okay."

"Whatever you do, don't let yourself be cornered at the far end of the island without a weapon because if you do, there will be no way out."

"But what if I am?" I ask, and he grips my hands in his.

"You cannot let it happen. Do you hear me, Nell? You cannot let it happen."

"I won't." There's a silence. "But at least in the kitchen it's never totally dark," I say. "Because of the light well."

"True."

I give him a look. "How do you know all this?"

"All what?"

"What you've just told me. Where to go, what to do?"

A haunted look comes into his eyes. "Ariane's murder had a terrible effect on me." He runs his hand over his chin, as if ashamed. "I became afraid and wherever I was, I always worked out a plan of action in case I had an intruder. That's why I began staying at Fifty-four Marlsborough rather than a hotel. I felt safe there."

I nod. "I'll be careful."

"I love you," he says.

And that's the irony. He knows everything there is to know about me and he still loves me.

Accepting that there's nothing more he can say or do, he leaves. He doesn't look back as he moves to the front door, nor when he pulls it shut behind him. I wait a beat, half expecting him to come back and when he doesn't, I sink onto the stairs, relieved to be on my own for the first time since Sadie died.

NELL

PRESENT

I couldn't speak for hours after I found her, the tip of a knife protruding from her stomach. The police found me slumped in the living room in a catatonic state and I remained that way until Superintendent Moss arrived and crouched down beside me. I remember asking them to call her and because she knew my story, I wasn't arrested on suspicion of murdering Sadie, which I could have been had she not intervened.

Things moved swiftly once Superintendent Moss was on the scene. I was taken to a police station to give a statement and then Alex was there. He took me to Béatrice and Victor's flat and we've been there ever since.

The police think that my stalker, the person who wants me dead, is connected to my past after all and are looking at anyone with a connection to the Parker family. But because of something that happened after Sadie's funeral, I know my stalker is closer to home.

The funeral took place yesterday. It was the first time I'd seen Simon since Sadie was murdered. He came and gave me a silent hug, and it meant more to me than any words could have, because in that hug was forgiveness. I didn't know how I was going to face Sadie's parents;

I was terrified they'd accuse me of being the cause of their daughter's death. But they were quietly dignified and thanked me for coming along, as they did to everyone. Maybe it was just that they didn't know who I was.

Alex, Béatrice, Victor, and Inès came to the funeral with me for moral support. Romy, Rob, and Marcus were also there because they'd met Sadie and wanted to pay their respects, and to support me. My surprise at Marcus being there when I'd been so ungracious about him buying the house across the road from mine disappeared the moment I saw Sadie's coffin, piled high with flowers. The grief I felt was unlike anything I'd ever known.

When the funeral was over, Béatrice and Victor invited Romy, Rob, and Marcus back to their flat because they wanted me to be surrounded by my friends after such a heartbreaking day. It was exactly what I needed; Béatrice, Victor, and Inès had never met Sadie and it felt good to tell them about her and raise a glass to her. But later, while we were talking among ourselves, my skin began prickling and I knew with a horrible, agonizing certainty that my stalker was there in the room.

I don't know how I managed to hide my internal agitation but I forced myself to continue talking to Béatrice while I tried to gauge who had eyes on me. No one seemed to be looking my way. My eyes fell on Alex, talking to Romy and Rob, and my mind returned to the deaths of Caitlin and Ariane. What if he had killed them and now wanted to kill me? What if he was a serial killer? What if he was my stalker? What if, when he said goodbye to me, he didn't go to the US but stayed in London and followed me? Or what if he was connected in some way to the Parker family? Or Bryony Sanders's family? What if he had known who I was all along and had targeted me from the beginning, when we first met at the media party?

My heart wouldn't let me believe it was him. I turned my gaze on Marcus, who was talking to Rob. It had to be him, why would he have bought the house across the road otherwise? I hoped it was him, I wanted it to be him, I didn't want it to be anyone else in the room.

I could cope with Marcus; if he came for me, I felt sure I'd be able to outwit him.

Along with the hatred I could feel directed at me, there was a terrible sense of suppressed rage and I guessed that they were furious at the mistake they'd made in killing Sadie instead of me and were desperate to put it right. And I realized that they would never be able to while I was staying with Béatrice and Victor. So I announced to the room that the following evening, I'd be going back to sleep at my house.

There were protests from everyone; they all professed shock that I could go back to the house where Sadie had been murdered. But I was adamant, telling them it was something I needed to do, a last farewell to my friend in the place where we'd spent such a happy evening together. Inside, I was trembling. I didn't know how I was going to be able to force myself over the threshold. But I knew that I had to; I needed for it to be over, once and for all.

I move to the sitting room and perch on the sofa, unable to relax. Alex, Victor, Béatrice, Inès, Romy, Rob, Marcus. I'll soon know which one of them wants to kill me. But I'll need help, the help of the only man I can trust.

I reach for my phone, telling myself that Sadie would understand. I can almost hear her saying, *Just do what you need to do, girl.*

Simon picks up immediately. "Nell?"

"I'll understand if you don't want to talk to me," I say, my words coming out in a rush.

"I don't blame you for Sadie, if that's what you're worried about. Is everything all right?"

"I'm back home," I tell him. "On my own."

"What? Where's Alex?"

"I sent him away. I don't trust him, I don't trust anyone."

"What's happened, Nell?"

"The police think that whoever wants me dead is connected to my past. But I know they're closer to home."

"What do you mean?"

"Yesterday, after Sadie's funeral . . ." My voice falters.

"Go on."

"We went back to Béatrice and Victor's and whoever wants to kill me was there, in the room. I know it sounds stupid but I could sense them."

"Not so stupid," he says. "I remember you saying the same thing when you called me and Sadie over that time, because you sensed someone had been in the house."

"The frightening thing is, everyone there was a friend. As well as Alex, Béatrice, and Victor, the only other people there were Romy, Rob, Marcus, and Inès."

"And your prime suspect is?"

"Marcus," I say. "Why would he have bought the house over the road otherwise? Anyway, the thing is, they all know that I'm here alone so I'm hoping that whoever it is will come for me, if not tonight, then soon."

"Nell, you can't do that." Simon is aghast. "There's no way you're staying there alone. I'm coming over, with Kintyre. I'll be there in half an hour."

"Simon, wait! Will you just hear me out? I've got an idea."

"It had better be good."

"Would you contact Marcus—I'll give you his number—and ask him if you can use his house, the one across the road, so that you can set up surveillance? I heard him say yesterday that he has the keys but he hasn't moved in yet. Tell him that you've heard I'm going to be home alone and that you want to keep watch on me. It will be interesting to see what he says. If he refuses to let you use his house, I'll know that it's him. If he agrees, then it probably isn't."

"It could still be," Simon warns.

"Let's see what he says."

Simon calls back twenty minutes later.

"Marcus is really happy for me to use the house, he's glad that I'm going to be looking out for you. He offered to keep watch with me but I told him it's a police operation so he can't be involved. He's bringing the keys over; I said I'd meet him halfway but he insisted on coming here."

My gut twists with anxiety. "Be careful, Simon."

"Don't worry, I have Kintyre with me."

"Call me when he's gone."

"I will."

I spend the next hour pacing the room, going over everything in my mind until my head aches with indecision. Even if Marcus hands over the keys without a problem, he could still be my stalker. And if he is, I've put Simon in danger by placing him in the house over the road.

My phone rings and I snatch it up. "Simon?"

"Marcus isn't your man, Nell. I made some inquiries while I was waiting for him to arrive. He was investigated following Sadie's murder but his alibi, that he was with his family that evening, checked out."

"Right," I say. "That's a good thing, I suppose. But who pointed the finger at him? Someone must have."

"It was Alex."

"Alex?"

"Yes." He waits for it to sink in. "Look, I'm coming over to Marcus's house now. Whatever happens tonight, or tomorrow, or whenever, I'll be there, keeping watch. Keep yourself safe."

"I've got a lock on my bedroom door now and when I go to bed, I'll push my dressing table in front of the door," I tell him.

"Good. If someone manages to get in without me seeing them, which I doubt, open your window and holler for me. Nobody will get past Kintyre." His voice becomes fierce. "We're going to get them, Nell, once and for all."

EXTRACT FROM NOTEBOOK 4

You sensed me yesterday, didn't you, Nell? You knew I was there, among you. It's why you said that today, you'd be going back to your house. It was an invitation, an invitation to me to come and kill you.

I know what you're doing, Nell. You think you're controlling the situation, you think you'll be prepared. But nothing can prepare you for what is going to happen. I'm tired of our game, I need it to be over.

I'll be leaving soon, Nell. You won't be on your guard yet, it's far too early in the evening. I've had to change other aspects of my game plan too. I won't be coming in through the front door but via your bathroom window. I can access it from the roof, where I need to be to make the last of my preparations. Perhaps I'll get a glimpse of you in the kitchen, making yourself a soothing cup of tea, before I come to kill you.

NELL

PRESENT

It's the lamp going out in the living room that alerts me the electricity has been cut. I jump to my feet, knocking my empty mug onto the floor. A crushing fear tightens my chest. It's too early, I'm not ready.

If they come for you, it will be in the dead of the night, Alex had told me.

But it's not the middle of the night, it's barely nine.

What if they come earlier, when I'm still downstairs? I'd asked.

Focus on getting to your bedroom where you can lock yourself in, Alex had said. *Don't let fear muddle your thinking.*

Remembering his words, I take a breath to calm myself, then grope my way to the door. The hall is in complete darkness. I'm about to run to the stairs when a dark shadow peels itself from the wall. I cry out in shock; they're already inside.

What if I can't get to my bedroom? I'd asked. *What if they're already inside?*

Scream, Alex had said. *Use your voice. Take a deep breath and scream as loud and as long as you can. You'll have a couple of seconds before fear numbs you. Use them well.*

I open my mouth to scream but fear has already wound its steely grip around my lungs, squeezing the breath from me. My eyes pick out a looming mass, advancing down the hall toward me. I scramble back as fast as I can and feel the kitchen door behind me.

If you can't get upstairs, don't let yourself be backed into the kitchen, Alex had said.

But what if there isn't anywhere else to go? I'd asked.

Then try and arm yourself with a weapon. You have knives on the workbench.

I grapple for the handle and as the door swings open, I stumble backward into the kitchen. They follow me in and kick the door shut. The room is in total darkness, confusing me for a moment, because there should be at least some light from the light well. I recover quickly and step to my right, visualizing the knife block next to the cooker. But as if they can read my mind, they bar my way, forcing me to move to the left, my feet tripping over each other as I back around the island, until I come to the far end and can go no farther.

Whatever you do, Alex had told me, *don't let yourself be cornered behind the island, because if you do, there will be no way out. You cannot let it happen. Do you hear me, Nell? You cannot let it happen.*

Yet here I am. My legs tremble at the implication. As my eyes adjust to the inky darkness, the looming mass defines itself as a black-clad figure standing on the other side of the island. There's a movement, followed by a swish in the air. My throat constricts; they have a blade.

"Stop!" My voice rings out and to my astonishment, the air stills.

"Before you kill me," I say, keeping my voice strong. "I need to know who you are."

I wait a beat then dig deep inside me for my greatest fear.

"Is it you, Alex?" I ask.

NELL

PRESENT

There's a snort of derision and relief courses through me; it isn't Alex. Then who? The silence and the stillness tells me that they've enjoyed the error I made. If I keep hazarding guesses, I might be able to buy myself the precious time that I need.

"It's you, isn't it, Marcus?" I say into the darkness, although I'm sure that it isn't him. On the underside of the island, my fingers find a strip of sticky tape and I begin to pick away at it, doing my best to keep my movements small. "I've suspected you all along."

There's no noise from the black-clad figure, so I press on. "But maybe I'm wrong. Just because you bought the house opposite mine doesn't mean you want me dead. So, if it's not you, it has to be Rob or Victor." I pause. "Rob, is it you? I can't think why it would be you, unless you're jealous of my relationship with Alex. But I know you love Romy, so I think you must be Victor."

I need more time, so I search for something more to say while I continue to pick away at the tape. "It was you who killed Caitlin, wasn't it? You went back to her on the slopes that day and forced over the edge to her death. And then, when Alex met Ariane, you killed her too."

"You're right." The hiss comes out of the dark, making me jump. "But you're also very wrong."

A female voice. Shock waves run through me. "*Inès?*" I stare into the darkness. "Is that you?"

She gives a wild laugh and I sense her crouch down, about to pounce. Ripping the last piece of sticky tape from the underside of the island, I grab the knife that I stuck there, swoop it up with both hands on the hilt, and thrust it forward. There's a grunt of surprise before the full weight of her body crashes down on me. My knees buckle and I stumble back against the wall. But the grunt tells me that the knife has gone in so I push her off me, pulling the knife out at the same time. She staggers back and I come round from behind the island, lashing out in the darkness with the knife, hoping to disable her further. There's another grunt as she falls to the floor and, hearing her go down, I lunge for the door, kicking out with my feet to stop her from grabbing on to me. She rolls her body forward, blocking my way, and grapples at my legs with her hands. I manage to pull the door open, kicking her hands away as she grabs on to my feet, and wriggling free, I charge down the hallway, already screaming for Simon.

"Simon!" I yell again, as the kitchen door opens behind me. I pull the front door open and tumble into the road. "Simon!"

Within seconds, the door of Marcus's house flies open and Simon comes charging out with Kintyre.

"Are you okay?" he asks urgently. "Are you hurt?"

"No." My breath comes in ragged gasps. "It's Inès! She's inside, she's injured!"

"Nell!" I spin around and see Alex. He pulls me into his arms. "Thank God you're safe."

I crumple against him. "It's Inès." There's a sob in my voice as the horror of it hits me.

"Inès? It can't be." He pulls back, searches my face. "Are you sure?"

"Yes." I shake my head. "I don't know, I don't understand."

Simon pulls out a flashlight and shines it into the hallway. It picks out the black-clad figure, the face masked by a balaclava, lying immobile in the kitchen doorway. Kintyre pulls on his lead, desperate to be inside.

"Be careful, she has a knife!" I warn.

"Police!" Simon calls, moving down the hallway. "Don't move!"

Alex keeps his arms around me as Simon crouches beside the prone figure. "She's dead," he says, turning his head toward us. Releasing Kintyre, who immediately sits next to the body, he eases the balaclava off and in the light, I see a shock of short brown hair.

"Wait!" I move from Alex's arms and walk unsteadily toward Simon. "It's not her, that's not her hair."

"Are you sure?"

Simon moves back so that I can see her face. Her eyes are wide open, her face and lips pallid. I'm about to ask Alex if he knows who she is, but then I look closer and imagine a glossy black wig covering the short brown hair and bright crimson lipstick on the pallid lips.

"Oh my God," I say, stunned. "It *is* her. It's Inès."

NELL

PRESENT—FOUR MONTHS LATER

"Shall we take a look?" Alex asks.

"It's up to you," I say, because it wasn't ever about me, it was always about him.

He lifts the small cardboard box onto his knees. When the police asked him, once their investigation was over, if he wanted the four notebooks they'd found in Inès's flat, in a box labeled *For Alex, in the unlikely event of my death*, he hadn't known whether to accept them or not. But because there's so much he still doesn't understand, he's hoping that whatever they contain might help him come to terms, even in a small way, with everything that happened.

He knows some of it. He knows that when the police raided Inès's flat, they found a room dedicated to him, its walls covered from floor to ceiling with hundreds of photographs, taken over the past four years. When the police told him that Inès's obsession with him began in Verbier in January 2021, Alex couldn't recall having met her there, and said that as far as he was concerned, the first time they'd met had been later that year, in November, at a dinner at Béatrice and Victor's, something which Béatrice confirmed. But as he opens the first notebook and begins reading, understanding dawns on his face.

"I'll make some coffee," I say, knowing it's going to be a long evening.

We're staying with Alex's dad while we look for a house in Washington. It's four months since we left the UK; we flew out of London two days before the story broke about Bryony Sanders's murder having been solved. Her killer, the lecturer at her university, died at the end of January, having clung on to life a few weeks longer than his doctors had expected him to. Superintendent Moss kept her promise and gave me enough time to leave the country before the story became breaking news.

I hoped that my role in the story of her murder wouldn't resurface but it did, and several news outlets ran headlines along the lines of "*Where is Elle Nugent now?*" I thought that my work colleagues from Drop In, or some of the regulars, would recognize me but so far no one has traced me to the US and with the story having run its course, I'm counting on being able to live the rest of my life without the shadow of the past hanging over me.

I'm not sure I'll ever get over killing Inès. I know it was a case of her or me, but I wish I'd only wounded her enough to be able to escape. Alex feels guilty too but not for the same reason. Inès had called him during the afternoon to make sure I would be on my own that night. He told her I'd refused to let him stay and that I wouldn't allow Victor to stay either. He'd also added that he intended to keep watch on the house from farther up the road. It was why she chose to break in via the roof and the bathroom window. In further proof of her meticulous planning, she'd thought to paint the light well black so that the kitchen would be in complete darkness.

"Thank God you had the foresight to have a knife ready," Alex had said, as he paced up and down, unable to sit still.

"It was what you said about not getting cornered at the back of the kitchen behind the island," I'd told him. "I knew I had to prepare for that possibility."

Alex and I had stayed with Béatrice and Victor during the police investigation into Inès. The findings were brutal; her flatmate had never existed—the room she had pointed out to me as belonging to "Cécile" was where she housed her shrine to Alex—and Maxime, her boyfriend, hadn't existed either. She had invented him once Alex had met me, pretending to Béatrice and Victor that she had already known him for a couple of months. It's not clear why she pretended to be in a relationship but maybe she thought it would provide her with extra cover once she started stalking me.

A black wig was found in her flat, along with several pairs of high-heeled shoes and boots. The scruffy sneakers I'd seen in her flat were hers, her preferred footwear for stalking me because not only did they make her a good four inches shorter than when she wore heels, they also enabled her to move fast. Because her face, devoid of heavy makeup and wig, was surprisingly bland, it had been easy for her to blend into the background whenever I turned around to see who was following me. And back then, I'd been so sure my stalker was Damon Parker that I'd always looked for a man, never a woman.

The contents of Inès's notebooks told the police what we'd already suspected by then, that she had killed both Caitlin and Ariane. But we didn't know how she had gotten there, how she had gone from being a young woman from a good background to being a murderer. Alex hopes the notebooks will provide the answer.

Alex's dad, Mike, has gone to bed so I make coffee for me and Alex and carry it through to where he's sitting. He doesn't look up as I sit down next to him, just passes me the notebook he's been reading, titled Notebook 1, and reaches for the next one. I scan the first pages; they're written in French but I know enough now to understand what I'm reading. It details how Inès first met Alex during a skiing trip to Verbier at the beginning of 2021. He'd been in a bar with his group of friends, including Béatrice and Victor, and she'd been there with a group of her friends, and the two groups had started talking. For Inès, it was love at first sight. There are pages devoted to physical descriptions of him, fantasizing in an almost schoolgirl way about what it would be like to be kissed by him, held by him, sleep with him. But Alex had barely noticed her.

I need to change my appearance, Inès had written. *Alex and his friends are all so glamorous and I am dull and mousey in comparison. No wonder he took no notice of me.*

Further diary entries show how she was determined to become part of Alex's life via Béatrice, even if it meant moving to London.

We met up with them again tonight and I made sure to sit next to Béatrice, his sister, because I need to find out what I can before they leave tomorrow. I dragged Mélanie, my friend, into the conversation so that I wouldn't seem too full on and I learned that Béatrice and her husband live in London. Alex lives in Washington, but he spends a week each month in London and Béatrice always sees him when he is there so I'm going to move to London, which will be easier than moving to Washington.

It would have seemed weird to ask Béatrice for her address so I asked about her life in London, if she knew other French people there and she'd laughed and said that South Kensington, where she lived, was an enclave for French expats. She also mentioned that she played tennis once a week at the tennis club in Hyde Park so my plan is to become a member and bump into her there. Not that she'll recognize me. I'm going to make sure of that.

After pages and pages of her dreams and fantasies about Alex, which both Alex and I skipped, and her annoyance at her plans not moving fast enough, I find this entry.

I'm going to London! It has taken months of harassing but Dad's friend has finally come through and I have a job at the French Consulate in South Kensington, starting in July.

And then, in September, after detailing her frustrations about not being able to find Béatrice and how lonely she felt without friends:

Result! I've found Béatrice. I've been playing tennis at the club in Hyde Park every weekend this summer, hoping to bump into her and today my dedication paid off. I managed to get chatting to her in the changing room. I told her that I worked at the French Consulate and that I was new to

London and didn't really know anyone. She immediately invited me to have a coffee with her. She's a journalist so maybe she thinks I can be useful to her through my job. Or maybe she's just a really nice person. Best of all, when she saw me in my street clothes, she told me she loved my look. I had a beautiful wig made because I wanted to leave my old mousey persona behind and also, I didn't want her to recognize me from when we met in Verbier. I've also taken to wearing red lipstick, high heels, and a lot of black, because it always looks chic. It gives me a slightly vampish look and a confidence I've never had before. It's like I'm a completely new person.

"I'm not sure I can read any more of this." Alex passes me the notebook he's been reading. "It's about Caitlin. I need a break." He gets up from the sofa and walks to the window, where he stands looking out. I open the notebook, titled Notebook 2, and see that the first entry is an excited account of how Inès managed to get invited on the skiing trip to Verbier by Béatrice, whom it seems she saw on a regular basis.

Alex and I are the only two in the group of ten who aren't coupled up but we soon will be, she wrote. *Only three more days until we're together!*

My eye is caught by a sudden change in the writing style, from neatly cursive to dark, scratchy capitals.

I DON'T UNDERSTAND. YOU MUST HAVE FORCED HIM TO BRING YOU ALONG, HE WOULD NEVER HAVE DONE IT OTHERWISE. YOU CAN'T EVEN SKI!!!

The entry is followed by two pages of abuse against Caitlin and a threat to kill her, followed by a detailed plan.

He's skied with you every day and there is so much rage inside me at times that I can hardly bear to speak to you when we meet up in the evenings. But I am good at hiding my feelings. Alex, not so much. I can see he's beginning to resent you, because I watch him so closely. This morning, when we all went to ski off-piste leaving him on the slopes with you, there was a look of real frustration on his face. But last night, you were making plans to see him next week in Washington and he seemed to be agreeing so maybe I've got it wrong and he likes you enough to continue the relationship. It's our last day tomorrow, so I need to act fast.

It's fine, I'm ready. Tonight, I'll whisper in your ear that out of fairness, because he has stayed by your side the whole week, you should let Alex ski with us on our last day. You're a people pleaser, so I know you'll agree. And once we set off, I'll double back and find you. Nobody will suspect me. I had intended to show off my excellent skiing skills to impress Alex but as soon as he turned up with you, Caitlin, I decided to keep them hidden until Alex and I are finally together. I know he'll be thrilled to have a partner who's a first-class skier, even if it means that I'm better than him. He's good but Victor is better and I could beat the pants off Victor in a race. That's how good I am.

There's no entry detailing how she maneuvered Caitlin into the ravine, just an almost childish entry the next day:

Easy peasy, lemon squeezy.

I close the notebook and go to join Alex at the window, sliding my arm around his waist.

"There was no reason for Caitlin to die," he says, his voice bleak. "I was going to break things off when we got back to Washington. If I'd told Béatrice, she might have told Inès and then Caitlin would still be alive. That's what I can't get over."

He can't bring himself to read the third notebook, which is about Ariane. I read the first few pages and am quickly sickened by Inès's rage toward a beautiful young woman simply because she was in a relationship with Alex. But there's a part of me that pities Inès. As Béatrice had already told me, Alex spent some weeks with her and Victor after Ariane's death and it's clear from the notebook that Inès believed she and Alex had a future together.

Béatrice says she's relying on me to cheer Alex up as he's still so upset about Ariane. She says I make him smile, that he brightens up when she tells him I'm coming over. I know she'll be happy when Alex and I get together. She told me today that I'm perfect for him because we have so much in common. She was referring to our taste in music, in films, in everything. If only she knew how hard I've worked to find out every little thing about him, through listening and discreet questioning, and pretend that I have exactly the same interests. I know more about him than anyone else does, which is why he finds me such easy company. Béatrice is right, I'm perfect for him and it won't be long before he realizes it too.

"Did you?" I ask him. "Find Inès easy company?"

Alex looks up from reading the last notebook, Notebook 4, which I've guessed is about me. "Yes, I did. We liked the same things and she had a great sense of humor. But I never thought of her as anything other than a friend and I never thought she saw me as anything other than a friend. That's what's so strange. How did I miss the signs?"

"Because she controlled her emotions too well?" I hazard. I go back to the notebook I'm reading. "I actually feel sorry for her. There was a dinner at Béatrice and Victor's and she was expecting it to be just the four of you. It was after Caitlin died and, according to Inès, she'd spent quite a bit of time in your company, so she thought she was getting somewhere. Then you turn up with Ariane."

"I remember that evening," he says, "because we'd barely arrived before Inès ran to the bathroom. She was there for a while and Béatrice kept going to check on her to see if she was okay. When she finally came out, she looked terrible. She said it must have been something she'd eaten the previous evening and Victor ordered a cab to take her home."

"Seeing you with Ariane made her physically sick," I say. "It's all here on the page, the rage and betrayal she felt. The next day she contacts you and asks for Ariane's number, saying she wants to apologize to her for leaving the dinner so abruptly when she'd only just been introduced to her. In reality, she wanted to befriend her and stalk her."

"And then kill her." Alex's voice is a mix of bitterness and anguish. "The frenzy of the attack still haunts me. I can't believe a woman could be so filled with rage toward another woman that she could kill her in such a violent manner."

"She lost control. She says it herself. It was the night Ariane told her you were going to get married. She had planned to get rid of Ariane, but not that night and not in that way. Remember what the police told us, about all the research she did into how to kill someone with a single stab wound and how to leave as little trace behind as possible?"

"Except that it's almost impossible to leave no trace," Alex says. "She was lucky that Ariane was working for the DGSE and that the police presumed she'd been killed because of her job and didn't ask too many questions. They just let the DGSE get on with it."

I move to sit next to him. "What I don't understand is how she could afford everything. The tennis club at Hyde Park, the lovely flat, the skiing trips—even learning the skills she needed to be able to cut the electricity supply to the house and pick the locks. It must have cost a lot."

"Family money. She told Béatrice she had a trust fund which matured when she was twenty-five," Alex says. "Did she tell you about her family?"

"Only that she was an only child. Was that a lie too?"

"No. Her father's a diplomat and so was his father before him. Her mother's a well-known French socialite but Inès barely knew them. She was sent to boarding school in England when she was seven years old and before that, she was brought up by a succession of nannies." He closes his notebook. "I'm done," he says. 'I don't want to read any more.'

"I'm not sure I want to read it," I say. "Not if it's about me."

"It's certainly taught me a lot about you." He turns to me. "Did you really think that I might be a spy?"

"Is that what it says?" I ask. He nods. "Okay, I admit, I did wonder at one point."

He raises his eyebrows. "You don't really know me very well, do you?"

I reach up and kiss him. "To be fair, we hadn't spent a lot of time together. And most of it had been pretty fraught."

"It's fine, I forgive you."

"Thank you." This time I kiss him for longer.

"And tell me, are you really learning French?" he asks.

"Does it say that too?"

He nods gravely. "It does. I did wonder how you were managing to read the notebooks."

"I wanted it to be a secret. I know your mother speaks perfect English but I thought she might like me a little better if I can speak French."

"My mother will love you anyway, but I can't tell you how much it means to me that you're learning my language."

"Good," I say, leaning into him. "If you've finished reading, can we go to bed now?"

"We can. But first, I just have one more question arising from what I read."

"Go on, then."

He wraps his arms around me. "How many children do you think we should have?" he asks.

ACKNOWLEDGMENTS

My amazing agent Camilla Bolton—thank you. You're equal parts guide, sounding board, and friend, and I can't imagine this journey without you.

I count myself lucky to have two outstanding editors, Catherine Richards at St. Martin's Press in the US and Kate Mills at HQ in the UK. As always, your suggestions and advice are invaluable. Thank you for your precious help in taking this book to the next level.

My grateful thanks go to the teams at St. Martin's Press and at HQ, who work tirelessly behind the scenes to polish my books and make sure they reach the shelves.

At SMP, Kelly Stone, Lauren Riebs, Brant Janeway, Marissa Sangiacomo, Katie Bassel, John Morrone, Omar Chapa, Catherine Turiano, Alexis Neuville, Chloe Nosan, Maria Snelling, Drew Kilman. Thank you too to copy editor Sabrina Roberts and proofreader Susan Barnett for catching my inconsistencies and errors, and to Danielle Christopher for the stunning cover. I would like to add a special thank-you to Jennifer Enderlin.

At HQ, Claire Brett, Becci Mansell, Emily Scorer, and Anna

Derkacz, with special thanks to Lisa Milton and Charlie Redmayne. Thank you for your continued faith in me, I'm thrilled to be home.

Every time I hold a foreign edition of one of my books, it feels like a small miracle. I am endlessly grateful to the dynamic Rights team at Darley Anderson Literary Agency—Georgia Fuller, Francesca Edwards, Ilaria Albani, and Sarah Brooks—who work diligently to find homes for my books abroad. I would also like to thank Rosanna Bellingham, Helen Dudley, and Georgia Schindler.

Thank you to my publishers and translators abroad, who bravely wrestle my sentences into forty-two other languages. I'm in awe of your talent.

Readers, you are everything. You take my books into your hearts and make them matter. Thank you for every page you've read, every word you've shared, and every review you've written.

Bloggers, your energy and passion are invaluable. You are the champions of stories, and I'm eternally grateful.

To my fellow authors: thank you for being my sounding boards, my allies, and my friends. And to my non-author friends—thank you for cheering me on and buying the books, even though you often hear about the plots long before anyone else does.

I would like to add special thanks to Phil Moss for his advice on police matters. Any mistakes are entirely my fault for not listening properly!

None of this would be possible without the encouragement and support of my family, especially Calum, our daughters, their partners, and the ever-growing band of tinies. You are my champions and I love you all.

ABOUT THE AUTHOR

Philippe Matsas

B. A. Paris is the *New York Times* bestselling author of *Behind Closed Doors*, *The Breakdown*, *Bring Me Back*, *The Dilemma*, *The Therapist*, *The Prisoner*, and *The Guest*. She grew up in England but spent most of her adult life in France. She has worked both in finance and as a teacher and now lives in the UK, where she writes from a cottage in the Hampshire countryside.